OUTRAGEOUS PRIDE

Book II in the Unlikely Gentlemen Series

GEM SIVAD

DARK MOUNTAIN BOOKS

OUTRAGEOUS PRIDE
Book II in the Unlikely Gentlemen Series
Copyright © 2013 Gem Sivad

ISBN 978-1-62622908-2
Published by Dark Mountain Books

Manufactured in the United States of America.

EDITOR
V.N. Johnson

COVER DESIGN
Michael Hart

PRAISE FOR THE
UNLIKELY GENTLEMEN SERIES

RIVER'S EDGE

2014 RONE AWARD NOMINEE,
AMERICAN HISTORICAL ROMANCE

*The author teases the reader's senses with her
descriptive writing... volcanic sexual tension...quirky
and distinctive characters and an appealing narrative...*

~ Danielle Hill, *InD'Tale Magazine*

OUTRAGEOUS PRIDE

*Kellan makes for a great hero who is not easily cowed: strong,
smart and willing to fight for what he wants. Natalia is a well-
bred young woman who deals admirably with the things life
throws at her. Together, they make for a perfect team.*

~ Ana Smith, *InD'Tale Magazine*

CERISE AMOUR

*Romance wrapped in Civil War history...
The characters were so well developed, I pictured many of them
in old daguerreotype photos. Very enjoyable read.*

~ Teresa Cypher, Review at Amazon

OTHER BOOKS BY GEM SIVAD

ECLIPSE HEAT

The Journal of Lucy Quince (free)
Destiny's Dream (free)
Quincy's Woman
Perfect Strangers

Five Card Stud
Wolf's Tender
Trouble in Disguise
Breed True

JINX

Cat Nip
Blood Stoned

MIZ

Call Me Miz
Hexual Healing

STAND-ALONE

Pinch of Naughty
A Staged Affair

UNLIKELY GENTLEMEN

River's Edge
Outrageous Pride
Cerise Amour
Acquisitions & Mergers (in 2015)

DEDICATION

To my husband, the inspiration for all my heroes.

PROLOGUE

*K*ell looked at the grim faced women waiting by the screened area and suppressed a groan. "Still time ta change yer mind, luv," he murmured but, obstinate to the end, Tali shook her head.

Ignoring the others in the room, he guided her toward the corner enclosure, and, hoping he'd be able to get his cockstand to the ready when called upon, braced himself for the coming do.

Bluidy fecking hell, I've never performed the deed for an audience let alone bedded a virgin. His glance swept over the lovely girl standing next to him and he pictured the moment he'd lie between Tali's sweet thighs.

A surge of heat settled in his groin, signaling his arousal—which under the circumstances was a bluidy miracle. Preparing for the task ahead, his shaft hardened into a solid length inside his trews. Kell concentrated on his bride and ignored their audience lest he shame his new wife by displaying a limp mackerel instead of a stiff rod.

As promised, Tali's friend Beth had assembled women to witness the event and now stood protectively beside the cot.

Once Tali lay with her skirts rolled up to her waist, she was no longer sure that publicly proving her virtue had been a good idea. After her peach colored drawers were removed, her naked lower region would be on view.

This will be over in no time. It's nothing. I'll just pretend I'm doing something else. That didn't help a bit when she heard the rustle of skirts as the ladies moved around the cot to get a better view. When Tali felt calloused hands remove her pantalettes, she recognized Kell's unmistakable touch.

I will never live this embarrassment down. The cot sagged under her and then he was there, pushing her legs apart.

"Natalia Lonigan, I'll be making ye me wife now." Tali shivered and looked up at the man kneeling over her who seemed barely more than a stranger. Panicked, she searched for a reassuring face in the crowd of witnesses.

Somebody stop this right now. The women's avid stares announced clearly they were not going to interrupt the proceedings. Celia Carter's eyes glittered with malice.

How did my safe world turn into this...?

CHAPTER I

"What the bluidy hell?" Kellan Lonigan dodged the knee aimed at crushing his family jewels but failed to duck the left cross that grazed his cheekbone.

"Objection," Liam called from Kell's corner. While the referee and umpire stood outside the ropes, conferring about the violation, the challenger ignored the protest and continued the fight.

Kell had participated in this exhibition match to work off his brother's gambling debt. The four rounds of showmanship sparring he'd agreed to perform with Handsome Jack Calloway had been replaced—as had Jack. Instead, Kell faced a big brawler dubbing himself Henderson's Hammer.

"Bets are down, I ken," Kell muttered.

"With you being the odds on favorite, Henderson stands to make a tidy sum when I rub your nose in the turf." The other man bragged about the plan as he ducked Kell's jab that became no more than a glancing blow sliding off his opponent's muscled shoulder.

"And the referee?"

"Has a family to feed." The challenger telegraphed his next move before he unleashed a left hook so powerful had it landed it would have ended the match and possibly Kell. Fortunately for Kell, the man was more mouth and brawn than skill.

"Enough of this, then, boyo." He landed two blows, right to left diagonally on the other man's chest. Instead of stepping back, the boxer lunged, and Kell used his own momentum against him.

"'Tis a shame to mar so pretty a mug." Kell pounded the other man's jaw and felt the jawbone pop out of its socket.

The bruiser shook his head, reeling from pain, and Kell delivered a right jab, satisfied to feel the crunch of cartilage as he mashed his fist against the lumbering giant's nose.

"Yer a *fecking* ox," Kell muttered when his opponent swayed on his feet but remained standing. Hit. Hit. Hit. Three blows to the solar plexus and the big man went to his knees, reeling and gasping for breath.

The time keepers started the thirty second count, and Kell took the moment to turn his back on his adversary and bow low in a theatrical sweep.

"Pride, Pride, Pride…" The crowd's jubilant chant changed to a warning. "Look out."

He doffed an imaginary cap and turned in time to deflect a meaty fist. Before he retreated, he delivered a kidney shot, taunting the bull of a man. His laughter had the desired effect, Henderson's secret weapon, though strong, lost his temper and forgot to use his brains.

Kellan, not as tall, but no slighter in build, matched the hulking brute for muscle power. He could have traded blow for blow with his opponent until he wore the man down. But he had no taste for hurting the fool. Henderson was the maggot bringing in an unknown fighter, intending to win a pile of cash when his man defeated Kell.

"Enough," Kell muttered, ending the match before it had really begun. He hammered another blow to the dislocated jaw and at the same time, nearly lifted the fellow off the floor with a fist to the gut.

The beast went to his knees, teetered for a moment, and then collapsed, gasping for air as his second rushed to the center of the four-and-twenty foot turf square. Kell raised his fists in victory and climbed over the ropes that enclosed the fighting area.

"'Twas a fine match," Liam said, grinning and holding out a towel.

"What happened to Calloway?" Kell accepted the proffered cloth and used it to wipe the sweat from his eyes. It was hotter than its namesake in Fort Worth's Hell's Half Acre.

"Jack was nowhere to be found beforehand. But as it turned out, the audience got the better show because of his defection."

Kell stared at him pensively. Though his brother had arrived before him to set up the night's gear, Liam had been mute about the new fighter Henderson had presented.

"And did you profit by Jack's absence?" Kell had been snookered into the fight because of his brother's gambling debts. Liam—*eejit* that he was—had been known to wager a bet on the outcome of two *crowlin' ferlies* scampering up a flop-house wall.

"I'll not repeat such as this again. No more saving ye from the likes of Henderson." Kell resisted the urge to knock his brother on his arse and looked past Liam, recognizing an old friend in the crowded room.

"Edge Grayson it is. Clear a path for me friend," he yelled at the mass. At Kell's request, the people between the ring and the outer door stepped to each side, making way for the gunslinger. In deference to the lass Grayson hovered over protectively, Kell donned a shirt to cover his bare chest.

"I hope ye were not lured to bet against me in this misbegotten affair," Kell called to Edge as the couple made their way to the roped area.

"Nope. We didn't bet," Edge answered when he arrived. "Kell, meet my wife, River Prescott Grayson. River, this is Kellan Lonigan, pugilist and friend."

"It's clear ye've been busy since we last met, lad." Kellan hid his astonishment and clapped the other man on the back.

"We saw a flyer advertising the exhibition match. It said, *Starring Pride Lonigan.* I bragged that I knew you and told River stories about you and me guarding the

Hatchet saloon together. After that, there wasn't any getting out of introducing the two of you."

The crowd once again jostled each other for space and queued before two different doors. The one lead to the exit, and the other led to Henderson's office. A loud disagreement nearby changed to a shoving match, and Edge wrapped his big frame protectively around his wee wife.

"I believe it would be best if we moved from this area, now," River said, showing remarkable intelligence as she peered up at Kell from fine green eyes.

Kell agreed, escorting them back through the milling horde. The place was about to descend into chaos if Henderson couldn't meet his payouts. Members of the audience stopped him to shake his hand on the way, and it took a bit of time to get to the exit.

When they finally reached the door at the back of the huge room, before he stepped through, Kell cast one glance back at his brother. Liam remained inside the roped fighting area, watching the throng disperse.

"After you freshen up, why don't you have dinner with us?" Edge's lady interrupted Kell's thoughts, reminding him that he was standing before her in sweat-stained fighting trews. Turning away from the ring and his brother, Kell nodded.

"But first, Edge, do ye still hire yourself out as a body guard? I need to collect from Henderson. Your company would no' be amiss."

"I don't sell my gun skills anymore," Grayson answered. "But I'm not opposed to accompanying an old friend during a business transaction."

Kell expected Grayson to escort his wife back to their hotel before they visited Henderson's office. But River disagreed, insisting she wanted to come along.

"Perhaps it would be best to visit him before he uses a back exit and disappears," River suggested. For someone her size, Edge's wife was a bold thinking lass. Her eyes sparkled with green fire as if cornering Henderson in his office was the greatest adventure she'd ever considered.

"Yep," Edge agreed. Grayson was clearly *bollocks over brains* ensnared by his missus because Edge agreed to whatever the woman said.

Has the man no sense? "I wouldna want yer bonny bride to be caught in a brawl," Kell reluctantly advised his friend.

"Nonsense. I trust my husband's ability to apply calm reason and logic without using violence." She beamed a confident smile as if that was the last word to be had on the subject. Not one to look a gift horse in the mouth, Kell accepted the wife's wisdom and led the way to Henderson's office.

"You've ruined me, you son of a bitch." Henderson's greeting when they entered didn't surprise

Kell. The office had been stripped of valuables and the room was in shambles. Nor did it surprise him to see the hotel-saloon-entrepreneur shifting the contents of the open safe into the satchel at his feet.

"Your prosperity is no' my concern. I'll take me payment for the match as we agreed—me brother's debts are to be wiped clean and we split the take from the door."

Henderson reluctantly pulled a stack of papers from his bag and laid them on the desk. Before he handed them over, Edge drawled, "Might want to write 'paid in full' on each, along with the date and your signature."

"Christ, Grayson. I thought you'd left the Acre. What the hell business is this of yours?" Henderson snarled.

"Does it matter?" Edge unbuttoned his suit jacket for better access to the holstered gun he wore, and as if they'd practiced the move, River stepped behind him.

Henderson glowered at his visitors but started writing. When he finished, he shoved the receipted i.o.u.s at Kell, grabbed his hat, and crossed to the back door.

"I think ye've forgotten my share of the night's payout," Kell reminded him before Henderson escaped.

"Here." Henderson retrieved a folded paper from his pocket, scribbled on the back of it, and tossed it at Kell. "It's all I have left—might as well take that too." Without further ado, he departed.

After he'd dealt with Henderson, Kell returned to his room to bathe and change clothes. Before he dined with the Graysons, he intended to have a talk with Liam. But when he looked for his brother, no surprise, the miscreant had disappeared among the gamblers, thugs, and prostitutes occupying the rough streets of the Acre.

Shrugging away his temper, Kell climbed on a street car and traveled across town to the Ellis Hotel. It was a grand accommodation and a far cry from the shabby room Kell shared with Liam. That, of course, was another bone of contention between the brothers. Liam knew to the penny how much Kell had socked away from his winnings and despised their frugal existence.

Someday, Kell intended to own a house and set up housekeeping with a decent woman. He'd explained to Liam time and time again that he saved the money he earned fighting toward getting them both to a better life.

Liam, being young and foolish, would have squandered all on drink and cards if allowed.

Kell stepped from the street car and walked toward the Ellis, hoping the suit he'd donned was splendid enough to get him in the place. He was pleasantly shocked when the doorman recognized and stopped him outside the entrance, not to question his visit but to shake his hand.

"I won a tidy packet on the last fight between you

and Calloway, son. Just want to tell you thanks."

Once inside, a hotel employee guided him to the Graysons who were waiting at a table in the restaurant.

After he was seated and the waiter had taken their orders and gone, Kell pulled from his pocket the document that Henderson had tossed his way.

"I doona ken whether this be worth spit or gold," he muttered, frowning at the paper that turned out to be a deed. It startled him a bit when Grayson's bride took charge.

"Let me see." River studied the title he handed her and then made her pronouncement. "I know exactly where this property lies. Your land is actually closer to the town of Isaca than to Annon. The buildings are sound, so, although Isaca has no hotel, you could stay in your own house while you're there."

"I inherited a ranch in the area," Edge told him. "That's how River and I met. We were neighbors."

"If yer no' selling your protection services now, what craft is it ye've pursued to afford such as this?" Kell asked, gesturing at the chandeliered dining room.

"Edge is now an author. I illustrate his stories." River Grayson pulled a dime novel from her reticule and thrust it at Kell.

"River's a famous artist," Edge told him and grinned. "She just lets me tag along."

Kell's jaw near fell to his knees as he gaped at the book she'd given him.

The title—*Kid Starks Rides Again*—appeared in bold letters across the front. Underneath, in a much more modest font, the words, *Story by Edge Grayson* and *Illustrations by River Prescott* appeared.

"That's me," she said, pointing at her name. "We're a team."

Before the meal was at an end, Kell teetered between admiration and jealousy toward Grayson. Instead of guarding payrolls or snooty muckety-mucks who wanted protection, his old friend had married a fine woman and given up the hard life.

"Let me give you letters of introduction to a few of our friends in the area since we won't be returning until the end of this month. They'll show you around Isaca and you can have a good look before you decide to sell or stay."

Kell hadn't been contemplating staying. In fact, he'd thought of trying San Francisco next. What he'd seen in Fort Worth's Hell's Half Acre didn't recommend itself to being any better than what he and Liam had left behind in any of the other cities they'd hit between Texas and Boston.

But, as he stared at the deed he'd won and then at the letters of introduction River Grayson had enthusiastically written, he changed his plan to sell the property and decided, instead, to give it a quick look-see before he parted with his prize.

It dazzled him a bit to realize that without parting with any of his cash, he already owned property. Even if the land wasn't worth much, it was his. The combination of

Grayson's good fortune and the possibilities of his own warmed his heart and put a spring in his step. He was suddenly anxious to see the prize.

Since his brother was still missing when Kell arrived at the boarding house where they roomed, he penned a note and left it for Liam. *Gone to the town of Annon to claim our winnings. Luck to you. Kell.*

"If that doona pique his curiosity and get him from this hellbent place..." Liam was a full twelve years his junior, and when Kell thought of the muck he'd made of raising his younger brother, his frown turned into a full scowl.

Grayson's luck turned to property, a wife, and a new endeavor. It didn't matter that, to Kell's way of thinking, the bride was a bit headstrong, or writing stories seemed a nancy way of making a go of things. Edge had a home and a lass who'd gone headers for him.

The wee bride gazed at her husband all night as if even his farts were made of gold. Kell grinned remembering and envied Edge something fierce.

With renewed determination, he gripped the deed and grimaced at the pain in his knuckles. His ribs were bruised, and his shoulder and neck already stiff. He touched his face and winced.

Edge's lady ne'er let on I must be a sight. Henderson's challenger had landed few good blows, but those few had done their damage.

CHAPTER II

*N*atalia Fitzwilliam laid her hat on the swing and stripped off her gardening gloves. The rambling roses, coddled into growing by her mother, were now under Tali's care and showed signs of blight. The wagon wheel, painted white and propped against the porch rail, had begun to peel.

Natalia Fitzwilliam laid her hat on the swing and stripped off her gardening gloves. The rambling roses, coddled into growing by her mother, were now under Tali's care and showed signs of blight. The wagon wheel, painted white and propped against the porch rail, had begun to peel.

Absently, she inhaled, filling her lungs with the blended scent of jasmine, honeysuckle and gardenias as she batted away midges that swarmed in the shade of the roof. Her upward glance caused another frown. Sooner than she could afford, the shingles would have to be patched or replaced. With the drought hitting the county so hard, she'd had little concern for rain, and had disregarded the problem. Her shoulders drooped. She'd been neglecting her home.

It wasn't that Tali lacked knowledge in how to treat the mold on the roses or whom to speak to about a new roof. Her mother, Cerise Fitzwilliam, had managed the repairs, hiring workmen when anything needed fixed. Though she was gone, she'd been an organized chatelaine who kept notes about all household business.

The bound book which held lists of names to contact for any household contingency—from catering to carpentry—had been tucked in her mother's files exactly where Tali had expected to find it. Six months before, she'd moved it from the bottom drawer to the top of the desk, dusted around it dutifully, and avoided reading the detailed records.

But the roof needed fixed, and the roses needed healed. She felt the familiar, clawing grief and forced back a sob. Taking charge of the necessities and management of the house was the final acknowledgement that she'd lost both her mother and her best friend.

So many times, they'd sat together in the swing, sipping sweet tea and sharing the beauty of the garden, the view of the river, and the utter enchantment of the place. Her mother had called it *homing*.

The backyard held too many bittersweet memories for Tali. Since her mother's death, she'd avoided lingering when she watered the plants that perfumed the morning air with exotic fragrance.

Determined to set aside her malaise, she went to the kitchen, poured a glass of tea, and returned to sit in the porch swing. Tali pushed the toe of her shoe against the floor and sent the swing into motion as she gazed with unseeing eyes at the backyard. In spite of the sunshine spilling across the terraced garden, Tali shivered.

"Mama, I feel so alone. I miss you so much." Tali murmured the words aloud and, then jolted by the sound, shook her head. "I'm now talking to myself for want of company. I'll speak to Beth this afternoon about getting a cat."

If Matthew and I marry... She gnawed her lower lip indecisively and then murmured with forced conviction, "*When* we marry I'm sure there will be room for one small kitten in our household."

If Mrs. Bodine likes cats, her traitorous thoughts intervened. Tali giggled, picturing a tussle with Mrs. Bodine over a kitten. Her humor faded and her smile changed to a frown.

Tali had never been clear about whether her mother liked Matthew. Cerise had supported Tali's interest, because as she'd acknowledged, "He owns the most successful ranching operation in the area and you will no doubt be well cared for."

But Matthew's devotion to Amelia Bodine's happiness was sometimes disconcerting. Tali had mentioned it once to her mother and been surprised at the arched brow and pragmatic response.

"If it's a docile man you want who does as he's told, fine. Just be prepared to lead on the dance floor. Amelia's trained her son well to take orders, but he can only bow and dip and glide on command."

"Mama, that's not …" *True?* Tali had stopped short of finishing her reprimand when a mental image of Amelia Bodine steering Matthew around a dance floor popped into her brain. She'd giggled and then felt disloyal.

Her mother had rolled her eyes and then laughed too. Cerise Fitzwilliam had avoided males in general and didn't mince words when she spoke of the few she knew. It had always surprised Tali that her mother had married at all.

"What was my father like?" The question had spilled from Tali unexpectedly, startling both daughter and mother. "Mama," Tali had continued hesitantly, "You never speak about my father. Did you love him?"

"Outrageously," Cerise had murmured and then stopped. It had always been thus; the topic of Tali's father was a taboo subject. This time, though, had been different. Cerise's expression had changed as she'd gazed at Tali. She'd spoken slowly, as if pulling the memories from a long locked vault.

"He rode with Walker's Greyhounds during the War Between the States, and we met after the Battle of Young's Point when he came to Madison Parish. I was a Northerner, stuck behind enemy lines and he was the enemy. I had no use then as now, for men who'd rather use swords than brains. He was a soldier in the God awful war that killed so many and could have been avoided."

Her mother never hid her disgust for the war that had pitted the North against the South. But Tali hadn't wanted her to talk about that.

"And my father?" Tali had asked, reminding her mother what topic they'd been discussing.

"He didn't take orders well," Cerise had quipped. Then, her laughter had disappeared. "We fell in love," she'd murmured, and her amused expression had melted into astonishment.

What did he look like?" It was a rare opportunity, and Tali had bombarded her with more questions.

"He was a tall, rugged, Texan, full of his own importance." She'd frowned as if still irritated by her late husband. "His thick dark hair was neither black nor brown, like yours, it was a lovely blend of each. He also had the prettiest deep blue eyes." Her mother had sighed and added, "He was a handsome devil."

"Do I look like him?" Tali had asked. She didn't favor her mother and assumed she'd inherited her father's features.

"You have his stubborn chin," her mother had responded. "More importantly, daughter, what color are Matthew's eyes?" When Tali couldn't answer, the question had affectively ended the conversation. After that day, Cerise resumed silence on the topic of her late husband, rebuffing Tali's attempts to open the subject again.

Tali reviewed the memory with a sinking heart. She

now knew that Matthew had brown eyes because she'd made a conscious effort to look. She'd comforted herself with the knowledge that, though Matthew would never set her emotions afire, he would be a dependable husband.

Tali groaned, closed her eyes, and leaned against the back of the swing, as she suddenly wondered if that was enough. She'd have preferred that Matthew sweep her off her feet and boldly romance her.

Unbidden, the picture of a man with wide powerful shoulders, thick curly blonde hair, and hands the size of dinner plates, sprang to mind. Tali had seen him at the livery stable in Isaca the last time she was in town. He'd been talking to a group of men, and she'd noticed the size of his hands because he'd had them balled into fists, holding them in front of him as if demonstrating something.

Whatever he'd been talking about, the discussion had ended with laughter, and the men had turned with interest to an arriving wagon, its contents covered from view by a tarp. Tali's curiosity about the wagon's contents had never been appeased. Nor had she forgotten the man.

Tali's cottage sat in a bend of the road, separating her from the other cluster of buildings in Isaca. Her mood lightened considerably, as she walked to town, anticipating a Thursday afternoon visiting with her friend Beth Harper who clerked at the Isaca General Store and Post Office.

When she passed the sheriff's office at the end of the street, the irony of its existence struck her. The town had been required to provide a lawman in order to set up receipt of mail in the general store. So they'd hired a local, unemployed cowboy for the job.

Now he was in jail for murder. So far, nobody in the county had suggested that they lose their post office so nobody had pushed to find a new sheriff. Tali passed the empty building and hurried toward the town mercantile.

The store would have received it's week's deliveries this morning, and helping Beth stock shelves had become a Thursday ritual. It gave the two friends time to exchange gossip while they unpacked the new products, priced them, and put them out for sale. Beth was probably already knee-deep in boxes of goods to shelve, so Tali hurried.

As soon as she arrived, Beth put her to work. Following on Tali's heels, Mrs. Pearson, the oldest woman in town and the finest hand with pastries, delivered bread and other baked goods still hot from her oven. Tali stood behind the counter arranging them when Horace Murdock, the town attorney, came through the front door.

"Ladies, I've been commissioned to hand-deliver these two letters from your mutual friend."

"Another letter from River," Beth crowed and snatched hers from Horace's hand.

"Yes. I'm sure it will be no surprise to you when I tell you that our town's resident artist is interfering with local business again."

Beth and Tali both grinned. The three girls had been friends forever, having grown up together. Well Beth and Tali had grown up. River had remained small, less than five foot and diminutive in stature. She'd made up for it though in her approach to life. She'd become an independent woman of means.

Tali admired the fact that rather than shrink from public opinion, River molded it or mocked it in the pictures she painted—and sold for astonishing amounts of money.

Until she'd married recently, the local men had quietly, and not so silently, named her *unnatural*.

Now that she'd married a famous gunman and gone on an extended honeymoon, most of the men didn't know what to say. All in all, since River had been gone, the town had been excessively quiet with only the depressing foreclosures disturbing daily life.

"And what has she done now?" Beth asked.

"She's sent an unlikely gentleman for us to vet. He's a friend of her husband's."

"Unlikely how?" Tali asked.

"Well he wears a three piece suit, a bowler hat, and his nails are clean, but—"

Tali laughed at the same time the bell up front rang, drawing her attention to the closing front door.

"Something in here smells mighty fine," Mathew Bodine announced and moved toward them.

"You hear that, Tali? He's tracking you," Beth teased.

Matthew smiled but made no comment, lingering instead by the canned goods, and picking up a few items before he sauntered over to where Tali stood behind the baked goods.

"Mother asked me to bring home one of Grandma Pearson's pies," Matthew drawled.

Tali noted his grin and the way he adeptly distanced himself from Beth's taunt without really denying anything—or confirming. It hurt Tali's feelings in a way she didn't want to explore.

"Here's your letter from River." Beth handed Tali the envelope, and she noticed Matthew's look of curiosity as she slipped it into her pocket.

"It will be no problem to drop you off at your cottage on my way home," he unexpectedly offered.

"That's very nice of you, Matthew. But, Beth and I have more work to complete. It would be best for you to go on. I'm sure your mother will be anticipating her pie." It felt good to refuse the ride, but when he readily accepted her decision, picked up his goods, and departed, Tali's satisfaction deflated.

She resisted the urge to read the letter in her pocket, electing instead to save it for her evening alone. It was another hour at least before she finished helping Beth and left the store to walk home. When she reached the edge of town, Matthew, apparently waiting for her, was sitting under a copse of trees on the front seat of Amelia Bodine's Coupe Brougham. When Tali came into view, he immediately jumped to the ground and motioned her over.

"No sense in you walking when I'm going your way." He swung her to the open box seat, wide enough for a driver and passenger. It sat in front of the enclosed portion of the carriage where Amelia rode in splendor to church each Sunday. It surprised Tali to see Matthew using the fancy rig with Amelia nowhere in sight.

After he lifted her to the front seat, he climbed up beside her, nudging her over with his hip. Though it was cushioned nicely, she thought the seat too narrow forcing uncomfortable contact as Matthew's leg pressed against hers. When she tried to make room for him, easing sideways, he moved too, and patted her arm.

"What did River have to say?"

"I haven't read her letter yet." Nor did she intend to until she was alone.

"I'm curious about what she's up to. Read it now."

Tali resented the intrusion into her privacy, but there really seemed no graceful way to refuse. Reluctantly she opened the envelope and pulled out the two pages inside. Before she'd scanned the first, intending to censor the contents as she shared, to her amazement, Matthew plucked the letter from her fingers and began reading it aloud. River talked about the art show she and her new husband had attended and the exciting adventures she and Edge were having on their honeymoon. Before she closed, she asked Tali to welcome a business acquaintance of her husband's to Isaca and help show him around. Typical of River, the man wasn't an ordinary citizen. Instead, he was a pugilist named Kellan Lonigan.

Dear God, for once, Matthew didn't need to confer with Amelia Bodine to devise an opinion. He was livid.

"Lonigan's another Eastern bloodsucker come to steal what he's too lazy to earn. Decent women avoid such as him." Matthew's virulence surprised her.

"Do you know him?"

"I don't want to know him."

"River's decent. She's vouched for Mr. Lonigan."

"And *she's* married to a notorious gunslinger. I think that's more than enough to know about her new *acquaintance.*"

Tali retreated from the argument startled by Matthew's vehemence. Displays of strong emotion from him were rare.

"I know you think I'm being high-handed. Forgive me if I seem overprotective, but your future will soon be part of mine, and I can't help but view the behavior of some of your associates with concern." Part of her wanted to jump for joy at the suggestion of their entwined tomorrows.

"Matthew, are you declaring yourself?" she asked.

"Haven't we always had an understanding?" He tucked River's letter back into Tali's pocket, answering evasively as always. His vague response was accompanied by a painful pinch that made her muscles tense and her body strain away from him.

He ignored her reaction and brushed his lips across hers, before he waited for her to climb from the buggy. As soon as her feet were on solid ground, he slapped the reins and drove away at a fast clip.

Your future will soon be part of mine. Haven't we always had an understanding? What exactly does that mean? Not for the first time, Matthew's way of implying something without actually saying *anything* irritated Tali.

Uneasily, she remembered the brush of his lips across hers and the way she'd withdrawn from his touch. She'd wanted him to be more attentive but…

Abruptly, she pulled the letter out to read by herself. The upper right hand corner bore a picture of a man with his hands fisted ready to brawl. It was a black and white sketch done in pencil, but nevertheless, Tali recognized the stranger she'd seen at the livery.

So that was Kellan Lonigan. Tali's cheeks heated and she snorted laughter as she viewed the taut muscles on the boxer's arms, the strong thighs, his brawny shoulders, and his bare chest. Then, she mentally compared the man in the picture to Matthew's rangy height and skinny frame. *No wonder he was upset.*

CHAPTER III

"**I** need ta acquire a horse," Kell had told the hotel clerk in Clarksville when he'd first arrived. Following the man's directions to a row of barns two streets away, he visited a livery, intending to rent a mount to complete the journey to his property.

"Nope, got nothin' left to rent," the first, second and third stablemen drawled. The stalls were empty of horses. One buggy with a broken wheel sat in front of the third barn, but the owner claimed it was already promised if he could get it fixed in time.

"In time for what?" Kell inquired. He'd seen no evidence of an impending parade or event.

"It's auction day in Annon." The stable owner scowled at Kell's bowler hat and suit. "Guess you'd know all about that."

"I have no auction to attend. I do need to get to the courthouse in Annon though."

"Thomas, down the row, might have a nag or two left. But that's doubtful." Following the barn owner's suggestion, Kell shrugged out of his jacket and carried it over his shoulder as he walked to the last building on the street.

"Got an old wagon and a buggy horse left," the old man at the last barn said. "But I'm selling not renting.

You want I should hook him up for you?"

"I'd intended to ride."

"Nope, horse and wagon go as one and then I'm done with my business."

Kell had planned to leave his bags at his hotel room in Clarksville. But after his option became buy the wagon or walk to Annon, he paid for the wagon and decided to take his gear with him.

"I'll eat a bite of food before I set out," Kell had told the stable owner as he peeled bills from his wallet to pay for his transportation. "If ye'll prepare the conveyance, I'll return for me rig when I'm through."

After breakfast, he checked out of his hotel room and carried his duffel with him to the barn. An old horse hitched between the shafts of an older wagon stood waiting for him. Without comment, he'd thrown his bag in the back and climbed onto the seat.

Before he'd driven more than two feet from the front of the livery, he acquired an additional passenger when a huge barn cat jumped into the back of the wagon. Kell had stopped. "Go on with ye now. I'll not be bringing ye back here tonight."

He'd tried to shoo the cat on its way and received no more than an arched back and hiss for his troubles.

"He goes with the horse," the old man had yelled from the barn. "Guess this is your lucky day."

It wasn't the grand conveyance he'd hoped for, and the cat had little to recommend itself for company. But, the wagon didn't break down as it rattled along behind the steadily plodding horse, and Kell arrived in Annon before midday.

Kell found the courthouse but was forced to wait for the ongoing auction to end before he could present his deed. He was jostled more than once as he made his way through the angry crowd of ranchers standing on the steps of the building.

After he shouldered his way inside, he understood the outside animus. Men, dressed in suits and wearing bowler hats—much like his own—stood bidding on parcels of ground that had gone into foreclosure.

Though Henderson had endorsed the title over to Kell, he didn't want to be accused of trespass, so he waited for the auction to end. Afterward, he approached one of the remaining men in the room to ask for guidance.

"No bloodshed today," the older man said, obviously relieved.

"And does the spilling of blood often happen at these affairs?" Kell asked.

"Too often. I'm Horace Murdock. I fill in as the town's attorney when I'm needed. Unfortunately today, I had to preside at the auction. How can I help you?"

The man's friendly greeting was a relief after the

outside hostility. Besides that, Murdock was one of the names on River Grayson's list. Kell pulled the letter of introduction from his pocket.

"And how are the newlyweds doing on their business trip?" Murdock had smiled fondly as he read the letter. "She's something of a celebrity in these parts; besides being an artist, she's a fine person. And how do you know our River?" The old lawyer had been filled with pride, and Kell hadn't needed to be a genius to see that Edge's wife was a well-respected lady.

"I've no' been acquainted with the wee lass but for our meeting in Fort Worth. It's her husband I'm known to."

"Yes, so the letter states. River's husband comes from good stock. I knew his grandfather well." The old man didn't elaborate on Edge's background and turned, instead, to the point of the meeting.

"Before the drought, the ranch you've obtained was a valuable property." Murdock transferred the title into Kell's name, talking the whole time.

"Rain has fallen in the past and will again," Kell said exhibiting a confidence he had no right to.

"I expect you're right," Murdock smiled. "It's just not easy on those who've lost their roots."

But fine for those who are putting down new ones. Kell had intended to rent a room in Annon, but the lawyer told him the only hotel was full of Eastern bankers and land speculators.

Not to be deterred once he'd gotten close, Kell obtained directions to his newly acquired ranch and once again set out in his wagon. The cat remained a fixture in the back.

"First things first, lads." He'd stopped his newly purchased old rig by the hitching post, climbed down, and studied the windmill. "Let's give the pump a try and see if we can get it ta spout a drink fer us."

Kell scratched the muzzle of the animal absently, taking in the size of the barn yard and the sturdiness of the buildings. His canteen held tepid water he could drink, but, no doubt, the horse was thirsty too.

He crossed the yard, grasped the pump handle, and begun pumping it up and down. He'd almost given up when drops of brackish water belched out, beading on top of the dirt.

Kell was inordinately pleased to discover he owned a working water pump in this desolate land. Afraid if he paused to search out a container the progress he'd made would be lost, when the drops turned into a clear stream, he drank straight from the pump, then filled his hat, and carried his improvised bucket to the horse.

The cat had deigned to move to the front of the wagon, expectantly waiting for his drink too. The beast was an old tom, battle-scarred and half-wild. Apparently though, he and the horse were friends.

"Well, it pleases me no end that ye've lowered yerself to meet me." Kell reached to pet the cat but drew back when his overture was greeted with a hiss, flattened ears, and sharp claws that swiped at him.

"So be it, then boyo." He set his bowler on the ground and stepped back, watching the cat lap thirstily at its contents. When the unfriendly feline finished, Kell refilled his hat twice more to water the horse.

I've finished tending me newly acquired livestock. Kell grinned at his foolish pride and enjoyed the trickle of water that cooled his brains when he set his bowler back on his head. Proceeding in his exploration, he walked to the house, mounted the steps, and traveled the length of the wide veranda before stopping.

He was surprised when he tested the flooring and found no weak spots. It was unnervingly satisfying to stand on a grand porch he could call his own and look out over land that belonged to him.

Nay, it belongs to the both of us. He'd intended to put Liam's name on the deed too; but upon remembering his brother's gambling debts, perhaps some yet unpaid, he'd recorded the property in his name alone.

He squinted at the sun causing the drought and then at the ranch yard. Parched clumps of grass defied nature by poking their way through iron hard soil, only to be burned to a crisp when each blade made it to the surface.

"'Tis a message in that somewhere, boyo," Kell muttered as he remembered the squalid Belfast tenement he'd fought his way out of. His hands clenched and he rotated his neck, working travel stiffness from his back and shoulder muscles.

But he was already picturing a line of wagons in front of the barn and horses filling the empty stalls.

Land, son. That be true wealth. 'Tis only so much ta go 'round, and those who own it be kings. His da's words rang clear in his head, and excitement swept over him as he looked at the beginning of his kingdom.

CHAPTER IV

Say little, and the little you say, say well . . .

"You have a letter," Beth said, waving a large square envelope at Tali as soon as she walked through the front door.

"I'll bet those are the designs for my wedding dress River's sending." Tali smiled and reached for it.

"So it's official? Mrs. Bodine is actually going to let Matthew free from her leading strings long enough to take a wife?"

"Matthew says we'll make a public announcement soon." Ignoring Beth's snide remark, Tali reached for the letter again.

"This isn't from River. Not unless she sent her drawings by way of the Annon Court House." Beth evaded her grasp and turned the envelope over in her hands, studying the seal on the back, before handing it to Tali. "This looks official."

They both stared at the envelope with the name Natalia Carter Fitzwilliam printed on the front.

A shout from outside brought both women's attention back to the window. Tali groaned and shook her head as she stared at the fracas in the middle of Isaca.

"That nincompoop is standing in the middle of the street, daring Matthew to ride over him."

The current male high jinks that had both women

staring out the window was a fight brewing between Isaca's newest property owner, Kellan Lonigan and Tali's beau.

Evidently, according to Mr. Murdock, Kellan Lonigan had won his first piece of Texas land in a pugilistic match. When he'd first visited Isaca a month before, local citizens had reserved judgment on the boxer, deeming him too temporary to bother getting acquainted.

It had been considered odd when he'd moved into the house on the ranch he'd acquired instead of staying in a hotel in nearby, Annon. It soon became clear that his stay was more than temporary.

When he used his ranch as headquarters and began attending the auctions to buy more foreclosed property, opinions varied from eager interest to irate. He had money to spend and did so, ingratiating himself with local business owners. Ranchers viewed him with disgust bordering on hatred.

He certainly wasn't difficult to spot since the three piece suit and bowler hat he always wore, made him stick out like a sore thumb.

Tali, gazed with Beth at the picture of adult males squaring off to fight, though one was on horseback and the other on his feet.

"Pride Lonigan will make a great character in one of Edge and River's make-believe stories." Beth pointed at the horse and rider blocking the brawny man from continuing down the main thoroughfare.

"But would he be the hero or the villain?" Tali frowned. "Mathew says he's an Irish lout.

"What do you say?" Beth asked.

Tali didn't know what she thought. It seemed to her that she'd been flustered ever since Kellan Lonigan had come to town, and she'd never even met him. When Horace Murdock, had visited the store to hand-deliver River's letters, Tali had intended to do as her friend requested: meet Kellan Lonigan and introduce him to other Isaca citizens.

After Matthew's vehement outburst, Tali dealt with the issue by staying at home to make certain she *couldn't* run into Mr. Lonigan unexpectedly. It had been a cowardly retreat. She'd only ended her self-imposed exile today because it was Thursday and auction day in Annon.

She'd emerged from seclusion, hoping that Mr. Lonigan and Matthew both attended the property sales in the next town over. Her reason for dodging the acquaintance of the former boxer was obvious. She didn't question her motives for avoiding Matthew.

"I say that since Mr. Lonigan's arrival, Isaca's been under siege." It vexed her that Beth wanted her to take sides. Tali had secured neutrality in the issue by neither defending Matthew's views nor championing River's friend.

"Not really. It's the land foreclosures that have

everyone upset. Nobody knows who'll topple next." As always, Beth's practical assessment rang true. "Anyway—I've heard that Kellan Lonigan intends to stay, which means he'll be your neighbor, and the females in town will have another single male to add to the slim pickings here."

"Mathew says he's of the same ilk as the bank's bully boys."

Drought stricken, long established ranchers had gone under and inevitably, land speculators converged on the weakened community, paying pennies on the dollar to buy once valuable ranch land.

Transactions had remained fairly anonymous at first, with local lawyers and bankers attending auctions, bidding on foreclosed properties, and transferring property titles to Eastern investors.

But, as the drought raged on, hostility toward the bankers and local lawyers became so great, they refused to risk bodily harm by attending the sales. Undeterred, the Eastern business interests sent armed guards to escort their representative to and from the auctions. Unfortunately, the guards wore three piece suits and bowler hats like Mr. Lonigan favored. It was easy to lump him in with the other bank thugs.

"What's your opinion? Oh, that's right, Matthew said you weren't allowed to meet him, so know him you don't." Beth rolled her eyes at Tali and shook her head.

Tali grimaced at her friend. She felt a twinge of

resentment at Beth's none too subtle jab at Tali's allegiance to Matthew. Since Beth remained devoted to the memory of her deceased husband, she shouldn't question Tali's loyalty to a live *almost* husband.

Turning back to the brewing street trouble, Tali focused on the man outside. She found especially ridiculous, his title: Pride of the Ring. *Matthew is right; a man who uses his fists to make a living can't possibly be a savory character.*

So far, she'd managed to avoid an introduction or accidental meeting during his month's stay, though Kell Lonigan frequently visited Isaca. As soon as she'd learned that the town had obtained the dubious distinction of becoming the cocky Irishman's postal address, and since he collected his correspondence on Saturdays, she'd eliminated that day from her town visits.

Now, here he was on Thursday, a day she'd expected him to be at the Annon auction.

"Why does he have to be in Isaca today?" Tali muttered, put out by the sight of him in the street.

"He's still living in the house he won. I don't know what he's doing with the two properties he's since bought," Beth promptly pointed out. "His official domicile is closer to Isaca than to Annon."

"I think River was mistaken in asking us to welcome an unknown man to Isaca," Tali muttered.

Beth rolled her eyes again. It wasn't the first

disagreement over their friend's request.

"Horse manure. That sounds like Amelia Bodine's opinion, not yours." Beth wore a grim expression as she handed Tali the letter.

"All right. *I* think Mr. Lonigan is a big fish in a very small barrel of water at the moment. I don't know what he's up to. He's a city person, and this is not the kind of place he'll flourish." Her censorious tone changed, and she grinned and added, "But he's certainly made things in Isaca interesting this summer."

"That's more like it," Beth murmured, "Since River's not here to see this, we'll have to watch like two busybodies and then tell her. In my letter, she said she's working on a painting of him fighting in a pugilistic contest she witnessed in Fort Worth."

"I miss her." Tali leaned close, her nose almost pressing against the glass in the window. "She confided in her letter to me that she and Edge had some family problems to deal with before they came home. What family?"

"I don't know. She told me the same thing. She doesn't have any relatives that I know of and Edge…"

"Right. Edge was born out of wedlock. You suppose he's discovered siblings?" Beth's question remained unanswered as the drama in the street continued to unfold. Matthew had effectively moved his horse so that he blocked Mr. Lonigan's path to his horse and buggy.

"Matthew's mother said Mr. Lonigan was a common

street fighter in Boston," Tali murmured, returning to gossip about Isaca's newest citizen.

"Not so common as all that," Beth laughed. "Joanne Miller said she was the teller on duty at the bank when he carried in a satchel of money and paid cash for Emmett Price's place."

"But that's…"

"Downright dumb. But impressive," Beth finished her sentence.

Tali's opinion on Mr. Lonigan's injudicious behavior remained unvoiced when the store bell jangled, signaling Beth had a customer. While her friend assumed her duties as store and postal clerk, Tali moved to the middle aisle and began shelving cans of peaches.

She was crawling on the floor, pushing the box of fruit before her when the customer spoke.

"Good day ta you. Might I have a word with ye, Postmistress Harper?"

Good Lord, it's him. Tali froze. After Matthew's edict forbidding her to meet Mr. Lonigan—as any red-blooded Texas woman would—she'd taken every opportunity to ogle the new man in town from afar.

She'd washed the church windows and admired his shoulders as he'd loaded grain on the old wagon he drove to town. A huge cat sitting in the wagonbed had reached for the Irishman's hat and tried to knock it off his head. Tali had laughed out loud and then ducked low, still chuckling at what she'd seen. Mr. Lonigan had straightened and looked around as if he'd heard her.

She'd spied on him another day when she'd seen him running on the river bank. It was her secret. She'd been standing in her backyard in early morning, frowning down at the river, disturbed at the low level of the water below when a man dressed in knee length breeches and a loose shirt had suddenly run into view.

She'd known immediately who it was, though his hair was unexpectedly blonde. She'd thought he'd be dark-headed or maybe even have red hair, but no, his hair was wheat gold and curly.

She had no idea why a grown man would exert energy running if there were no emergency. But that's what he'd been doing.

She'd also listened to the varying opinions of Isaca citizens. Mr. Lonigan's past pugilistic exploits were enthusiastically rehashed by local males. Local females seemed more interested in his wide shouldered, burly figure. Both genders discussed the wealth he was reputed to have stashed somewhere close.

"Rich as Croesus and muscled like a prime bull." Laura Styles, the minister's wife, had worn an odd expression as she'd confided her opinion last Sunday.

Unfamiliar though she was with the attributes of bulls or other male animals, Tali still tended to disagree with the assessment. Even from a distance, there was no denying the former boxer's magnificent size and conformation but he moved with the sinewy grace of a cougar not a bull. As for his wealth, in this drought stricken area anyone with more than two nickels to rub together could call themselves rich.

But now here he was, inside the store, two feet from where Tali crouched on the floor behind the shelves. She wanted to jump up and greet him, having missed meeting him because of Matthew's silliness. On the other hand, Matthew was in the street outside. Feeling pangs of guilt for even considering such disloyalty, she didn't move and remained hidden between the rows.

"Good day to you, Mr. Lonigan. What can I help you with today?" Beth answered using her mid–friendly tone reserved for better than slight acquaintances.

"Ahhh…'tis fine ta see that ye remember me. And as to what I need, I've been told you can fix a man up with an account that lets him run a tic to pay at month's end."

Tali had never been close enough to hear him speak, so she was unprepared for the deep tone of his rumbled words or his speed of delivery. The effect his voice had on her was startling. The rich timbre brushed over her senses like warm molasses, and the lilting quality was even more lethal, making heat curl in her belly and air stutter in her lungs.

Tali had absolutely no place to hide when he stepped to the front of the canned-goods aisle and peered down at her.

"And is it a helper you have today?"

.ෛ ෙ.

"Tá tú iontach álainn," *you are verra beautiful*, Kell muttered in Gaelic when he looked upon the vision of loveliness crouched on the floor.

"What?" she asked, giving him a perplexed stare from eyes the sweet, clear blue of a summer sky over the River Lagan. Instead of accurately translating, Kell squatted in front of her and brushed his fingers across the smudge on her nose.

"A wee speck of dirt has taken up residence here." He could see the incongruity of his scarred knuckles against her delicate flesh, and it surprised him that she didn't flinch from his big paw. When he removed the streak of dust and unnecessarily dragged the back of his hand across her flushed cheek, nothing had ever felt as exquisite as the silken skin beneath his calloused touch.

At his finest moment, he wasn't a pretty man, but since he'd hammered Henderson's challenger in Fort Worth and taken a few blows himself, his face wasn't at its best.

"You're Kellan Lonigan, Edge Grayson's friend," she said in a husky whisper.

"That I am," he agreed. "And you would be...?" He waited for her response, watching rose colored lips form her answer.

"Tali. Natalia Fitzwilliam." Her dark brows and darker lashes accented the warmth in her expressive eyes as she introduced herself.

"Ye would be the wee sprite's other friend," Kell murmured, feeling almost breathless as her smile smote him a mighty blow, knocking him back on his heels.

*Bluidy hell. A*s Kell savored the look of her moist pink lips, the dimples that indented each rosy cheek and the tiny creased laugh lines fanning from the corners of her beautiful eyes, his usually quite sensible cock became unruly. And then the miscreant reared its foolish head, unfurled into full stance, and left him shifting from thigh to thigh, trying to disguise his condition.

"*An bhfuil tu posta?* " he murmured.

"That's very rude you know," she scolded him. His face flooded with color and then he almost collapsed in relief when she added, "Speaking in a language I can't understand."

"Is it now?" He felt a bit hoarse and struggled to get out something sensible that wouldn't scare her away. "I've lived by meself for a bit and forgotten the niceties of getting along. Are you married is what I ask."

"I'm not wed yet, but will be soon." Her cheeks took on an even rosier glow as she shook her head.

"So yer betrothed; what is the name of this lucky man?" Insanely, he thought of hunting the fellow down and persuading him to move on. Then, of course, he cast that idea aside as barbaric and unworthy of such as her. Still…

Her blush deepened. "My engagement isn't official."

"Ahh…" He looked at her thoughtfully. *Reprieve.* She hadn't spoken a name, so perhaps some gobshite bastard was toying with her affections.

"Bluidy fool to let one such as yerself go unclaimed. Were you mine…" He stopped, realizing that he'd said too much, leaned too close, and blabbered the wrong things.

"Will you be attending the dance this weekend?" she asked. Instead of recoiling from his proximity, she tilted her chin, waiting expectantly for his answer.

"Dance?" He was incapable of uttering more as her husky tone and sweet warm breath fuddled his senses. His dancing didn't amount to more than a shuffle from foot to foot, but the thought of holding her in his arms— even if a stately distance from his body—made his cockstand throb painfully. This, in turn, reminded him that he needed a graceful way of exiting before he revealed the state of his groin.

When she didn't elaborate, Kell grunted, picked up the nearly full crate of canned peaches and held it before the thick erection tenting his trews.

"The *First Annual Annon Ice Cream Social and Dance* is Friday—tomorrow," she told him in a rush. He had no idea of what she spoke but he'd find out.

Feeling light-headed with lust, he walked to the payment counter where the Postmistress, *Beth-something-or-other,   the-wee-sprite's-second-friend*, stood waiting.

"These," he managed to spit out.

"Do you want me to create an account for you?"

He nodded.

"You're taking the whole box of peaches?"

"Aye." After being so gob-smacked by the lass hiding in the grocery aisle, he praised his ability to use the pencil and paid no heed to what he signed. When he scribbled his name to the bill the clerk presented, he might easily have been guaranteeing payment for the town's yearly expenses.

Holding the box of tinned fruit before him, he crossed to the door. His lust cooled considerably and his prick deflated in size when he saw the bluidy arse blocking the exit.

"Can I help you with something, Matthew?" the lass who'd just waited on Kell asked the cretin standing in the doorway.

"I saw a coyote slink in here," Bodine said and nodded at Kell.

Many a time a man's mouth broke his nose, Kell thought. It wasn't Kell's first run-in with Matthew Bodine even today. The local rancher attended most of the Thursday auctions in Annon the same as Kell. And he bid on many of the same properties as well.

"I stopped in to make certain no harm had befallen you, Beth."

Ye've bollocks for brains if ye think ye'll provoke a fight with me before the lassies. "Move out of my path,"

Kell said gruffly.

"Make me," Bodine growled, settling back and tilting his chin, preparing to suffer the blow that would convince citizens of Isaca that Kell was a lout.

Suddenly, a head appeared above the row of canned goods and Kell's vision of loveliness stood from her hiding spot, glided to where the men faced each other, and put a cautionary hand on the cowboy's arm.

"Matthew, I don't believe you've been formally introduced. This is Mr. Lonigan, River and Edge Grayson's friend."

Bodine's sneer changed to tight-lipped fury but he moved from blocking the door.

Before he stepped outside Kell smiled at River's two friends. "I look forward to a dance with each of ye in Annon at the social."

Glad that he'd exited the store without rearranging Bodine's face, Kell managed to get himself back to his wagon without falling down.

Are you married, I asked her. He'd never acted such a fool and felt the scald of red in his cheeks just remembering his gauche question. He'd been no better than a tongue-tied eejit.

After he read the flyer left on his wagon seat, Kell's big head resumed command. Instead of home, he drove to Annon. Once there, he talked to Horace Murdock and waited on the answer to a wire the old lawyer sent.

CHAPTER V

Three things that run swiftest;
fire, water, and falsehood . . .

*T*o Tali's way of thinking, the business people of Annon deserved to collectively be thrashed. They'd wanted and found a way to capitalize on the *Special Friday Property Sales* flyer that had been printed by the banks. Store owners quickly coordinated their own event, designed to begin when the auction ended.

The decision was made to hold the festivities for several reasons. The three ranches on the auction block were closer to Isaca, and the loss seemed less personal to Annon citizens. Also, because each parcel of land being sold either had water on it, or contracted water access rights, the parcels were considered prime acquisitions, and the sale itself was expected to attract huge crowds.

Gossips claimed that the bankers were so heartless they'd allowed one of the families a week longer in their home if their young son delivered the foreclosure advertisement to every breathing person in the area. Times were hard, and Tali thought it possible.

The number of anticipated buyers and interested spectators was so great the bankers had rented a giant tent from a traveling revivalist. Some of the businesses in Annon had decided to capitalize on other's misery and set up booths outside the canvas dome. The town restaurant owner had helpers shaving ice for cups of sweet tea, and the local gunsmith had his merchandise on display.

Other, more discreet business owners had browbeaten the council members into sponsoring an old fashioned ice cream social with an evening box supper and dance to entice town visitors into staying longer. Spirits in the area were low, and it was feared they'd be even lower after Friday.

Tali had planned to avoid the occasion since she knew members of all three ranch families and didn't want to witness their loss. But the official letter she'd received requested that she be in attendance on Friday at the Annon Courthouse for the private reading of Jeb Carter's will.

"I'll accompany you since I think it would be best to have a male presence with you. There will be more than a few ruffians roaming in town," Matthew had asserted.

Tali had mixed feelings about his new aggressive interest in their relationship. As he had been with River's letter, his actions now were again rather dictatorial. On the other hand, after years of tepid wooing, his boldness was almost a relief.

But for all his concern about attending the will reading with her, Matthew hadn't been available to drive her to Annon. He'd left in the early hours this morning in order to secure a spot in the auction tent.

Yesterday afternoon he'd stopped in the store and

asked Beth to relay the message. Since everyone would be in Annon for the day, Beth had decided to close the Isaca mercantile at noon and driven the store wagon to Tali's cottage, delivering Matthew's message and the offer of a ride to the courthouse there. They gossiped most of the way and arrived in Annon by mid-afternoon.

"I doubt that I'll stay for the dance, but it will give me a chance to stock up on supplies." Beth grinned at her, obviously excited to have a reprieve from store tending for an afternoon.

Although she'd previously considered Matthew's concern exaggerated, when Tali saw the crowded town, she was glad she and Beth had come together.

The stables were packed but Beth drove her wagon behind the town's general store and parked. "I told Abel to expect me for a pickup today. We'll leave the wagon here to be loaded." They unhitched the horse and led him to a stall in the shed across the alley from the store.

They entered the back of the Annon Mercantile to find the aisles overflowing with customers. Abel nodded at Beth and yelled, "Your supplies are crated and on the wood pallet back there."

Beside Tali, Beth nodded but led the way toward the front door anyway. "I'm going to see the sites. I'll stay with you until you get into the courthouse through all this mess."

Tali headed for the courthouse steps and sighted Mathew's tall lanky frame among other men loitering there. She needed only one look at Matthew's scowl to know he'd been unsuccessful in obtaining the properties he'd wanted.

"I'm not the only one upset that Lonigan stole all three parcels right out from under us."

"Surely not stolen," Tali protested. "He bid—"

"We thought we had enough to outbid him. He brought in outside money, had a promissory note to back up his offer. We couldn't scrape together the funds in time." Matthew's anger was palpable.

"What is he doing with all this land?" Tali asked.

"Nothing good, that's for sure. He now holds title to a third of the access points for water around here."

"No," Tali corrected him. "River owns the actual river front property. She allows access rights on all three of those ranches. Why would that change?"

"Explain that to Clement Tolbert. Hell he went belly-up waiting on your friend, River, to give him access."

That wasn't an accurate account of what happened, and Tali opened her mouth ready to set the record straight. But with the fevered expression Matthew now wore, she decided to leave it for another time. Arguing wouldn't fix anything.

A boisterous mix of bank representatives, their security guards, cowboys affected by the sale, and ranchers riled that more locals had gone under, all milled in surly groups on the courthouse steps.

Matthew held her arm and escorted her through the crowd, into the building, and to the designated meeting room.

•๑๑ ๑๑•

Kell turned from speaking to Horace Murdock in time to see Bodine escort Miss Fitzwilliam into a side room.

Good, me lass is here today. He frowned at Bodine's hand on her arm at the same time he planned what he'd say to her when they danced.

"I'll take care of the paperwork later," Murdock said, interrupting Kell's thoughts. "Right now, I have another matter to attend." He left Kell standing alone and entered the same room where Bodine and Miss Fitzwilliam had gone.

Kell's attention was pulled from wondering what kind of meeting the object of his lust was attending, to startled incredulities when he saw his brother Liam, accompanied by Jack Calloway, enter the courthouse.

Ignoring the foul names and rough shoves directed at him, he crossed the room to meet the two men.

"What in bluidy hell are ye doing here?" he asked Jack at the same time he swept Liam into a bear hug. "And did ye lose yer way to Henderson's fight?"

Jack's usual lazy grin appeared and he drawled, "Henderson bashed me on the head, tied me up, and threatened to do worse if I got loose before the fight."

"I found him in Henderson's closet, trussed up like a turkey and gagged. 'Twas tempting to leave him there, but since we made out like bandits," Liam paused to wave his hand at the courtroom, grinned, and added, "I set Handsome Jack free."

"And the two of you miscreants are here now because?" Kell asked.

"Family business," Jack said and frowned. "Maybe I'll see you later. Liam claims you're amassing a kingdom hereabouts. I'd enjoy hearing about it." Without further discussion, he left Liam with Kell and entered the same room Murdock, Bodine, and Miss Fitzwilliam now occupied.

Kell's attention was forced back to commerce when Clement Tolbert went berserk and attacked him with his fists.

"Leave off, ye gobshite fool," Kell ducked a blow from the other man and dodged in low, pinning this arms. "Murdock was supposed to tidy things with you. But since the bluidy lawyer's abandoned us, come with me."

"Find us a spare corner fer privacy," Kell snarled at Liam when he spied his brother lingering at the edge of the gathering crowd. "They'll be no fight today. Tolbert, Morgan, and Sinclair, ye'll join me for our talk and then I doona want to see ye the rest of the day."

Kell led the way to the room Liam found open and empty. He didn't waste time on niceties. As soon as the door was closed he began.

ﻭﻟﻖ ﺟﻖ

Tali felt almost grateful for the argument taking place beyond the judge's chambers. It gave her a chance to study the other people in the room since all eyes were trained on the thick, closed door. In spite of a ceiling fan stirring the air, the judge's chambers were stifling.

A lawyer, who had been introduced as Anthony Simmons, mopped his brow and shuffled his papers, looking nervously around, as if at any moment the author of the expletives on the other side of the door might somehow breach the entrance.

"Special Auction today," Horace Murdock, the county attorney explained. "Ranchers losing their land tend to be upset."

"The external court proceedings have nothing to do with our reason for being in Annon. We've arrived to hear the reading of Jeb's will. Get on with it," a well-dressed woman demanded from her chair on the other side of the room.

"Miss Fitzwilliam, Mrs. Carter, Mr. Carter, I believe we can begin." Mr. Simmons bowed awkwardly as he addressed each person.

Though Tali recognized the surname of the deceased, she remained puzzled about why she had been asked to attend. She felt reassured by Matthew's presence next to her and wished for a moment he'd take her hand. Instead, he sat ramrod straight on his chair, frowning at the noise from outside the room.

Discreet glances at the living Mr. Carter in attendance confirmed striking similarities between her features and his. This, plus the fact that she bore the middle name Carter, caused Tali to speculate that these people were cousins of her late mother, Cerise Fitzwilliam.

The two lawyers seemed at odds and Judge Stanley openly irritated. "Get on with things. My wife and daughter are waiting for me to get home and escort them to the ice cream social."

"With all due respect, Judge," Lawyer Simmons interrupted. "Mr. Murdock doesn't need to be present. This is a private family matter."

"As an officer of the county where property is being dispersed, I've been authorized to sit in on this meeting. Besides, I was a friend of both of the deceased."

When Horace Murdock claimed his right to remain, using the words *family matter* and *property,* Tali had an uneasy sense that more was going on than she understood.

"I daresay there were many men who knew Cerise Fitzwilliam *well.*" Mrs. Carter's tone left no doubt of her meaning.

"What an outrageous thing to say," Tali gasped in shock staring hard at the other woman.

"Your mother was once my…" she paused delicately and then continued, "Jeb Carter's mistress." She glared at Tali with ill concealed rage. "You are his bastard. Let us not try to wrap soiled goods in clean linen.

"But that's not true. My father died shortly after I was born. I've always lived here. I have no idea why you have come here today to make such slanderous accusations." Tali alternated between burning anger and chilled fear.

"We didn't meet today to engage in insults," Judge Stanley announced. "Get on with the matter at hand: the bequest for Miss Fitzwilliam."

Tali met Mr. Murdock's gaze. Her mother's attorney and friend looked grim as, without further prompting, the portion of the will pertaining to Tali was read.

"In trust for my daughter, Natalia Fitzwilliam, born of Cerise Fitzwilliam…" That stunning revelation blotted out much of the next part. When Tali focused on the reading again, the attorney was saying, "…leaving my daughter the house I provided for her mother to live in at the edge of the town of Isaca. With the deed to the house is to be included the plot of ground it sits upon, the water rights and other minerals beneath, and the land and trees that adjoin it extending to the river below."

Tall, spare, Cerise Fitzwilliam a light skirt? Her mother hadn't owned the cottage? Ridiculous. Tali tried to concentrate on the contents of the will but the information about her mother left her stunned and reeling. When the Carter's attorney stopped speaking, only two things seemed clear. Tali didn't own the cottage and never would unless she married.

Until then, Jeb Carter had provided money for her expenses and orders for his estate to pay the upkeep on the property. She could remain there as long as she lived in a chaste and respectable manner. *Only* if she married and lived with her husband was the deed to be signed over to her. That part made little sense to her. Mr. Simmons read the details aloud carefully.

"Only after my daughter marries and lives as a proper wife to her husband for a time no less than a year, shall she claim title to the river's edge property. If her husband chooses to live with her in her cottage, then at the end of a year, the title becomes hers. Likewise, should she live in a home provided by her husband, at the end of a year's time, the title will become hers. Once the property has been claimed, she may dispense with it as she chooses."

By the end of the meeting, Tali had discovered that her life had been built on a huge lie. Her mother had not been a widow, and her father was only recently dead. The irony of his requirement that she remain chaste and respectable in order to stay in the cottage until marriage didn't escape her.

Her head was pounding as Matthew escorted her from the courthouse. She regretted asking him to attend the meeting with her, since instead of lost cousins she'd met a sibling who no doubt despised her, and an outraged widow who wanted her gone from Texas if not dead.

"Miss Fitzwilliam." The lawyer representing Jeb Carter's family joined them as they reached the buggy. "The Carter family is contesting the will. If you want to avoid unpleasantness, they're offering a generous price to buy the property in question, on the condition of course that you leave the state."

"Not now, Mr. Simmons. Miss Fitzwilliam needs time to consider what's been revealed today." Thankfully, Mr. Murdock had walked her outside. While he engaged the other lawyer, deflecting attention from Tali, she was left staring at Jeb Carter, Jr., her half-brother.

"You look like me," he muttered. "Who would have thought the old man had it in him." His appraisal was more wonder than condemnation. Tali stared back at him.

"I assure you this is a mistake. My mother was not any man's mistress, my father died shortly after my birth, and..." His face, though bruised on the upper left cheek, was shaped like hers. His hair was the same shade of brown not quite black, as hers. His eyes, almond shaped and heavily fringed with dark lashes, were the same cerulean blue as hers.

Matthew's defection when he slipped away from Tali's side was insignificant next to her mother's betrayal. It was both incomprehensible and only too believable when she gazed at her own features worn by another.

Beth suddenly appeared at her side and took charge, guiding Tali away from the arguing attorneys and the brother she'd just met.

"Let's have a bowl of ice cream before we go home, Tali. Then we'll decide whether to stay for the dance or drive to Isaca."

Tali followed her friend gratefully. "Just get me away from here," she murmured. "Matthew has disappeared for the moment, and I have no inclination to suffer this crowd in order to find him. If it's not too much trouble, may I ride home with you later?" It wasn't what they'd planned. Tali had assumed Matthew would see her home.

"I'll be glad for the company," Beth agreed readily. "There will be plenty of people on the road to Isaca, and not all will be in a happy frame of mind. I was going to ask you to stay with me tonight, anyway."

Relief flooded Tali as she accepted the offer to stay overnight with Beth. At the moment, being alone tonight in her mother's cottage seemed impossible.

"I'll go home tomorrow after I've collected my wits." When Beth raised a questioning brow, Tali added quickly, "I really don't understand yet what just happened. When we get back to Isaca, maybe I'll have it sorted enough in my head to explain it all to you."

CHAPTER VI

*Spend your wealth before your enemy
spends it for you . . .*

*A*nnon business interests had predicted correctly. Instead of going home after the foreclosure sales, the monied bank representatives, security guards, lawyers, and their companions, lingered to watch scheduled afternoon races. By late day, the crowd had swelled in anticipation of the evening's entertainment, a blind auction featuring boxed suppers and a dance afterward.

While Tali had been in the courthouse, the big tent had been swept and decorated by the Annon Gardening Ladies, and the floor of the area had fresh sawdust covering the ground. The auctioneer's platform had beribboned boxes and colorful baskets, each numbered but otherwise anonymous, sitting side by side on the long table at the front of the stage.

At five o'clock, the auctioneer would start the second auction of the day, selling each boxed meal to the highest bidder. Tali thought that given the nature of his job earlier in the day, using the same man to preside over the evening's entertainment seemed in poor taste.

But, nobody quarreled with the choice since the proceeds from selling the boxed suppers went to the *Annon Drought Crisis Fund,* something anyone of the Annon citizens might need to tap into soon. Hopefully, the mood of the crowd would lighten when the afternoon's drama transitioned to evening fun, beginning with the picnic boxes and baskets being sold.

In theory, when a man tendered a bid on one of the boxes, he didn't know which woman had prepared it. Since buying the basket of food insured the man a companion during his meal, and also guaranteed him the first dance with her later in the evening, bidding was expected to be fierce.

But most single men didn't like buying a pig in a poke, or taking chances on who they'd be sharing a meal and dancing with later. Married men paid a minimum fee, all in a good cause, and purchased the baskets their wives had them carry in. Mistakes were rarely made since each participant decorated her box or basket lavishly and uniquely, whispering the secret of which was hers to the man of choice.

As she walked with Beth, she watched the crowd, rehearsing what she'd say to Matthew when he returned. She'd forgotten to tell him that her basket was adorned by a polka dot ribbon and matching napkin tucked over the contents.

During their meal together, they could discuss what to do about her cottage. Perhaps it would be best to accept the Carter's offer to buy her property since once wed, she'd live with Matthew.

She frowned. The offer had been conditioned on her leaving the state which she certainly had no intentions of doing. But then again, why give up her cottage when she could claim title to it after her first year of marriage. Her mother's marital state had nothing to do with her own. She focused on the conditions of the will because thinking about her mother brought too much anxiety and pain.

Beth spied an unoccupied bale of straw outside the big tent. It was on the fringe of the crowd but out of the main body of people. Tali hurried to it before someone else claimed it, sinking down on the rough seat to ponder her new circumstance.

When Matthew's mother spotted them and called to her, Tali waved her over.

"I'm so glad I saw you in the crowd. What a crush," Amelia murmured when she'd made her way to the temporary oasis of calm surrounding their bale of straw.

"Yes, I'm glad you found me. Somehow, Matthew and I got separated." Tali smiled and scooted closer to Beth, making room for the older woman.

"My, isn't it hot today?" Amelia fanned herself with a lace handkerchief and smiled benignly at them. "Beth, I'm sure I saw someone selling sweet tea. Be a dear and fetch me a glass." As soon as she'd sent Beth on her errand, Matthew's mother spread her kerchief over the rough straw and sat next to Tali, coming to the point immediately.

"My son has a future in politics in this state. I

approved a possible match with you long ago when I recognized the Carter in your name. Since the Carters are powerful people, if all had been well and your connections to the family legitimate…" she paused delicately than continued. "I'm afraid your current situation eliminates you from any possible future with Matthew. I'm sorry my dear. We wish you well." Without further discussion, Amelia gathered her reticule and departed.

Tali shivered in spite of the heat. Mrs. Bodine's conversation left her in no doubt others would also quickly see her in a less favorable light. She didn't realize she was twisting the polka dot napkin in her hands until words spoken in a lilting baritone interrupted her panic.

"Ye seem a bit distracted Miss Fitzwilliam. Might I be of assistance?"

Tali didn't realize how chilled she was until the sound of his voice blanketed her in warmth. She didn't intend to do more than smile. But when her gaze met his, her eyes welled, and she had to blink back tears.

"Come, walk with me," he said instantly, offering her his hand.

Without hesitation, she reached for him and let him draw her to her feet. He was a big man, not towering like some males, but wide of shoulder and all parts of him muscled strength. She'd often felt overwhelmed by taller men, even Matthew, but as soon as Tali laid her hand on

Mr. Lonigan's arm, he covered it with his big palm, and she felt protected.

They did not speak at first. He closed the space between them when they passed one boisterous group and did not open it again as they silently walked together, taking in the sights. Gradually, he guided her toward a more open area, past the tent, past the ice cream being churned, toward the one tree in the open field.

"Thank you." She halted and managed a small laugh. "I think I might be ruined. But if we sneak away to that tree over there, I know I will be."

Mr. Lonigan nodded and squeezed her hand as she withdrew it from its place on his arm. She immediately missed the contact. As if he understood, he turned to face her, standing at ease in a three-quarter-turn, protectively shielding her from the view of others.

"Now lass, explain to me this ruin." His mouth drew her attention as he spoke. He had a scar slashing from his nose to his top lip, not wide, but rather deep. Her eyes skated upward, touching the bruise on his left cheek.

"You've been hurt," she murmured.

"Nay, I've been hit, 'tis a difference. But I'm scarred for certain. Do ye find me scary, battered as I am?"

It was a mistake to meet his gaze. His expression, so gentle, almost tender, made her want to weep all over again.

"Of course you don't frighten me." She frowned at the idea.

"Then what ails ye lass? Have ye learned ye are to be dead by the morrow?"

"No."

"Then Postmistress Beth has decided yer no longer her friend." He shook his head and gave her a stern look. "I'll speak with Mistress Beth and—"

"You're being ridiculous. Of course Beth and I are still friends," Tali interrupted him but he swerved right into another suggested disaster.

"Ye've invested your funds in a scurrilous business and now yer pockets are all to let?" His recital of one dramatic possibility after another in an exaggerated brogue had her trying to decipher words and meanings and laughing when she did. He finally ended his litany of foolishness and waited.

That quickly she remembered the afternoon's incredible revelations, swallowed a sob, and stared at his chest trying to compose herself.

He tilted her chin, forcing her to meet his gaze once more. "Will ye no' trust me lass?"

ॐ

The poor lass had had some kind of shock for certain. Kell wanted to haul her into his arms and cuddle her to his chest. Instead, he walked beside her, coaxing her to tell her story.

"Me mum would say ye need to share yer misery and lessen the load."

She winced at his words, apparently not wanting to hear about his mother. But then she asked, "Is your mother still living?"

"Nay, Liam and me lost both da and her before we set out for this land."

"How old were you?"

"Hmmm." He had to stop and think a bit. "'Twas no more than a decade ago, and I already a man."

"Why did you leave your home?"

"'Twas no' future there for Liam and me," he told her, feeling the familiar wash of bitter regret.

"And who is Liam?"

"Me brother, and hard-headed as a brick he is," he said gruffly, realizing that she'd turned the tables and was interrogating him.

"If we look sharp, we might see him. He arrived earlier in the day and then disappeared." Kell resettled her hand on his arm, managing to narrow the space between them at the same time.

It wasn't his brother that his gaze encountered when he cast it over the crowd. Matthew Bodine glared balefully at him from where he stood outside the tent.

"I think yer friend is not pleased to see ye on me arm," he murmured. "Ye dinna say what lad ye've fixed yer future with when we last spoke. Might it be yon, Bodine?"

"No," she answered quickly. "Matthew and I are no more than friends." Her grip tightened on his arm, but she gave no other indication that she cared a whit for the other man.

Kell had managed to lead her to a less populated area and again stopped and faced her. "Then, if no' Bodine, who?"

"What difference does it make?" she said sharply, her smile changing to a frown.

Because I've set me sights on ye, lass. "I wouldna want to get in the way of another man's courting," he lied smoothly. As a matter of fact, he intended to warn off any other contender who planned to, might be thinking about, or had ever in the past shown interest, in Miss Fitzwilliam. *I plan to wed ye before another can steal ye away.*

"I was wrong to imply otherwise in our earlier conversation. There is no one courting me, Mr. Lonigan." He wasn't sure who was more affected by this declaration—himself—or the lovely colleen with flushed cheeks and trembling lips.

I was right. Some gobshite arse has toyed with her affections. Mayhap this calls for a bold move. Anything to erase the woebegone look in her eyes. "Well, nay, that's no' quite the case. I'm greatly interested in pursuing your acquaintance, lass."

Without realizing it, he settled into a fighting stance, fists clenched, waiting to parry the coming verbal blow. Breath squeezed through his constricted lungs and he resisted the urge to loosen his tie.

This will be where she tells me I'm no' fit to carry her hem. He tilted his head, rolling his shoulders a bit to ease the strain. Vertebrae stretched against muscles as he flexed his neck and the subject of his insane desire flinched at the cracking sound.

"Mr. Lonigan, are you all right?"

"Kellan," he said wanting to hear her speak his name. "I was christened Kellan Aloysius Lonigan; birthed by parents Adele O'Shay Lonigan and Kevin Riley Lonigan. I wish to include me brother in our household until he has sense to be on his own."

He stopped his recitation to draw breath, waiting hopefully for her to say something. When she didn't so much as blink, he added, "I am thirty-two and financially able to care for a wife and bairns if we should be so blessed."

.യ ഇൈ.

He was serious. He'd met her only once before, walked her around the grounds of the social today, and then proposed.

At the time, she hadn't agreed with the phrase *bull of a man* that Laura Styles had used to describe the pugilist. Now, observing his clenched fists and belligerent stance, Tali changed her mind.

What does one say to an erstwhile suitor who pops the question amidst a teeming crowd? She was saved from answering when Beth arrived.

"Tali, I'm not feeling well. I'd like to—"

"Yes, of course," Tali interrupted. "We need to get you home." Thank goodness she had something to focus on besides the fire-breathing dragon standing before her.

"I'll help ye ladies to yer buggy then. I would no' want ye to feel any more distress Postmistress Beth." Lonigan nodded as if things were settled between them, took Tali's arm again, and offered Beth his other.

The three of them walked arm-in-arm to the stables where Beth had left the horse and store wagon. It wasn't elegant, but Tali was inordinately happy to see the old conveyance. Their escort lifted Beth to the seat, and then before Tali could scramble up, he wrapped his big hands around her waist and stared down at her.

"I've no' forgotten our discussion. I'll be visiting ye lass. When might be a good time for our next words?"

She had the awful feeling that if she didn't give him a concrete time, he might simply hold onto her and not let her leave. His hands remained settled around her middle and his heat seeped through her dress, warming her body beneath her clothes.

"Mr. Lonigan," she whispered in a husky voice she barely recognized. "Beth is ill and we need to be on our way."

"Me name's Kellan. I'd be pleased if ye'd try saying it, lass. And, aye, ye'll be on yer way as soon as ye give me a day to come calling on ye."

"Tomorrow," Beth unexpectedly answered. "She'll

be at the store with me. Now we really have to go." Tali's usually amiable friend wore a fierce expression and had already taken up the reins.

"Tomorrow it is then, ladies. And do no' think I've forgotten ye both owe me a dance," he said, swinging Tali to the seat and relinquishing his hold on her.

"Hang on," Beth muttered and slapped the reins against the horse's rump, setting a fast pace for home.

Had Tali not clung to the wooden bench, she might easily have bounced from her perch. Beth urged the store horse into a fast pace and they sped from Annon as if the hounds of hell were chasing them.

Glancing over her shoulder for a last look at Mr. Lonigan, she saw that he'd been joined by two other men. All three stood watching as she and Beth drove away. One of them, Tali's newly discovered brother, wore a pensive expression as he stared at their retreating backs.

After asking Beth if she should take over the reins and being rebuffed, Tali sank into her own thoughts on the ride back to Isaca. The day had been one horrible nightmare after another—until Mr. Lonigan had come to her rescue. Somehow, that leavened the Carter family's insults, Matthew's treachery, and Mrs. Bodine's practical application of the rules of society.

Kellan is completely unacceptable as a beau, of course. She tested his name in her mind and found it pleasing. *But, how flattering his attentions were to my bruised ego.*

She smiled, remembering his clenched fists, pugilistic stance and determined stare. *I believe I frighten him.*

Her thought entertained her until they reached Isaca where she helped Beth stable the horse. Before they left the barn, Beth stood in the darkened interior and peered outside.

"Are you hiding from someone?" Tali asked. Her friend seemed more upset than ill.

"Of course not." But when they left the building, Beth's usual saunter had changed to rapid strides that left Tali racing to keep up.

Once inside, Beth seemed almost to collapse with fatigue. "I'm sorry Tali. I just feel terrible. I need to lie down." She retreated to her bedroom, brought out a blanket and sheet, and left Tali in the sitting room alone the rest of the night.

She didn't expect to rest, but fell asleep immediately. It was early the next morning when Beth woke her.

"If you intend to avoid Mr. Lonigan, we need to get you home now before he shows up at the store. I have deliveries out past your way, so I'll put the sign in the door to let customers know I'll be late."

After Tali hurried into her clothes and followed Beth, she was surprised to see that her friend had already hitched the horse, loaded the wagon, and was ready to make her deliveries.

Tali looked forward eagerly to returning to the comfort of her own home. She was certain that once there, she'd be able to calmly think through the events of the previous day and make sense of them.

When they rounded the curve in the road and Beth stopped the wagon in front of Tali's cottage, she hugged her friend and jumped from the bench to the ground. It was then she saw splashes of red on her porch and read the one word written on her front door—*whore*.

CHAPTER VII

Even a small thorn causes festering . . .

"Who would do such a thing?" Tali gasped.

"Tali, get back in the wagon. There's no way you're going into that house alone."

"I'm not alone. You're with me," she answered grimly. Suddenly, all the chaos of the past twenty-four hours coalesced into rage. "And I know you carry a shotgun under the wagon seat. I would like to borrow it, so I'm armed when I go inside and investigate."

"Alrighty, then, here we go," Beth murmured and jumped from the wagon, handing Tali a rifle and keeping the shotgun for herself.

The red proved to be paint, still tacky to the touch which meant the vandals had visited sometime during the night. The front door was still locked and after Tali fumbled with the key and entered her home, nothing inside appeared to have been touched.

She and Beth searched each of the five rooms carefully, locking the front door behind them as they traveled through the house. Tali breathed a sigh of relief to see that the kitchen door was still secured. But when she and Beth continued to the back porch overlooking her mother's garden, they saw the rest of the damage.

The swing where she and her mother had spent so many beautiful moments together had been smashed into pieces. The backyard was littered with its broken slats, shards from broken clay pots, and the dying remains of uprooted flowers. More red paint coated the larger bushes and plants.

"If we had a sheriff in town, I'd drive in and report this but…" Beth's expression of horror mirrored Tali's.

"I'll deal with the flowers later. Right now, I need to scrub the front porch," Tali said, shoving aside her fear to deal with the immediate problem. "I can't let other people see this. It's disgusting."

"But whoever did this could still be around," Beth said.

"Then I'll shoot them if they come back." Tali's mother had kept a rifle in the corner of the kitchen pantry but couldn't remember ever having seen it used. "Mama's varmint gun will work just fine."

Tali filled a bucket with water and Beth followed her to the front of the house. They propped their rifles on the front porch and spent the next hour scraping and scrubbing the filth from the door. Though most of the paint came off, it left a pink stain behind.

"Do you still have tins of paint at the store?" Tali finally quit trying to erase the remnants and admitted she'd have to cover it with a new coat of white.

"Yes. And I'm late, late, late. I won't be able to make the deliveries now. I need to get the store open." Beth tried to persuade Tali to return to Isaca with her, but she refused.

"I'm not leaving. Whoever did this might come again."

"Exactly," Beth answered wryly. "Lock yourself in the house, and I'll find someone in Isaca to deliver the paint. Meanwhile, we'll have to report it to the Annon sheriff if we want anything done about it."

The chances were very slim that the vandals would ever be caught. Tali thought of the fouled backyard still waiting to be faced.

"Send a message to the Annon sheriff if anyone is going that way today. But more importantly, send paint."

After Beth had gone, Tali continued her futile efforts to remove the red stains marring the once beautiful front door. Try as she might, she couldn't erase the outline of the word *whore.*

She was still scrubbing the porch with soap and a rag and hadn't worked up the courage to face the damaged back yard when she heard the creak of a wagon as it rounded the bend in the road. Hastily, she stood and grabbed the rifle.

๑๑ ๑๑

"'Tis paint I've brought ye, lass. But it looks to me as though ye need a strong arm to help ye set yer place to rights." Kell hid his anger at the mess before him.

The bonny Miss Fitzwilliam stood before her front door, her hair loosened from its usual tame coiffure and curling in tendrils around her face. In her arms she cradled a rifle, which at the moment was pointed at him.

"How did you know...why are you here?" she stammered but he was happy to see her remove her finger from the trigger and lower the gun.

"Yer friend Beth sent me to assist. She tells me that while ye enjoyed a night at her abode, yer house suffered a crime." He picked up the bucket of paint and assorted brushes the store clerk had bundled for him and eased from the wagon to the ground.

"Would ye let me help ye, lass?"

She nibbled her bottom lip uncertainly, clearly bollixed by the attack on her property. When she nodded assent, he carried the paint to the porch. Closer inspection showed him that her hands were reddened and chapped from the work she'd already performed.

And, although she'd made a valiant attempt to obliterate it, Kell could still read the foul word that had been written on her door. Unexpected fury made him clench his fists, and he could see it wasn't sympathy but a protector she needed.

"I'd rather others not know what was written there," she murmured as he stared at the word.

"Doona fash yerself, lass. A bit of paint will cover the insult and the word will be as never there." Matching his actions to his promise, he pried the lid from the tin of paint and stirred it to creamy perfection.

You'll get paint on your good clothes," she warned him.

"Nay, 'tis a careful man I am. Ye'll see." Before she could protest more, Kell shrugged from his suit coat and rolled up the sleeves of his shirt.

She held her brush ready, and before he'd even stepped back, she'd filled it with paint and attacked the door. He dabbed a second brush in the bucket and then took his place by her side.

They worked silently, erasing the pink remnants of violence and restoring the porch to pristine white. When they were finished, he recapped the left-over paint, and she cleaned the brushes.

With that completed, he had no further excuse to linger. He looked at the paint spatters on his hands and grinned wryly. "I dinna soil my suit but I canna say the same for me hands. Might ye have a pump in the back I could use for a good wash?"

"Yes," she whispered. Her pleased smile at the improved porch disappeared, replaced by angry sorrow. "I don't want to start there yet, but you'll find a pump by the back flower bed."

She ushered the way around the porch, following a path to the back of the cottage. Once there she stalled as if she couldn't go on.

For the love of all things holy, when he saw the retched condition of what had once obviously been a small piece of heaven, he wanted to pound someone into the ground. But she needed bracing, not bellicosity.

"Well now. 'Tis good I haven't rolled down me

sleeves quite yet." Not waiting for her permission, he strode into the backyard and began picking up pieces of broken flower pots and removing the other signs of devastation.

"When you're finished, would you like some tea?" she asked, this time not jumping into help. She'd radiated anger while slapping paint on the front porch, but this despoilment had violated her spirit, far exceeding the hurt inflicted by the front door slander. This had the lovely woman so white-faced he feared she might swoon.

"A spot of tea would be grand," he agreed.

Without further words, she took herself off, presumably to the kitchen. He continued piling the loose debris next to a compost pile. The uprooted flowers he had no knowledge of how to treat. But he was certain that leaving their roots to fry under the increasing heat of the sun could not be a wise thing.

So, when he came upon any plants with roots still intact, he carried them to the shade by the small pool to wet them. The water itself had been fouled with more paint, as had the rose bushes and holly hedge that bordered it.

Kell was glad the lass didn't return to the yard while he worked. It was a nasty act of cruelty that had been wrought upon her. After he'd skimmed the oily paint from the water's surface and scrubbed the interior's rock sides, nature joined with him to clear the tiny pool. It seemed to be fed by an artesian well, because once the weight of the oily paint was removed, the surface rippled and began to regain its clarity.

Standing at the back of the yard, he took a moment to study the overgrown path that meandered down the slope to the river below. Oddly enough, he'd taken his morning run along the lower course many times, never knowing that Miss Fitzwilliam resided on the bluff above. The grass and weeds sprouting from the trail downward didn't look as if they had been trod upon, but he marked the access as a weakness in her defense.

By the time he heard the slam of the backdoor, he'd set most things right. But nothing could disguise the plants torn asunder or the swing missing from the porch. When he'd carried the broken rails and slats to the throw away pile, he'd understood what they'd once been.

Back and forth, gliding up and down... His groin tightened as he pictured Natalia swinging gently on her porch surrounded with the sweet scents still clinging to the air.

"I've brought your tea," she announced, interrupting his lascivious thoughts.

He crossed to the porch where she'd set two straight back chairs, a small wooden table holding two glasses, and a plate covered with a polka dot napkin.

She must have seen his expression change, though he'd tried to disguise his grimace. He didn't have a taste for the cold brew served locally.

"You don't care for tea?" she asked.

"Aye, I like a cuppa in the afternoon. Hot, ye understand. Perhaps a dollop of cream to cool it a bit and a wee sprinkle of sugar. Nothing more. But 'tis fine what ye've provided," he assured her and sat down on a chair, picked up the glass, and chugged its contents.

Kell felt a niggle of concern when her head tilted sideways and she viewed him as something she'd never seen before.

"Lass, did I offend?"

"No, I find the sound of your voice very musical, but sometimes it takes me a moment to be certain what you've said." And bluidy hell didn't she go and flash him one of her wondrous smiles and the unruly piece of flesh between his legs sprang to life—again.

"Aye, ye'll ken the way of me speech as we progress," he assured her, easing the napkin from the table. "Ah, biscuits," he murmured and nonchalantly laid the polka dotted cloth across his lap before helping himself to her offering on the plate.

"We call them cookies," she answered.

"So yer skilled in culinary arts as well as being so bonny," he bit into the flakey dessert with relish.

"Not really," she answered. "My mother said this recipe for sugar drops is infallible." At the mention of her mother, the companionable moment ended. She frowned and closed her eyes.

Kell could see her knuckles turn white as she clenched her fingers together. The poor colleen needed to have a change of thoughts. He offered a taunt to get her attention.

"I have cause to differ with yer opinion when it concerns yer food, lass." He consumed the last chunk of biscuit, chewing it thoroughly, and openly savoring it before he brushed his hands and smiled at her. "A point of complaint I have though. Ye've promised me a dance which yet remains uncollected."

"I couldn't stay. I.I..." Her lips trembled as she spoke and her voice, always husky, became a broken whisper.

Kell wanted to scoop her from her chair, hold her on his lap, and make all of her troubles go away.

"Enough of yer silent misery. 'Tis time to share with me what has happened. Oh, I can see some terrible miscreant has invaded yer private bower. But methinks there's more afoot to yer troubles than that. Tell me."

His frustration rendered him blustery. His voice, even to his own ears, was gruff. If she wondered at his audacity in making such a demand, she didn't say as much. Instead, she drew a deep breath and began her story.

"My mother was a pillar of society. I've always thought that such an inelegant description of an honorable person, but in Mama's case, it was apt." She began the telling in an anguished voice that changed to reminiscence as she spoke.

"And do you favor her in your looks?" he asked,

expecting her to extol her mother's beauty. Instead, her lovely smile showed itself and she shook her head.

"Mama was very tall and very thin. Her hair, when she was younger, was light brown. She always called it dishwater blonde. As she grew older, she'd begun to get silver in her hair."

"And did this cause her distress?"

"Not at all," Tali said quickly. "She claimed white hair would make her look venerable. Mama had a peculiar sense of humor."

"Then, I conclude that ye, Miss Natalia Fitzwilliam must take after yer da'," he stated the obvious, saying her full name and edging closer to being less formal.

Anger flashed in her eyes, and she fair snarled, "I wouldn't know. I thought he was dead. Well, I guess he is now. But my mother told me that he'd died right after I was born." She calmed enough to relate the events of the will reading the day before, finally ending the telling with a sigh.

"It appears I didn't know my mother at all. It was a shock. I can't believe it. If you had met my mother even once, you would understand how bizarre this claim is. I keep thinking they've confused me with someone else."

"If there's no real evidence to the contrary, lass, perhaps they have."

"I have a brother," she stated baldly. "We look very much alike." She paused and then continued. "You evidently know him. His name is Jack. He was standing with you when Beth and I drove home."

"Jack Calloway is yer brother?" Kell said, startled by the idea, and yet, as soon as she mentioned Jack, Kell saw the resemblance: same eyes, hair color, bone structure, nose, though Jack's had been broken more than once.

Shite, they look enough alike to be twins. Kell could see why she seemed confused. To be presented with evidence of her mother's falsehoods and a brother ta boot seemed enough to set most on their arse.

"He was presented to me as Jeb Carter, Jr. but their family attorney did call him Jack when he spoke to him."

"And this brother ye've had thrust upon ye, what age would he be?"

"I have no idea. You must understand, I've never seen him before today."

Kell tucked that information away to be investigated as soon as he caught up with the rowdy brawler he knew as Handsome Jack. "Might there be a question of ye inheriting a wee bit more than this cottage?"

"Mr. Murdock was there. If that were the case he…" Her eyebrows went up at the notion, but her frown told him she was at least thinking.

He recognized it had been an indelicate question to be asking. But bluidy hell, someone had just broadsided the lass's domain. Things needed to be sorted out.

"Apparently, I haven't inherited this cottage as much as I'm being allowed to continue to live here until I'm wed. Of course there were all kinds of ridiculous conditions put on even that."

"Doona fash yerself about it. In due course, ye'll unravel these mysteries. The question that comes to me is, where will ye be staying now that yer home is no longer safe?"

"This is my home, and this is where I'll be," she said tartly, rejecting his suggestion that she leave her cottage.

"Well then, will Miss Beth or another trusted friend be staying with ye?"

"Beth can't. It wouldn't be practical since she lives in rooms over the mercantile, so she can open the store early."

"And another?"

"There is no one else I'd ask." Her eyes held a militant gleam as she stared back at him.

"I doona approve of yer plan to stay alone." Kell delivered his opinion and crossed his arms, ready to argue if necessary. Only after he'd made his declaration, he remembered he had no standing at all in her life, and she might whack him over the head for his temerity.

"I appreciate your concern and all of your help today, Mr. Lonigan. I'm sure I'll manage fine. I don't expect more trouble. Perhaps it was no more than vandals playing a prank because I wasn't home."

"And if ye had been here?" he asked, incredulous at her words.

"I would have shot them," she answered. "And if

they come back, I'll be ready."

"Lass, ye've no' got a battalion of men to protect ye here, and yer cottage doesna sit so close ta town that others might hear yer distress." He fair stuttered over the words, worry making his speech thick as he tried to convey the danger she invited by remaining unprotected in her home.

"I will be fine." She stood, clearly signaling that their interlude had ended.

Unsettled but determined to find a way to insure her safety, Kell finally left. His own house was not so far away that he couldn't travel there, talk to his brother, and still return by nightfall to guard the cottage, whether Miss Fitzwilliam—*who wouldn't call him by his given name*—approved or not.

He'd worked security with Edge Grayson many a time and knew the ins and outs of protecting someone. And now, whether Miss Fitzwilliam knew it or not, she'd have a professional guard who would not let her face peril alone.

The truth was, he'd been at a loss at how to proceed with his future, which for the first time in his memory, offered choices. He'd hung his punching bag from the barn rafters, using it to keep fit, while he mulled over possible businesses, knowing that he'd never climb into a boxing ring again.

When he worked out, he couldn't help but notice the fine quality of his barn, which had led him to consider how to make money using the buildings on the place, more than the land he now owned.

He had no skills in ranching, but his short stay in his newly acquired house had confirmed in his mind that he had a fondness for the quiet of the place. And that was all before he'd ever set eyes on the lass; after that he'd lost all thought of moving on.

Kell grinned, his mood lightened as he drove back to Isaca. He stopped in the store to inform Beth of Natalia's plan to stay alone, and conveyed his disapproval of that idea. Then, he returned to the ranch, hoping to find his brother there.

CHAPTER VIII

---❖---

Fear is worse than fighting . . .

*T*he devastation in the backyard had to be dealt with but, after Mr. Lonigan departed, Tali retreated to the interior of her home. Once there, the emptiness she found proved even more depressing. She wandered from room to room viewing each place as if she'd not lived there her entire life.

The couch, resplendent in velvet, the ornate back made from carved and laminated rosewood, was a Rococo Revival sofa by John Henry Belter, its solid understructure, varnished chestnut. It had been terribly expensive when purchased, but that had been twenty years before. She knew this because her mother had told her so. Cerise had taught her daughter the practicality of investing in quality furniture that would age well.

The large antique French armoire standing with imposing elegance in the cottage foyer, also represented an acquisition of great cost. The fine English Bone China and sterling silver cutlery stored inside were antique, unflawed, and equally priceless.

Her focused review of the contents of the cottage confirmed their circumspect affluence. Tali had never questioned her mother about the source of her funds, assuming that her late father's estate had provided the money for all of the luxury.

Now it would seem, though provided by my father grudgingly, they are my funds. She grimaced, embarrassed at the churlish tone of her sire in his will. He'd clearly resented her existence and taken one last opportunity, albeit from the grave, to express his disdain. She'd grown to womanhood believing her father a loving man who would have cherished her had he lived.

The events of yesterday had dispelled that childish fiction. And, she admitted it had been her own. Her mother simply had not discussed Tali's father other than to smile when he was mentioned and move the conversation in another direction.

Tali turned slowly, eyeing the Queen Ann leg desk in the corner. Memories flooded her. Not long before her mother's death, Tali had expressed impatience at Beth's loyalty to her deceased husband. Cerise had looked up from doing the monthly accounts and reprimanded her.

"There is no measure to love. Not even death can stop eternal devotion. To think that is foolish."

"Is that how it was with my father?" Tali had asked. The romantic notion seemed foreign to her mother's dry humor and usual acerbic wit.

"In a way, I suppose." Her mother had pushed her reading glasses higher on her nose and looked thoughtful. "It's hard for you to imagine, I'm sure, but your father captured my heart. Just as Beth still cares for her lost husband, after your father was gone, I remained faithful to his memory." But she'd waved away more conversation, returning to her accounting journal and ignoring Tali's pleas to tell her more.

To escape the house that had once been her sanctuary but had now become the author of more torment, Tali returned to the ravished garden. It was when she discovered the salvaged plants by the rock pool, that she found relief from despair.

The stone basin of water had been scrubbed, not a speck of red paint left to be seen. The crevices through which the water fed, burped liquid that was never pure enough to drink but usually ran clear. The gentle draw and infusion below spread ripples across the surface. Ravaged foliage lay on the flat rock behind the tiny pond, the plants had been separated, stacked atop each other, and the roots carefully wrapped in her linen napkins after they'd been thoroughly wet.

Tali frowned. One of the scraps of linen had been over the plate of cookies she'd served Mr. Lonigan. The other she'd taken to the auction the day before. The bright polka dots embroidered in a whimsy pattern on each corner of the cloth made it easily identifiable. Of course, she'd tied a more flamboyant ribbon matching the bright colors on the basket handle. Her message had been received, but the recipient unexpected.

Tali pondered that thought. After Amelia Bodine's *te-ta-te* with her, she'd had no illusions. Even had she stayed for the auction, Matthew wouldn't have been the man enjoying her fried chicken and peach cobbler surprise.

"At least my basket wasn't sitting woebegone and lonely at the end of the sale, testifying to my unwanted status."

But I'm not unwanted, her mind whispered. *Mr. Lonigan is… Different? Disturbing?* She chewed her bottom lip, distracted by trying to find the appropriate description.

He's sees everything. She pictured his piercing glance given from gray eyes so light in color they appeared silver. Tali shivered, recognizing the dissonance between the Irishman's affable smile and predatory gaze.

Matthew despises him. Tali's jaw hurt from gritting her teeth. The thought of Matthew made her wince. At the moment, her former beau's loathing almost acted as a recommendation for Mr. Lonigan.

He said he had reason to know I'm a good cook. A smile curved her lips, and her mood changed as she thought of Kellan buying her box supper.

"That public demonstration of his interest will set the gossips ablaze," she murmured. "Never mind that he remains determined that I'll address him by his given name. He is polite and incredibly gentle for being so…"

Tali paused, searching for the correct word to describe Mr. Lonigan. She didn't quite know how to define the aura of potent sexuality and power surrounding him. When it came to her, she swallowed nervously and then said it aloud.

"Virile." He gave the appearance of being temperate and calm, at the same time his visage was battered, and he exuded male dominance.

Objectively, she numbered his scars: one on his forehead, evidence of a deep gash once cutting through the eyebrow itself; a second on his left cheek, small, more akin to a dent; right ear torn; jagged mark on his jaw; an obviously recent split lip; and a faint scar above his mouth that traced a white line to his nostril.

His nose... She sighed, wondering how many times its broad expanse had been broken.

"The scars on the back of his hands count at least twenty more marks left by brutality," she said aloud. But instead of being repelled, she was fascinated. On their first meeting, the brush of his calloused knuckles across her cheek had roused her in some inexplicable way.

"And he is persistent. 'Me name is Kellan Aloysius Lonigan'," she murmured, mocking his brogue. Yet there was something quite thrilling about Lonigan. She pictured the Irishman with his sleeves rolled high and the corded muscles in his arms on display.

The memory distracted her from the debris she'd watched him remove from her yard. She'd stared through the kitchen window, admiring the flex of his thighs as he'd bent over the compost pile. Tali moistened her lips. The memory of how his trousers had drawn taut across his rump rendered her mouth dry and her throat constricted.

Inhaling, she imagined she could smell Kell Lonigan's scent, mingling with the exotic fragrance of jasmine. She likened it to a mix of maple candy and crisp, autumn air with a large dash of male musk added.

A flush of heat that had nothing to do with the sun surged through her. Uneasily, she fled back to the house to escape the tantalizing aroma.

"I'll replant you when it's cooler this evening," she promised the uprooted foliage, carrying them to the porch and laying them in the shade.

⋆·❦·⋆

It was nearing dark when Kell followed the trail that led to the riverbank below Tali's house. The cat ran ahead, having insisted on accompanying his friend, the horse. Once Kell had situated the horse, leaving it comfortably contented with nosebag on and saddle loosened, he carried his rifle with him as he climbed the slope to Tali's backyard. The cat disappeared, probably to hunt grizzly bear.

The beast was a terrible thing. More than once, the snarling ball of ragged fur had swiped his claws across Kell's hand, or leg, or whatever appendage presented a likely target.

The animal often crouched in the hay mow of the

barn, watching Kell fight the punching bag he'd strung from the rafters. Kell had feared an attack more than once when the monster stalked across the high beams, presumably trying to decide if he could strike a killing blow from above.

The cat was long gone by the time Kell reached the copse of trees behind *her* house. He had problems saying Natalia, her given name, not having been given permission to use it. But thinking of her as Miss Fitzwilliam was impossible.

His plans included changing her last name as quickly as possible. She was too fine a lassie to bear the scourge of such an English sound. No daughter of Ireland had ever had more beautiful features, lovely voice, or sweet innocence. Meeting her had acted as an aphrodisiac on his soul.

Not that it was attendance on his spirit that drove his interest. His cock had proven rowdy, stirred to desire by her comeliness, each time Kell had seen her.

Natalia was much too fine for the likes of him, but then again, he owned property when others were losing theirs and she had been delivered a mighty blow that set her world a kilter; stranger things had happened.

Ye'll never plough a field by turning it over in yer mind, lad, he chastised his self doubt, studying the house, looking for intruders or signs of discord as he got comfortable and thought of ways to win his heart's desire. And then, he saw the cat. The beast stalked across the yard and jumped on her porch, then onto the seat of one of the chairs she'd brought earlier.

Kell clenched his fists, ready to strangle the monster and be done with him. But he couldn't call him, or fetch him. It occurred to him that the object of his desire would think he was a *fecking pervert* if she found him loitering in her backyard.

The cat stared through the night, its beady gaze fixed on the spot where Kell knelt in the weeds. *I'm on watch. Protecting the lass ye bluidy beast.*

Arrogantly, the mangy feline jumped from his perch, thumping loudly against the floor when he landed. Kell tensed when the backdoor swung open.

"I have a gun, and I'll shoot if you—" She stared at the furred monster and lowered the rifle. "Why hello."

Kneeling on the porch, she held out her hand. "Here kitty, kitty, kitty."

No, no, no... Kell prepared to charge to her rescue, praying she wouldn't lose her arm to the ferocious bastard. But his lunge toward the porch was stalled when the treacherous devil strutted to her, ducked his head under her hand, and began to purr. Kell could hear the miscreant's rumbled pleasure all the way to the trees.

It's pretending to be civilized, he is. Just to cop a feel. Indignantly, Kell watched the crazed wild cat he knew so well, pretend to be a tame tabby, winding himself around her ankles, arching his back against her skirts, and purring so loudly the good citizens of Isaca could probably hear.

"You sweet thing. You must be hungry." Natalia gave him a pat on the head and retreated into her house, no doubt to fetch a meal for the miserable sod.

While she was absent from the porch, the bluidy fool jumped back on the chair and commenced grooming himself, pausing now and then to cast a smug look in Kell's direction.

Sure enough, it wasn't more than a few moments before Natalia reemerged carrying a saucer.

"For you," she said and set it on the floor by the chair. "I crumbled some bread and soaked it in the warm milk. You do like milk don't you?" she asked, as if she expected an answer.

Obligingly, the wicked pretender jumped back to the porch, sniffed the offering, and then began to lap.

Natalia sat down on one of the chairs and proceeded to observe her guest dine on the fine meal. Kell's stomach growled. He hadn't taken the time to sup before he'd hurried back to protect her. As a matter of fact, he hadn't eaten since he and Liam had shared the contents of her box supper the night before.

After she and her friend, Beth, had departed, Kell attended the basket sale. When he'd seen Natalia in the courthouse, she'd worn a perky white kerchief with colorful dots peeking from her pocket. He'd questioned Horace, and the old attorney had explained how the box supper worked.

Armed with the image of polka dots, Kell had inspected the baskets before the sale, discovered that number eight wore a polka dot ribbon on its handle, and bribed the auctioneer to switch the number to one. When the sale had begun, he'd shouldered his way to the front and commandeered the event.

"Twenty dollars I'll give ye," he'd growled loud enough for the auctioneer's ears. Kell had known the amount was a bit high. He'd meant to dissuade his rival, whoever he might be, from bidding and secure the basket for himself with no falderal.

She'd said they were only friends, but from the way Bodine had glowered when he'd seen Natalia and Kell together, Kell thought there was more than friendship between them.

Bodine was an arse, not worthy of River Grayson's sweet friend. Kell contented himself with luring her attentions from the miscreant, knowing that he was doing her a service. Though, he had a sinking feeling that he'd made a right gom of himself, hanging onto her until the last before she departed from the Annon fray.

Bluidy hell, his brain was banjaxed beyond all help. He hadn't a clear thought in his head since he'd first set eyes on her lovely face. Holding her arm as they'd strolled through the festivities had been heaven, but he'd felt desolate, yearning for more of her company as soon as she'd gone.

After he'd secured the basket, he'd hunted until he'd

located Liam hanging around the horse barn and left the festivities with his brother to return to their house. Once there, it had given him great pleasure to introduce Liam to their grand estate.

Together, they'd inspected the property, or as much as could be seen that late at night. He'd held a lantern aloft and proudly pointed out the solid structure of the barn and the sturdy fence ringing the paddock. They'd walk the land another day.

Liam seemed unimpressed with the acquisition until he learned that Kell considered them partners in the enterprise. Immediately, his brother had become animated and eager to liquidate their asset.

"This must be worth a pretty penny. I heard the amounts you paid today on the three parcels you've newly obtained." Liam's enthusiasm had carried them into the house, to the makeshift bench Kell had rigged. They sat side by side on a moldy bale of hay retrieved from the barn and inspected the contents of the basket together.

"I was no more than an agent acting for another who could no' attend," Kell had explained. "And aye, someday I ken this land that we do have will be worth even more. 'Tis the lack of rain that's driven it ta auction. Mark it well, Liam, the same fate that ended the good fortune of the previous owner, has blessed us with this chance."

"All the better to let someone else share in the gift.

The person we sell to will reap the bounty of future rain. But even so, now, the money the land brings us is all profit. As soon as we sell, privately if you think that best, then we can move on."

"'Tis a bluidy politician ye've become, lad, smoothing the way fer yer own purposes. I doona want ta move on." His tone had been a bit defensive when he'd added, "I intend ta keep it."

Kell had removed the fancy linen cloaking the basket and shared the contents, but even that had caused a dispute between the brothers. Discovering that fried chicken was the main course, Kell had handed Liam a wing and taken the drumstick for himself.

"As it is in everything, I see." His brother had held the bony bit of fowl next to the plump leg and scowled.

"I need the sustenance to recover from the bruises I incurred redeeming yer gambling debts." Kell had resisted the urge to snatch the wing back, ungrateful cur that his brother seemed. They'd not had a rousing brawl for a time but Kell could see one brewing on the near horizon.

But he'd been content to trade his leg for the wing and let his brother's snide remark pass. He'd been more concerned with having the basket to return to her when they next met than eating the meal within it. But when he and Liam had shared her dessert, they'd reached accord on at least one subject.

Kell had found two fancy plates tucked in the basket,

each holding a slice of peach cobbler wrapped in paper. His brother had set aside his hostility to sample the pastry; after he'd taken a big bite, closed his eyes, chewed, and swallowed, he'd smiled beatifically.

"Are ye courting this woman, then?" Liam had asked, falling into the Irish lilt seldom heard in his voice in the recent past.

Kell had nodded, suddenly self-conscious under his brother's stare.

"And suddenly yer arse has grown roots to this spot?"

Kell nodded again, bracing for more derision.

"Good to know she can cook," Liam had grunted, finishing his cobbler and scraping the plate of crumbs. "I'll not move on until I see you situated." For a moment Liam adopted the paternal role, reminding Kell that his brother was a full grown man, now.

"I'd not expected the contents to be so delightful, meself," Kell had admitted, focusing on the food and avoiding further discussion of future plans. He'd praised the peach treat, feeling possessive pride in Natalia's skill; but he'd been uncomfortably aware that no doubt, she'd prepared the basket of food for other than him.

And beneath it all, he'd wanted to grab his brother and keep him safe, lest the boy who had grown to manhood on Kell's watch, blunder into the world and get beaten to a pulp.

CHAPTER IX

Dry soles won't catch fish . . .

*K*ell crouched amidst the weeds, watching the cat lap milk and wishing he could be the trespasser being stroked with such a loving hand. The bluidy flea-bitten beast finished its snack and had the audacity to leap onto the chair to snuggle against Natalia for more cosseting.

"You are such a friendly animal. I bet you're lost and afraid aren't you?"

Kell nearly choked when he heard her opinion. Mesmerized, he watched the animal sprawl in her lap, languishing in pleasure as she scratched his belly.

"Or did some horrible person toss you out to live in the wild?" she asked, tipping up the cat's chin as if expecting him to answer.

Kell knew he was in trouble while he watched her fondle and pet the cat. She was a delight, was Miss Fitzwilliam. Upon first seeing the vision of loveliness—days before she deigned to introduce herself and only then at his prodding—he'd begun gathering information about her. Discreetly of course.

As he'd transacted his business, he'd needed an attorney and shared many a visit with Horace Murdock. Gradually the professional demeanor of the man had relaxed and he'd begun to enjoy their conversations, sprinkling his stories with those of a more personal nature. Eventually, River Grayson's lawyer had become Kell's attorney, and as such, proved to be as gossipy as an old woman.

"'Twill make a grand home and lucky I am ta have happened on it," Kell had declared after he'd signed legal documents on the first day. "I doona ken whether ta thank God or pray the devil doesna see my good fortune."

Murdock had beetled his brows and looked over his glasses at Kell. "An older couple, friends of mine, owned the place. They lived there, raised their family, the children grew up, the kids had no interest in ranching and moved on. The drought hit, the taxes came due, the kids ignored the situation, and the ranch was facing foreclosure. The woman took sick and died. Her husband hung himself in the barn two days later."

The old lawyer had recited the events in a hard voice, still angry, Kell understood. Family stupidity could make a man snarl.

"I'm sorry ta hear such sorrow came to those who lived in the place afore me. But I'll no' be deterred from sinking my roots in the ground there, just the same." The why of how Kell now owned it, was a bit gruesome, but only a fool stopped to count the coin when he found a bag of gold at the end of the rainbow.

"You'll not like it there. Too lonely for a man who's always lived in crowds his whole life," Murdock had declared, sitting back in his chair and studying Kell. He'd opened a tin of tobacco, filled his pipe, lit it, and drew deep on the stem as if he'd not just predicted Kell's failure.

"Aye, 'tis a big place after having lived in rooms most of me life. 'Twill make a fine home for a family, though. I'll no' be lonely long. I intend to wed, soon."

"And how will you support a wife and pay your taxes? Surely not by ranching or resuming your pugilistic career." The older man had prodded him for details that hadn't yet been well-developed, but Kell understood he, himself was being vetted, so he'd taken the lawyer's questions in stride.

"Mind ye, the paperwork is no' done on the deal yet, but I've investors interested in establishing a freight company on this side of the railhead. Since shipping will surely require guarding, it's ta be a Freight and Security firm that will feed me family."

"Lot of work starting a company by yourself."

"Aye, 'tis glad I am that me brother and others will be sharing the load."

"You seem to have done everything else. Have you selected a bride, yet?" Murdock had smiled, replacing his sad mood of moments before, with inquisitive interest.

"'Twould help me greatly if ye wrote a list of names I might consider. I have furnishings to buy and would no' want a new missus ta find me taste wanting. 'Tis in me mind ta let my lady line the nest and make it a bonny place."

Murdock had laughed aloud, though Kell had told him the truth. He wanted a woman to furnish the house because he'd decided that this place would be his home. The permanent kind. And he bluidy well needed a woman to share it with him.

He'd been, subconsciously at first, then, deliberately assessing the women he met. Annon females were plentiful, some of them not single but available just the same. But none of them were quite what he had in mind when he thought of his wide veranda. He was proud of that porch. It was as elegantly detailed and constructed as any fine home he'd seen in Belfast as a lad.

"I wish you well," the old man had said that day, and gone on to scribble a list of names Kell still had in his pocket. The first two names proved to be River's friends, and he'd already met one of them.

Beth Harper had welcomed Kell to Isaca, even trading Edge and River Grayson stories with him. The postmistress was a lovely woman and he could easily see why River Grayson called her friend. But it was also quite clear to him that Mistress Beth still pined for a lost love and that knocked her off Kell's list, immediately.

Natalia Fitzwilliam, on the other hand, he'd had a devil of a time meeting. He'd expected to greet River's other friend, accept her welcome, and continue down the list, methodically interviewing each candidate for his bride. Of course they wouldn't know his plan. He'd felt certain once he'd made his selection, the wooing would fall into place and he'd soon be a married man.

But he'd been in front of the livery, inspecting the bed he'd ordered, when he felt the gaze of another locked on him. He'd found it best through the years to identify lurkers and their intentions, so Kell had taken his time loading his wagon and then driven it behind the livery to make it appear he'd left town. He'd then loitered in the barn, discussing the merits of draft horses versus mules with the men there, all the while watching the buildings across the way.

When a young woman had emerged, Kell had asked the stable owner her name.

"That's Miss Fitzwilliam. She'll be in town to help out Beth Harper. It's delivery day at the store," one of the men had volunteered precious information.

She was the very same woman he'd been trying to meet. Again that day, she'd somehow dodged him. Likewise the avoidance continued until he began to wonder if somehow he'd inadvertently offended her. Did she not like the cut of his suit? Perhaps she favored the wide brimmed Stetsons the local men wore, instead of the bowler hat Kell preferred.

He'd questioned Murdock and learned that Natalia had grown up in Isaca and her mother was recently deceased. The older man smiled benignly when he spoke about the girl and assured Kell that she was chaste, refined, and single. The final aspect—her being single that is—had been the most important information revealed.

He'd then begun his own watch, coming to town more often than necessary and tarrying when and where he thought she might appear; that of course was no hardship, for, as Murdock had pointed out, the ranch was a lonely place with nothing but a cat for company.

He'd fixed his attention on the elusive Miss Fitzwilliam at first because it piqued his interest that she didn't want to meet him.

She was very well-liked and highly thought of. More than one of his informants mentioned her volunteer work for the church and for the town. He learned that she was twenty-five—which seemed the perfect age to begin a family with him.

When Kell had finally cornered her between the aisles of the Isaca Post Office & General Store, heard her voice, saw her dimples, her lovely smile, her vivid eyes and beautiful face, he'd been gobsmacked by everything about her. Bluidy ruined for any other. Lusting after her like a desperate shite.

"You are a ragged beast. You remind me of River's friend," the object of Kell's insanity said to the cat. "If you stay, I believe I'll name you Aloysius."

Her words to the cat brought Kell back to the present.

Fecking hell. The wretched feline reminds her of me. Still, she was scratching the animal's belly. Kell swallowed his groan and shifted the thick wedge of arousal begging to be released from his trews.

He couldn't reveal himself, and he couldn't leave. He'd come to make certain she was safe. The attack on her home didn't seem random to him. The ugly word on her door indicated that the perpetrators had known a woman lived in the cottage by the road.

Also, the flowers in the backyard had been viciously destroyed, the swing wrecked and the pool fouled. The extent of the damage indicated to Kell that someone had taken a strong dislike to the lovely owner of the cottage.

It wasn't safe for her to be alone, so Kell nestled in nettles and other weeds, stifled his urge to scratch, sneeze, and whine, and settled down for a long night.

On the porch, Natalia urged the cat from her lap and stood. "Goodnight, my furry friend. It was very nice meeting you. I hope to see you again."

She went inside, and after a brief period, during which Kell imagined her donning her pretty nightwear, she extinguished the light.

٭٭٭

Someone was outside, crouched in the weeds at the back of the yard. She'd heard sounds, set the cat on the floor and casually retreated. Tali felt proud of her ability to keep calm until she shut and bolted the back door and realized she'd left the rifle behind. The front door was locked as well, and had been all evening while she'd sat on her back porch petting a cat and feeling safe.

Tali didn't know what to do now. She was absolutely certain she'd seen the weeds move, and then she'd heard a groan. Animals didn't make that sound.

She felt safer sitting on a chair in the dark of the kitchen than stepping back outside to retrieve her gun. Part of her wanted to give into terror, hide in a closet, and... *What? I've lived in this house all my life. It's always been safe. I've never had to hide.*

Her attention was diverted to the front of the house. She heard voices, then a loud knocking on her door.

"You sure this is the place, Jim? Don't look like she's home." The words came from the front porch. He'd obviously been the one banging on the door.

"Shack at the edge of town, right around the bend in the road." Another man, presumably Jim, answered. He was loud. She didn't have to leave her seat to hear his slurred words.

"Does not look like a shack ta me." As well as unease in his tone, Tali heard a tinge of an Irish accent similar to Mr. Lonigan's. Dear God there were three men prowling around the front of her house. Had they been in the weeds earlier?

"The best brothels don't look like whorehouses. This place is discreet. The woman probably does a good business." A fourth man spoke confidently as if he knew Tali and had visited her often. It was horrifying. She needed her gun just so she could shoot him.

She almost recognized the voice. The other three

men, even the one with the Irish tones, were clearly Easterners with their broad vowels and fast speech. But the last man was an educated Texan.

Anger gave her courage. She slid to the floor, crawled to the kitchen exit, unbarred it, eased it open, moved to the porch on her hands and knees, and pulled the door closed behind her. The rifle was where she'd left it. The cat was gone. *Good, I'd hate to shoot him by mistake.*

Tali could hear the rowdies in front who didn't seem inclined to believe that she wasn't home. She remained crouched, holding the rifle while she peered at the weeds she'd targeted before. The spot seemed empty. She felt certain that the former threat was gone, probably having moved to the front yard.

Quietly, she eased her way to the far edge of the porch and ducked under the side rail, slipping down to the strip of bushes that led to the front. She was thin enough to make her way between house and shrubs to the corner of the cottage, where she remained hidden, but near enough to see the faces of the trespassers.

And then from the other side of the house, a familiar voice interrupted the men's conversations.

"'Twould be a favor to me, lads, if ye'd cease making yer racket. 'Tis no one ta home and ye've been misled in coming here ta boot."

Tali didn't need to see the owner of the Irish brogue to recognize Mr. Lonigan's presence. Her fear receded, replaced by renewed anger tinged with relief. She didn't know why he was present, but he'd made it clear he wasn't with the others.

"Ah, Jack's friend. You beat the rest of us here," the educated Texan said. "I heard you were sniffing around her."

Now that she could see his face, Tali recognized Simmons, the Carter family attorney. Her hands tightened on the rifle as she lifted it, pointing it in his direction.

"Desist with yer malicious suggestions. I'm on a job. What might be yer reason fer disturbing the night's peace? And I'll warn ye, more than one rifle is pointed at ye so deliver yer answer fast and then depart."

"What kind of job brings you to the home of a beautiful woman in the middle of the night, Lonigan?" the lawyer asked suspiciously. He shifted in his saddle, sounding less confident as he faced a real opponent.

"Security, lad. Handsome Jack, me brother, Liam, and me have formed LLC Security. Miss Fitzwilliam—a respectable young woman I assure ye—is our first client. It seems her cottage was vandalized last night, and fearing the miscreants might come again, she's hired our company to protect her house."

"Bluidy hell, I knew it was too good ta be true." The man who'd earlier pounded on her door, moved from the porch, blaming the lawyer for the mistake. "Simmons said a light skirt lived here."

"Seamus," Mr. Lonigan called to the man leaving her yard. "Lawyer Simmons is full of shite. When ye quit fecking around with the arses ye've been selling yer services to, boyo, come see me."

My brother is partners with Mr. Lonigan? That information wasn't reassuring. But the men were leaving. She'd deal with her Irishman when they were gone.

Tali gasped, startled when she felt a warm body pressing against her ankles. Then it was gone, leaving her shuddering in the dark and contemplating what she'd just encountered. She didn't have to wonder long.

"What the hell?" The stray cat she'd earlier fed, raced across the yard, snarling and hissing as it launched itself at Seamus, first clinging to his pants, then climbing his leg. The thug who'd earlier been brazenly pounding on her door, screamed in terror, then pried the cat loose and threw it to the ground. "Shoot the creature," he yelled.

One of the men on horseback pulled his gun.

"That's enough." Tali stepped from her hiding place, her rifle cocked and aimed at the lawyer. Simmons tipped his hat at Tali.

"Miss Fitzwilliam, you've chosen your protector well. I congratulate you."

"Get off my property. Now. All of you." Her finger itched to pull the trigger but that would have attracted Isaca citizens, something she didn't want.

"Lonigan, you were holding out on us." Simmons

called as he gathered his reins, preparing to leave. "Trust a brawler like you to beat us all to the prize." He nodded at his companions and said, "I've got what I needed. Have fun boys."

Tali watched with a sinking heart as Simmons rode away, laughing.

CHAPTER X

*U*ntil they were certain the thugs were gone, the lass remained out front, pointing her gun at the troublesome rowdies, as did Kell. After Simmons departed, it wasn't difficult persuading the other three to be on their way, but Kell feared the damage was already irreparable.

When the last had withdrawn, Natalia returned to the back yard. He followed.

"I shouldna have claimed ye were gone from home," Kell said, standing next to her on the porch, regretting the lie that had seemed expedient at the time.

"If we're exchanging *should-haves*, I should have stayed unnoticed by the corner and kept my mouth shut," Natalia said, heaving a sigh and blowing a tendril of hair from her eyes. Kell resisted agreeing with her. Her expression was already bleak.

"Would you care for tea?"

"I would," he'd answered immediately, hoping she'd remember he liked it hot.

She disappeared into the house and he sat on the same chair the cat had perched upon earlier. The mangy beast came slinking between the porch slats to join him.

"Doona think to claim the other seat, boyo," Kell warned, glad that he'd not said worse ta the pesky feline when Natalia reappeared through the door.

"Oh, you've met my cat," she said and carried a tray to the small table between the chairs, and set it down.

"He's certainly an impressive rascal," she said, her smile of approval directed at the cat. The demon cast a smug expression at Kell. Before she took her chair, Natalia rewarded the cat with his own serving of cream. He sampled the cuisine, and then ignored all else while he guzzled his bounty.

As if nothing untoward had just happened, she turned to the table where steam rose from the china teapot. Two delicate cups with saucers sat between a small pitcher of cream and a bowl of sugar.

She filled Kell's cup, and handed it to him with a napkin, and a spoon. "I'll leave you to cream and sugar your own tea, Mr. Lonigan."

The lass is taking it well, all things considered. He stirred in the cream and a bit of sweet, waiting for an indication of what might come next. She appeared very calm, perhaps a wee bit too calm, as she sat on the other chair and served herself, draping a napkin across her lap, and sipping the hot liquid.

"A dram of spirits in yer tea would no' be amiss, lass. Ye've had a shock."

"If I kept spirits in the house, Mr. Lonigan, I would agree."

"Kellan," he corrected, congratulating himself on his distraction.

She sighed and brushed her hand across her

forehead. It was the first indication that she might be less than serene. "Unfortunately, I don't." Her inner turmoil began to crack the calm façade. "Keep spirits in the house, I mean," she said in a rush. She squinted at him accusingly. "Why were you spying on me earlier in the evening?"

Shite. He'd hoped she'd forgotten about his bluidy lurking in the weeds with all the rest of the fuss that had followed, but it wasn't to be.

"Protecting ye," he answered stoically.

They stared across the table at each other a moment longer. Miss Fitzwilliam's gaze remained steady when she asked, "What is the worst thing that can happen?"

"Well now. 'Tis a bed in me house, but no' much more," he answered glibly. "Ye might find things a bit rough fer a time." He emptied his cup and set it on its saucer.

"Mind, I doona have chairs and such, yet. Nor have I the ready to make it so," he confessed. She'd as well understand from the start, he wasn't a rich man. Until he got his business going she might have to wait a bit for the grand furnishings he planned.

"What are you talking about?" she asked, her tone exasperated.

"Lass, 'tis no' how I intended to woo ye. But it would have come to this in the end if I had me way. We've no' had the time ta get acquainted but…" She gazed at him from eyes as big as the saucers under the wee teacups; but as he could see no threatening tears, he ploughed on.

"Marriage, lass. And we'd best be at it quickly for I'm certain Lawyer Simmons is spinning dross into gold as we speak." Kell was inordinately pleased that his intended barely flinched at the notion of being his bride.

Think Lonigan, think. Ye've made it to the final round, the prize is near yours but yet to be claimed. He could see she needed more convincing and prepared himself to do the thing right. He would bend his knee to her, offer insight into his business plans, promise her blooming flowers under a purple moon—anything it would take to get her from the chair to a wedding bed.

⚬⚬ ⚬⚬

Tali studied Mr. Lonigan as he waited patiently for her to answer. Though she tried to appear composed, her hand shook when she refilled his cup. "I have to think about this."

She should have objected to his plan but she had none of her own. Marry he suggested. Quickly would be best, he said. The Carter attorney was up to no good, which she did not doubt.

It was early Sunday morning, dawn not even close yet, but she felt as if she'd lived years since the cataclysmic events of Friday's meeting. Her normally calm existence had been pummeled with threats, name calling, vandals, character assassinations, and the revelation that her entire life had been a lie. Panic threatened to suffocate her. Her guest no doubt sensed her distress.

"If I could give ye but one wish lass, what would ye have from me?" he asked earnestly before taking the teapot from her, setting it on the table, and catching her hand between his.

What would ye have from me? Suddenly, Tali knew. She'd not cared for Matthew's caresses and been glad that they'd been infrequent and brief. Before she really considered Mr. Lonigan's offer, there were many things she'd like to know about him. But only one seemed important at the moment.

She leaned closer and murmured against his lips, "A kiss." He remained absolutely still as she brushed her mouth across his. She closed her eyes to better savor the experience, noticing first how dry his lips were under hers. When she felt a rough indentation on the upper one, she tentatively touched it with her tongue, identifying it as the scar she'd noticed there.

His breath was warm and tea-scented when he huffed in surprise. And then it was her turn to be startled as his big palms moved from holding her hand, to drawing her to her feet, and then to his lap. All without breaking the kiss.

"Open for me, *mo chroi,*" he growled. Keeping one big paw cradling the back of her head, he used the other to tilt her chin, bettering his access to her mouth, and nipping her bottom lip. Hesitantly, she parted for him; then stiffened, trying to pull away, shocked when his tongue penetrated the opening.

But his hand, though gentle, firmly held her head in place not allowing her escape. Tali's nipples tingled and her breasts ached, so she pressed her front to his chest, hoping to ease that distress. The contact was better, but still not enough.

Her frame, seemingly weakened by his nearness, could no longer support the heavy weight of turgid breasts grown fuller in response to him. Needing to be yet closer, she wrapped her arms around his neck. He groaned and the reverberation tickled her, raising goose bumps on her arms and heating a pool of desire in her depths.

She'd begun the intimacy as an experiment to discover if she could stand his touch. When Mr. Lonigan finally abandoned her lips, nibbling from the corner of her mouth, up her jaw, across her cheek, and back to her lips to capture them again beneath his, she was satisfied that she'd resolved that issue.

"You've completely muddled my senses," she whispered, blinking up at him when she could finally speak after the kiss ended.

"Have I now?" he rumbled. Slashes of bright red tinged his high cheekbones, his eyes were molten silver, and his teeth flashed in a white grin.

She shifted on his lap, uneasily feeling his erection

beneath her rump. Hastily, she removed her arms from his neck and sat up straighter, inadvertently grinding against the elongated proof of his arousal. It should have been embarrassing, but Tali had to resist the urge to rock against *it* as the ache spread from her breasts to her womb.

She scrambled to her feet, bending over the tray, preparing to carry it to the kitchen and lock herself in the house. While she organized the contents, she kept her gaze fixed firmly on the teapot.

"I greatly enjoyed yer supper the night of the auction."

She tore her glance from the tray to stare at him. As if nothing had passed between them, he continued his conversation. "Ta be sure, the meal would have been more pleasant had ye been with me at the time."

"You bought my box supper?" She'd found the napkins he'd returned. He'd used them to wrap her plants. But pretending surprise helped her gather her wits.

"That I did. So doona claim agin in my presence that ye have no hand fer feeding a man. My stomach will testify 'tis no' the case."

His awkward compliment delivered in a gruff scold drew her smile. She inhaled, bracing herself to face what she wanted to avoid.

"What was the purpose of Mr. Simmons' visit tonight," she asked, although she dreaded hearing the answer.

"To besmirch yer character and steal yer house," he growled.

"And you're offering to marry me because…?" She forced herself to look at him. The ruddiness of his complexion had faded to normal tan and his silver gaze was once more gray.

"You'll look good on me veranda," he answered.

"You want me for a decoration on your porch?" His reason was so ludicrous that she laughed out loud, only moments after she'd thought to never smile again.

"Aye, yer a lovely lass ta greet a man when he's done a day's work. I'm asking to be that man fer ye, Natalia." He continued to hold her gaze, showing her nothing but unruffled calm consideration.

"Mr. Murdock is a Justice of the Peace for the county," she murmured before she could lose her nerve.

"And he is empowered to perform weddings?"

"Yes."

"Then, lass, we need ta go see our friend and ask him ta help us upset the enemy's plans."

⚬ꗃ⚬

Simmons was a smarmy bastard and Kell expected the worst from him. This was, he told himself, his reason for hurrying the courtship and herding Miss Fitzwilliam toward his goal. The kiss had been the last thing he'd expected from her and had truly knocked him for a loop.

Repeating the experience had now listed itself as his top priority.

Before, it hadn't even been on his list of possibilities for the near future. He'd planned to woo the lass slowly, getting to know her and letting her come to trust him while he ingratiated himself with the local establishments and grew his prosperity.

He'd intended to build a freight business, starting with two wagons, ready to carry loaded merchandise, grain, or produce to the railhead in Clarksville, unload at the train depot and reload with new merchandise to transport to customers in the underserved areas south and west of Isaca. To be sure, much of that merchandise would require protection, as well.

But all his business ideas were blown from his head when the lass brushed her lips across his. It had been all he could do to keep still for her exploration. When she'd touched his scar with her tongue, his cock had surged to life, and lust had fought for control.

For all his guise of self-assurance he proceeded with caution. It was an ugly situation. Although she'd done nothing amiss, by the time Simmons finished telling his tale, she'd be labeled a doxy and Kell would be the man who ruined her.

"We've time to negate mistruths if we use our brains," he told her and hoped his words proved true. "But first, there are things to settle between us."

"What?" Her gaze slid sideways to meet his, her

stance uneasy. Aye, he'd scared her, prodding her with his tongue the way he had.

"Yer name is Natalia. I asked leave to call you such, or the more diminutive form, Tali, as I've heard you addressed by yer friends."

"Oh, I…of course."

"Which?" he persisted.

"I prefer Tali," she answered.

He did not trust the day to be without incident, though it was Sunday. Nor did he deem Tali safe in her cottage alone.

"We'll depart together," he announced. When he explained their need to see Murdock before others could work their mischief, her expression was grim, but she nodded her head gamely.

"He attends church in town. If we hurry we can catch him before he leaves his house." She picked up the tray, looking around with a puzzled expression. "Earlier, how did you get here?"

And didn't he feel like a bluidy arse. He'd left his poor horse tied below by the river and only remembered it when she asked. Of course anyone spying on her might recognize the old animal as his and draw the conclusion he was an illicit lover sneaking in and out under cover of darkness.

He fetched the horse, leading it up the steep slope while she made her preparations for their visit to Murdock. When he led the animal through her backyard to the road in front, she stood waiting on her porch.

"I'd like to stop at the store and ask Beth to attend also," she said.

He'd been feeling the wrongness of the situation but cheered some when he saw she'd chosen to wear a pretty dress the color of rich cream.

"I would have liked to have me brother with me for the event," he admitted.

"Where is he?"

"More than likely sleeping in me bed."

She looked askance at him and he hastened to explain. "We've only the one. With me gone, no doubt he took the opportunity to enjoy it."

"I have furniture," she offered timidly.

Now that was a thought he'd not considered. The house seemed in question but the contents did not appear to be in dispute.

"I'll accompany ye to yer friend's, but after that, perhaps there's a better order to this happening."

They made their way to town. Rather than make a muck of her dress, Tali walked beside him as he led the horse. The cat, finding the empty saddle to his liking, jumped on board and rode to Isaca like a prince on his steed.

"And ye'll call me Kellan, now," he said, half way to the town.

"All right," she said.

He dinna care much for the way she held her head,

rigid as she walked, as if afraid to look the one way or the other. She was fair scared to death, putting a good face on things, but…

Will ye no' say my name, lass? But she didn't have anything more to say to him, breaking her silence only when they reached the store, and leading the way then to the back where she advised him, "I'll be fine from here."

"I'll wait here at the steps 'til I see ye enter," he told her stubbornly.

"Thank you…Kellan," she said, patting his arm reassuringly. "I'll wait with Beth until you return."

CHAPTER XI

Bare is the companionless shoulder.

Kellan, she said and 'twas a sweet sound spilling from her lips. It was an auspicious beginning, Kell felt. She'd finally said his name. He played the sound of it over in his head as he appropriated the saddle from the cat and rode from town to his ranch.

He arrived to fetch his brother to attend his wedding and found three men waiting on his porch, ready to tear his limbs from his body. It was easy to see the three displaced ranchers had decided to take action against him, though what they'd planned, he didn't intend to find out. Before he'd cleared the top step, one of them stepped forward.

"Lonigan, we need to work something out. I'll be damned if I'm turned into a sharecropper on my own land." It was the one named Neal Sinclair growling at him, but they all followed him into his house and the empty front room. Empty that is save for Jack Calloway sitting on the floor, resting his back against the wall, and Liam lounging on the bale of straw they used for furniture.

"'Tis good yer here," Kell told his brother and Jack. "We've business to conduct."

He turned then to his uninvited guests. "Mark what I say and then keep it to yerselves. I dinna buy yer land

Thursday for meself. I merely am the representative of the new owner and the new owner intends for ye to stay right where ye be."

"If not you, then who? What's the name of this mysterious buyer?" Adam Morgan asked.

But the third rancher, a man named Clement Tolbert interjected a low comment. "You bought Emmet Price's old place, too."

"Aye, that I did," Kell agreed. "Again, I was acting as agent fer another."

"I heard River Prescott is sponsoring you in Isaca. She had you buy the parcels, didn't she?"

Adam Morgan shook his head. "Why the hell would…?"

Sinclair muttered, "I don't understand."

"Whilst, boyos. The banks got their blood money for yer debts, so yer starting clean. Pray fer rain and work out the rest when Edge and his wee lady get home. I'm just the messenger."

"But it's done. We have a chance." Tolbert began to smile; the worry drained from his face, and he stood taller, shedding the extra fifty years he'd carried when he'd entered the room.

"Exactly." Kell watched the three ranchers assimilate the news. One by one, they shook his hand and started for the door.

"One thing ye can do for me. I've need of a sturdy wagon today. Might one of ye have one to lease?"

And though it took an extra bit of time, he walked the men back to their horses, worked out the details of the borrowed wagon, and ended the siege with a cordial farewell, encouraging them to use his freight service if they ever had need.

"Hell Lonigan," Sinclair said as he mounted his horse. "You're borrowing equipment from Tolbert today. What kind of a freight business has no wagons?"

"A new one, boyo," Kell admitted and laughed with them as they rode away.

"What are ye, now, the good fairy?" Liam drawled from his spot on the porch where he'd moved to unabashedly eavesdrop on the conversation.

"As I told the three of them, I'm just the messenger. 'Tis no' often in life a man gets to help set things straight," Kell confided, feeling satisfaction settle in his bones.

Remembering how lovely Tali had looked in her cream colored dress, Kell decided he had time to change his crumpled clothes for a set of unstained. He sent Liam to the closet upstairs for clean longjohns, a tie, white shirt, and Kell's second suit.

While he waited, Kell stood in the kitchen, squinted in the square mirror hanging on a nail in the wall, and shaved. After he'd scraped the whiskers from his face, he washed the sweat of the previous day's labors from his body.

Upon his brother's return with the pile of clothes,

Kell answered questions the other two men threw at him, and interjected his own when they paused.

Kell could see Jack's uncertainty, though he tried to mask it behind nonchalance when he took up residence in the kitchen.

"Tell me, which name 'tis real—Calloway or Carter?" Kell asked, catching the glance of the man, leaning against the wall.

"Carter. Calloway is my stage name," Jack answered and smirked.

Kell nodded. "And did ye Jack Carter, paint foul words on yer sister's door? Did ye creep into her garden under dark of night and damage her flowers? Hire men to destroy her reputation? Conspire with others in yer family to steal her property?"

"Good Christ no," Jack snapped, standing at attention and losing the smile. "Explain."

He detailed the events since Thursday's legal hearing and listened to Jack swear his ignorance of the happenings. "'Tis a good thing, I won't have ta beat ye to death since ye'll soon be me brother. Now as ta that…"

Changing the subject he gave Liam a stern appraisal. "Now lad, 'tis sorry news I have ta tell ye. Ye'll have ta take yer share of our winnings in company stock."

"What company," Liam asked looking suspicious.

"LLC Freight and Security. Jack, I've included yer name to lend support to yer sister's precarious position. Until she is safe from yer family's machinations, ye'll keep yer mouth shut about it not being true."

To Liam he said, "For now, I've come ta fetch ye ta stand with me at me wedding. The rest we'll see to later."

"You're really marrying the girl I met Thursday," Jack asked.

"Yer sister. Aye, I've talked her into it. Now doona hold me up with more blather. I've already tarried so long she may have changed her mind."

He'd handled the ranchers, his brother, the swift organization of the business, and the allocation of current resources with aplomb. But at the thought of Tali waiting—or perhaps not—his veneer of calm cracked.

"I need a bluidy ring and have none," he confessed. "With it being the Sabbath, I have no where ta buy one today."

Liam offered him a cigar band and for want of anything better, he tucked it in his shirt, then gave it back and said, "Ye'll be my best man. 'Tis fer ye to keep on the ready."

He frowned at the bale of straw on the floor and shook his head. "I canna let her know we've shared the beasties bed. Jack, after ye've removed the pitiful furnishing, take yerself from the house fer a time."

"I'm coming along," Jack suddenly announced. "Someone has to give the bride away. Why not her brother?"

Kell cast a hard look at the other man. "No foolishness now. Whate'er ye need to work out with yer family will be done another day. My bride will no' be plagued with more ill will."

"Understood."

Before they reached the door, Kell froze and turned to Liam. "Assure me ye dinna foul me bed in me absence."

"Never touched it," his brother said.

"Then we're ready. I dinna wish to linger lest my bride change her mind."

"You said that before. Does she not want to marry you?"

Kell thought of the kiss and answered quickly. "Aye, but any lass would like more pomp and circumstance than what I can offer today." He tried to keep his thoughts from the image of his big bed with the fine mattress waiting in the room above stairs. His brain skated obligingly from that to the feel of Tali's mouth when he'd stuck his tongue inside.

Wet, hot, tight... Bluidy hell such thoughts overwhelmed him, and by the time they reached Isaca and tied up their horses behind the General Store, Kell was a mess. *A fecking truncheon in my pants, I'm sporting.*

৩৫ ৩৯৹

Kellan she said his name in her head testing the sound of it and liking it. Tali felt both more secure, and less, as soon as he left. It made no sense, but sometimes when he was near her, he radiated more of that virility she'd ascribed to him than at other times.

He'd seemed even more potently male than usual during the kiss—and after. Her own response had been woefully uninhibited. At the time he'd aroused desire in her, a delicious wanting for more of his touch. Upon their separation, and the absence of all that virility, she felt vulnerable and more than slightly embarrassed.

Beth fixed her a cup of coffee and listened, inserting observations and a few questions during the telling. She was much more concerned about Tali's decision to marry Kellan Lonigan, than in the possibility of Tali's reputation being torn asunder.

"People here all know you. And, the Bodines excepted, no one in Isaca will turn away from you or believe lurid stories about your mother. You're being influenced by the vile words of a family you don't know nor want to know—correct?" Beth paused until Tali nodded. Then she continued. "Matthew is a noodle. If his mother had told him to slap on a six gun and protect your honor, that's what he would have done."

Tali smiled, sharing Beth's opinion, but glad to have her own confirmed. The sudden cooling of their already tepid relationship wasn't personal with Matthew, or for that matter, Amelia Bodine.

"The Carter family sounds as if they are predatory animals. You're well away from such as them. There's little credibility in the slander they've spoken. Your mother was not a downtrodden, mistreated convenience for a man, nor was she a siren, seducing unwary males to her door. She was a woman of dignity and poise. Have you forgotten that?"

It had taken that not so gentle reminder from her friend to get past the character abuse that had been heaped on Cerise Fitzwilliam.

"Setting that aside, what other reason do you have to rush into a marriage with Mr. Lonigan."

"His name is Kellan," Tali said. "He asked me some time ago to call him that."

"You never spoke to him before last Thursday," Beth said dryly. "Granted, I thought I might have to place a fire guard around the peaches to control the sparks flying in the aisle."

Tali blushed, wondering what her friend would say if she knew about the kiss.

"Aside from the obvious physical attraction between the two of you, why must you marry today and drag Mr. Murdock from the minister's Sunday sermon?"

It was a very rational question though, in Mr. Lonigan's presence, marrying quickly had seemed the answer to all of her problems.

"Marry in haste repent in leisure," Beth cautioned, quoting the old adage.

Tali had always recognized that both of her friends were smarter than her. Her mother had also been exceedingly intelligent, considered a bluestocking with a shade too much feminine logic for refined behavior. River Prescott had really been more of a reflection of her mother than had Tali.

Cerise Fitzwilliam had laughed, more than once calling herself a wren who'd birthed a swan. Beauty had been Tali's talent or gift, her looks fine enough to marry well. Nothing else had ever seemed expected of her.

Though she'd accustomed herself to deferring to the opinions of her mother and her friends, when Beth suggested that Tali take longer to consider different options than marrying Mr. Lonigan, she astonished herself when her answer came without hesitation.

"As soon as I marry I'll own my house. That is the condition of the bequest. I want my mother's cottage. You're absolutely right when you say that her reputation precedes her and no one will condemn her for ancient, unwitnessed sins after an unblemished record of good works.

"But she's gone and I'm here and mud sticks. I don't want to be alone, facing crazed men in the middle of the night, or worrying about my home being attacked while I'm helping you at the store. This is a way to stop the insanity."

"Whatever decision you make now you'll have to live with. Keep in mind, Mr. Lonigan is a very tangible outcome. Besides a house, you'll have a husband."

"You said you like him."

"I do, as much as I know of him, and honestly, that's not a lot."

"River vouched for him."

"Yes, and I trust her judgment. But saying hello on Saturday's when he comes into shop is a lot different from marrying the man."

"On Thursday, Matthew tried to provoke a fight, and Kellan refused; on Friday, Kellan comforted me after I'd received crushing news; on Saturday, as I scrubbed evidence of an attack from my house, he helped me put things right; last night, he protected me when strangers threatened me in the middle of the night. What more do I need to know?"

As Tali watched, her friend blinked, her mouth opened, then closed, as if she couldn't find the right words, which was unusual for Beth.

"Beth, I *want* to marry him. I'm worried that if he has too long to consider me, he'll change his mind," Tali confessed in a rush, then, out of breath, stopped speaking.

"If you know you want him, then grab him." Beth's look of concern was replaced by a smile. "How can I help?"

"Go to church this morning and ask Mr. Murdock if he will return home and wait for a visit from us this morning."

"Should I explain why if he asks?"

"I fear it won't be necessary. Mr. Simmons was very

pleased when he left last night. I'm terrified that his smear campaign has already begun."

"Maybe you should go to church with me," Beth suggested hesitantly.

"I can't." Tali felt as if she'd explode if she experienced one more attack, whether verbal or physical.

Beth agreed to be Tali's messenger and after dressing in her Sunday finest, walked to the Isaca Church of God on the corner of the main street in town.

Left alone, two thoughts were fixed firmly in Tali's mind. No one was stealing her mother's house from her, and marrying Kellan Lonigan was the means to achieve that goal. The kiss, though, remained in the background of all her thoughts.

Before Beth returned from church, Tali heard heavy steps ascending the outer stairs leading to the small apartment above the store. When she peered outside, Tali breathed a sigh of relief to see Kellan. She'd really feared he might recant at the last moment.

CHAPTER XII

❈

Good luck trickles when it comes at all;
ill luck comes in torrents . . .

*H*e'd changed his clothes and shaved. Tali knew
this because he had a nick on his neck above the
clean collar of his white shirt. She'd never really
considered men's clothing of interest, but found Kellan's
suit a relief from the monotony of blue denims and red
cotton favored by local ranchers.

Her glance roved everywhere else as she avoided
meeting his gaze, lest he see how desperate she felt. He
must have sensed it, for he came to stand beside her
without speaking.

Two other men filed inside and followed behind him
into Beth's kitchen. For want of avoiding Kell's gaze,
Tali's eyes slid over the last man coming into the room.

"That's…" she managed and then stopped.

"Aye, 'tis plain for any to see yer related."

"Why—"

"He discovered my intentions and counted himself
into the plan. He says he's no' responsible for the
damage to yer property, nor for sending the miscreants to
yer house last night."

"That lawyer—"

"Works fer the Carter family, which as ye ken, Jack
is no' in good standing with." Kellan anticipated each

thought she had with a ready answer.

Tali shoved aside her irritation, and let Mr. Lonigan take charge, though in her mind, she resumed the more formal address. Almost immediately, following in their footsteps, Beth returned, her expression anxious.

"You were right. I don't know how the vile man managed it, but there are rumors already circulating," she announced as soon as she walked through the door.

Ignoring the large male bodies in her kitchen, Beth navigated through them to reach Tali's side. "I spoke to Horace before he went into church," she murmured. "He made his excuses to the minister and he'll be home if you decide…"

"And have ye decided?" Tali's erstwhile bridegroom asked, placing his hand on her shoulder, turning her to face him, and tilting her chin so she had to meet his gaze.

The Irishman exuded tension as he waited. Wishing she could feel happier about getting married, she nodded.

In the background she heard Kell's brother murmur, "Brave lass."

Some of the apprehension receded from Kell's expression and his eyes crinkled at the corners, the usual laugh lines showing again.

"He suggested that you not tarry and be discreet when you visit," Beth murmured.

And then as if not enough had been thrown her way, Tali had one more giant decision to make when she descended to the alley and saw the Bodine carriage, black curtains lowered for privacy, waiting below.

As soon as her foot left the last step, Matthew jumped to the ground from where he'd been perched on the open box driver's seat.

He ignored Kellan behind her and crossed to Tali. "I've come to offer you my name. I heard stories this morning and—" His expression was grimmer than Tali had ever seen before.

The low sound of the others descending the steps ceased as everyone waited for her response.

"I will find a way to kill him, if you want," Matthew muttered, promising, she feared, to engineer Kellan's death.

"Thank you, Matthew," Tali answered, seeing him brace at her response. "But Mr. Lonigan and I are affianced. We hadn't planned to culminate our relationship so precipitously but it seems our plans have changed. And, I would prefer that you not arrange his death."

She smiled up at him, liking him better in that moment than ever before. Matthew, nodded stiffly, but relaxed when she rejected his offer.

"If it's help ye be offering, the loan of yer covered carriage would be a grand aid to our enterprise," Kellan growled behind them.

"I'll drive with you inside," Matthew said immediately. "Where to?"

It was a lovely gesture on her former beau's part that

Tali greatly appreciated. She took a spot next to Beth with Kellan trying to shrink his size to fit the fold away seat he pulled down from the front corner. The carriage's maroon and black velvet interior, with its dark curtains covering the glazed windows for maximum privacy, was exceedingly elegant, but terribly warm.

"It's a good thing we have only a short distance to go. It's like an oven in here," Beth whispered, mirroring Tali's thoughts.

.಄ ಄.

He'd made a fair muck of himself when he'd returned to Tali in the apartment above, crowding her too close, and speaking for her. Kell was surprised and gratified when the lass rejected Bodine's offer.

Pleased though he was, he wasn't foolish; Kell deemed it prudent to move the events forward, not giving his bride time to rethink her choice.

Beth accompanied them in the carriage as Matthew set a fast pace, driving them from one side of Isaca to the other, his passengers hidden inside.

Once he'd delivered them to Mr. Murdock's residence, he tendered his best wishes and jumped to the ground. "I'll leave the buggy for your use. Park it behind the store when you've no more need of it."

After he left, walking toward Isaca, Kell escorted Tali up the steps of the lawyer's house, with Beth and the Lonigan entourage accompanying them.

Horace Murdock proved unflappable when he met them at his front entrance. "I've performed more than one ceremony," he said. "Before we were blessed with having a minister in Isaca there used to be a steady troop of couples knocking at my door."

He ushered them to his den and once there, questioned Tali, studying her expression. "Are you sure you want to marry this man?"

"I am," she said, her answer a husky whisper that made Kell's groin tighten.

Murdock turned to Kell and said, "You're a lucky man in winning her hand. Congratulations. Now guard her heart."

The ceremony was brief, but to Kell's way of thinking, a sweet joining. Tali's friend, Beth, stood beside her and Liam stood up with Kell. The only jarring moment came when Jack Carter stepped forward to give the bride away. And even that seemed providential when, as the brother of the bride, he was asked to stand witness to the ceremony.

When that was done, Murdock said, "Now a word with you two, alone."

Beth hastily declared she had things to attend to at her home and begged a ride back to the store from Jack and Liam. They had Kell's business to attend, and left immediately.

"I think a toast is in order," the old lawyer said and produced a bottle and three globe glasses.

Murdock took a key from his pocket and unlocked the cabinet behind them, which was interesting, Kell thought, considering the room and the rest of the house was filled with fine furniture and paintings surely worth a poor man's year of labor.

When the lawyer turned back to them, he cradled a bottle of spirits in his hands as if he held the holy child.

"Ah…" Kell murmured, understanding the caution when he saw the 1811 date on the label. "'Tis a bottle of the *Comet Vintage* ye have there. No wonder ye lock it up like a priceless jewel."

"Not too many understand or appreciate that I hold a miracle in my hands." Murdock smiled and nodded approval at Kell. Then he turned to Tali.

"Your mother did, Natalia. She was a fascinating woman and a dear friend." He paused to pour a generous amount in each snifter, handed one to Tali, the other to Kell, and resumed his story. "I would have married your mother if she would have had me."

His expression was pained as he gazed at the child of the woman he'd evidently loved deeply. "You looked just like him. A constant reminder to me, and, of course," his voice became wry, "to Cerise. She never stopped loving the surly bastard." Humor rather than hatred coated the ugly name.

"Suffice it to say, I loved them both, called them both friend, and watched them hate each other for twenty-five years." He patted Tali's arm affectionately and promised, "Another day when we have longer, my dear, I'll sit with both you and your brother and tell you it all. But today is for you and your groom."

He brought his glass high and said, "May the two of you be happily one."

Following the toast and clink of the three glasses, they each drank the rare and expensive cognac. Kell's focus was purely tuned to his bride as she sipped the golden liquid from the balloon shaped goblet.

He was afraid he disappointed Murdock with his indifference to the taste. As he watched Tali savor the flavor, her eyes drifting shut, her tongue peeking out from her lovely mouth and rubbing against soft, pink lips, he could have been swallowing rot gut from the local pub for all he knew or cared.

"Exquisite," Tali pronounced. After the first sip, she tipped the glass bottom up, swallowing the contents greedily.

"Aye, 'tis that ye are," Kell murmured, finished his drink, and took Tali's empty glass from her fingers, setting both of the goblets on the table. "We thank you, Mr. Murdock for your assistance this day. And we'll be off now."

Murdock walked them to the front door, exuding mellow benevolence. Unfortunately before they made their exit, he reverted to being legal counsel. He handed Kell his copy of the marriage documents.

"First thing tomorrow, I'll register this at the Annon

Courthouse." Then he turned to Tali and said, "Natalia, we can't erase whatever foul gossip Simmons has already dispensed, but your wedding at least secures your property."

Kell had been pleased at the day's progress until Murdock's reminders of why they'd married so hastily had served to dampen any nuptial bliss that might have been blossoming. It was a situation he intended to rectify. He escorted Tali from the house, lifting her into the backseat of the carriage Bodine had obligingly left for their use.

"I doona want ye to think me a bluidy savage, but 'tis a moment together we'll have before we continue," he said. Climbing in behind her, he scooped her from the cushioned velvet, and deposited her on his lap, intending to claim a kiss within the intimacy of the closed buggy.

"There's room for both of us to sit," she said, squirming to get free.

"Nay, yer where I've wanted ye since I spied ye in yer finery, Mrs. Lonigan." He bent his head, brushing his lips against the sensitive spot behind her ear, savoring the fragrance of roses mingling with the scent of her. All he could think about was getting her home, into his big bed, and under him.

She shivered in his arms when he kissed his way to her temple, then her eyelids, then her mouth. "Natalia Lonigan, me sweet wife," he groaned against her lips. Her hands left where they pressed against his chest and slid them upward until her arms twined around his neck and she relaxed in his embrace, opening her lips for the thrust of his tongue as he'd taught her.

He could not control the swell of his cock beneath her bottom or the way his one hand crept from his side to cup her plump, firm breast, and the other surreptitiously found its way beneath her petticoat and skirt.

Who knows how far upward his fingers might have crept if the sound of riders outside the carriage hadn't interrupted them.

"I think church must be out," Tali said breathlessly, sliding from his lap to the seat, her cheeks rosy pink with a blush.

"Stay seated where ye are, wife," he murmured, planting one last quick kiss on her forehead. "I'll take the front seat to drive us home."

His smile of anticipation became a scowl when he climbed out of the buggy and faced the Carter family lawyer and the three men who had accompanied him the night before.

"Lonigan, we meet again. What brings you here today?"

"I might ask ye the same. But I've no interest in yer scurvy affairs, nor are mine any of yer business."

Simmons laughed out loud. "You're an uppity mick for a street brawler. If you think that marrying Miss Fitzwilliam will save her house, think again. For all that she's a pretty girl, I fear you're the only fool to offer for her though there are many who've already had her."

Kell crossed to where the bluidy bastard sat on his horse spouting lies and grabbed the cretin. Simmons jerked his reins, turning his mount in a tight circle, slamming the shoulder of his horse into Kell. As he reeled backward Kell held tight to the lawyer's arm, unseating him, and leaving him in a sprawling heap on the ground.

Being on his arse in the dirt did not seem to appeal to the lawyer. Simmons was livid. "It's time you learned your place, you Irish sonofabitch," he snarled. To the other men, he said, "Don't kill him, just teach him some manners."

The biggest of the three thugs the lawyer had hired for security, slid out of his coat, and dismounted, smiling. "I saw you take down Henderson's Hammer in Fort Worth and lost a packet. It'll feel good beating the piss out of you."

The other two hung back, waiting their turn, it seemed. But then again, maybe not. The second hireling slid to the ground and grinned. "I'm going to enjoy this."

Kell had no time to divest himself of his own suit jacket before the first man lunged at him. The miscreant landed a kick on Kell's knee, and he felt it buckle.

"So it's dirty ye want ta fight," he roared at the man.

Simmons scrambled to his feet and away from the coming brawl. "As long as I'm up, what say I have a look inside the carriage?"

Kell shifted most of his weight to his left side, favoring the right leg and keeping his back toward the buggy, blocking Simmons, and facing two of his brutes.

"And would ye still be offering an Irish mick a job," Seamus McGill called to him.

"Aye," Kell yelled, ducking the meaty fist coming at him.

"Wages and a place ta sleep?"

"Aye," Kell snarled. "Ye bluidy gobshite if 'tis help yer offering, I accept."

"Terms," McGill called, but as Kell landed a blow to the first *culchie* and dodged away from the second, it relieved him to see Seamus dismount.

"Aye, I'll meet yer terms," Kell yelled and then muttered, "within reason."

"Quit yer blatherin' ye eejit, we've a fight ta win," Seamus yelled and jumped into the brawl, taking on the second man.

It would have felt good to work off his anger on Simmons' tool, but Kell limited his enjoyment.

"'Tis sorry I am ta end this teaching affair," Kell said to the bruiser he faced, letting a glancing blow slide off his shoulder.

"What the hell?" the man grunted.

"No time fer lessons, boyo," Kell said and punched the brawler soundly in his gut, following with an upper cut to his jaw, and a roundhouse jarring blow that caught him on the temple. He went down.

Not waiting to see if he stayed down, Kell left Seamus tending the second hireling and limped to the buggy where Simmons stood pounding on its door.

"Cease and desist ye bluidy maniac," Kell said, jerking the lawyer around to face him.

"Simmons," Murdock called from his steps. "If we had a sheriff in Isaca I'd have you arrested for disturbing the peace on a Sunday."

"You have the wrong of it, Horace. I stopped here this morning to inform you of a new hearing set for tomorrow morning concerning the Carter bequest. As a courtesy, one attorney to another, of course."

At that moment Kell became aware of another buggy approaching, followed by a second.

Simmons straightened his suit and ran his hand over his hair, for all the world, primping as if ready to face an audience.

"Miss Fitzwilliam, I know you're in there. I simply want to deliver your summons."

And didn't she open the door as the slimy sleeveen had known she would. The poor lass was ruddy from the heat trapped inside, her once lovely dress drenched from perspiration, near transparent, and clinging to her curves.

Her lips trembled as she asked, "What do you want, Mr. Simmons?" Her hair, which Kell himself had mussed a bit with his burst of uncontrolled lust earlier, now hung about her face in wet tendrils.

"My felicitations on your recent nuptials," Simmons

smiled, showing white teeth in a shark's face. "Or did I interrupt? Has your gallant protector yet to give you his name?"

"Watch yer tongue, Simmons. The lady is me wife and I'll no' stand fer more of yer slander." Kell lifted Simmons by his shirt front and shook him. Unfortunately they'd gathered the audience Simmons craved. Kell should have broken the man's jaw to prevent his speech. But he didn't.

"Murdock," Simmons gave a strangled yell. "Explain to Mr. Lonigan that if he doesn't release me, I'll see to it that he rots in the Annon jail. I'm here as a sworn officer of the court."

CHAPTER XIII

---❖---

Honor cannot be patched . . .

Tali cringed as riders on horseback milled among the wagons and buggies clogging the only thoroughfare in and out of Isaca. Church had let out and the attendees all stared in amazement at the events taking place in the county prosecutor's front yard. Remnants of the brawl remained as men staggered to their feet and Kellan manhandled the horrible Carter attorney, threatening to strangle him.

Kell moved Simmons further from the buggy before he released his grasp. Then he stepped back to stand next to Tali.

"Are ye well," he asked, concern showing on his face.

"I'm fine," she murmured. By comparison to him, she was *very* well, since his suit was ripped, his tie missing, and bruises were already blossoming beneath his right eye.

Mr. Simmons by contrast, had brushed the wrinkles from his clothes and looked, if not impeccable, at least tidy. On the porch, Mr. Murdock glowered at all of them.

"Whatever you think you've achieved, Simmons, your scheming is done. I performed the union of Miss Fitzwilliam and Mr. Lonigan this morning. By the terms of the bequest, the property is hers."

Tali doubted that many of the listeners understood the exchange. But Mr. Simmons announced his rebuttal in loud tones designed to reach the back of a courtroom or in this case, all the loiterers on the road.

"The terms of the will obligated Miss Fitzwilliam to lead a chaste and respectable life while she resided in the river's edge property. Last night, I was led to her home by business colleagues visiting a light skirt in town. Imagine my surprise when it turned out to be the very cottage in dispute."

Tali watched in horror as he pointed at two of the three men who had arrived with him. "Their sworn testimony will be delivered tomorrow. I would have preferred for Miss Fitzwilliam's sake to keep the affair private, of course, but since this attack on me today…" he paused and shrugged.

"My colleagues will swear they both lay with Natalia last night, as they have on several other occasions. As a matter of fact, when I arrived, Mr. Lonigan was already there, no doubt, having already partaken of the local delight."

"Ye bluidy, fecking, gobshite, arse," Kell snarled, reaching for Simmons.

"I understand your humiliation, Lonigan. You married above yourself and, even so, still ended up with a whore." Simmons taunted him deliberately and Tali realized the Carter's lawyer held a derringer in his hand, pointing it at Kell's heart.

Without giving it a second thought, Tali launched herself from where she crouched in the carriage, landing on Simmons' back. His arm came up defensively, and his intended shot went wild.

Kell caught Tali in his arms before she followed Simmons to the ground. The lawyer sprawled in the dirt for the second time in the day.

"You bitch," he snarled, forgetting his audience for the moment. "I'll have you locked up for—"

"Nothing. You fell. Go along, Simmons. You've delivered your message and served your summons. You'll accomplish no more today," the old lawyer announced.

"I have witnesses…" Simmons persisted.

"Did anyone see anything untoward here?" Horace Murdock asked the crowd.

"I didn't see anything but an Eastern lawyer fall on his ass and make a fool of himself," Clement Tolbert drawled from his wagon seat. "Anyone else see other than that?" he asked. No one volunteered a different story.

"Lonigan," he called to Kell. "I was delivering your requested wagon. Of course, it would be a mite easier if the street into town wasn't filled with gawkers."

The observation, coming from an older, greatly respected rancher from the area, galvanized the drivers of the vehicles clogging the artery and the crowd began to disperse.

"You can take it from here, I'd say." Tolbert parked the wagon at the side of the road, jumped down, retrieved the horse tied to the back, and mounted.

"Best wishes on your marriage, ma'am." He pulled the brim of his Stetson in a gesture of respect before giving Kell a half smile. "Better ice that eye, son, before it turns black on your wedding day."

Wondering what else could possibly go wrong, Tali watched the rancher ride away. And then Horace Murdock interrupted her thoughts with the assurance that worse was yet to come.

"I'm sorry, Natalia. Everyone who matters will know it's a lie. But it will be your word against the witnesses. I'm afraid after this morning's brawl, and Simmons' no doubt colorful version delivered to the court tomorrow, the testimony of two Eastern businessmen will probably be enough."

"They're no' businessmen. They're paid muscle, hired bully boys," Kell argued.

"He'll have them prettied up, in nice suits, looking respectable. And you…"

Tali's heart sank as she retrieved her handkerchief. "Bend down," she ordered her groom.

Kell frowned but did her bidding. Trying to be gentle, she blotted the cut that oozed red on his chin.

"Aye," he muttered, seeing the blood on her kerchief. "I felt his ring split me skin."

He stood before her, a bloodied warrior, wounded in

her defense, and she had no idea what to say, so she said nothing.

༝ଡ଼ ௐ

Kell hadn't discussed his plans with her and knew already that she'd not be happy with his meddling; but, 'twas done.

Oblivious to the goings on in town, at his direction, Liam and Jack had already set a fair amount of Tali's furniture in the front yard of her cottage. The top of a highboy was the first thing to be seen as they rounded the bend in the road.

"Now what?" she muttered from her perch next to him on the wagon seat. He was glad to hear her speak since it was the first thing she'd managed since she'd knocked the lawyer to the ground.

"And on the back of the miscreant ye jumped, saving me life," he pronounced proudly. "I've married me own Boudicca."

"Who?"

"A bonny Celtic Queen, smiting the Roman's at *Camulodunum*," he exclaimed and threw an arm around his bride's shoulders, giving her a fierce hug.

"I'd rather have had a sword," she grumbled, rolling her blue eyes at him. But the lass seemed no worse for wear other than being thoroughly disheveled and out of sorts from the bluidy ill deeds of the day.

She's me wife now. In spite of all the interruptions since the wedding and the grand kiss he'd begun after, Kell's desire to have her alone, simmered beneath the immediate necessity of resolving problems.

"How did he know where I was?" she asked, interrupting another of her prolonged silences. Before he could respond, she answered her own question.

"Matthew. Simmons didn't know if we'd already been wed. Your brother and mine attended the wedding." She closed her eyes and shook her head. "Matthew told the Carter's lawyer where we were and what we were doing didn't he?"

"Aye, so it would seem." Kell had surmised as much. He hated adding more hurt to her already tender feelings, so he merely nodded, rather than tell her how lucky she was to be shut of the gobshite bastard she'd called friend.

Liam and Jack diverted her attention when they emerged from her house carrying a huge piece of furniture.

"That's an antique French armoire," she called to both of them, preparing to hop from the wagon to assist. "Please be careful handling it."

"Be easy, lass." To his brother he yelled, "Stay still whilst I back the wagonbed closer." He'd not been in her cottage, but from the furnishing already on the lawn, she must have had every nook and cranny crammed full to overflowing.

"I'll back mine in too," Beth called, driving up in the store wagon she'd brought to help with the move.

With three brawny men carrying and the ladies tying down each piece as it was loaded, the house was quickly emptied of everything but two bedrooms of furniture. It was going on dusk and by the time they hauled what they had to the ranch house, it would be dark.

"Finish tomorrow?" Liam suggested, leaning on the side of the wagon.

She'd been quiet about the happenings of before in the day, but now answered Liam's words with a grim response.

"I won't own the cottage after tomorrow. If I don't get my things tonight, I doubt I ever will."

"We'll nay stop 'til all is transferred, lass. 'Tis time to carry the first batch to yer new home, where ye and Mistress Beth can sit on the veranda whilst we unload. Then we'll return for the rest."

His knee hurt like bejezus where the miscreant had kicked him earlier, but the grand smile she gifted him erased the pain, shifting it to a throb in his groin, reminding him that soon the furnishings would be reset, Beth would be escorted to town by Liam and Jack, and Kell and his bride would be alone.

ᦟᦞᦞᦟ

They arrived at Tali's new *home*, which did, as Kell

had claimed, have a very nice front porch. It also had empty space to fill with the furnishings the men carted through the front door.

She and Beth consulted with each other, directing the placement of each piece as it was brought in. The stove and icebox were the last items to be unloaded, and once the men carried the cast iron appliances to the kitchen, her enthusiasm began to wane, and she desired more than anything else to have a cup of coffee.

There seemed no limit to what she could ask of him. When she eyed the coffee pot wistfully, Kell, Liam, and Jack squatted on the floor, connecting the vent and fiddling with the stove until it was ready for the coal he carried in. Once properly working, Kell was off again, taking the other two with him.

"We'll be ta get the bedrooms now, lass," he announced, sweeping Tali in an embrace, planting a kiss on her nose, and then striding from the kitchen and taking the other two men with him.

Mr. Lonigan seems to be a very nice man," Beth said hesitantly, once they were alone.

"Yes," Tali agreed.

"Are you all right?"

"Not really," Tali admitted. Wearily, she filled Beth in on the disastrous Simmons encounter. She finished her tale of woe, glad at least to see the coffee perking and ready to drink. "It was all for nothing. In spite of marrying today, tomorrow, Mama's house is gone."

"But you have a fine husband. You won't be alone tomorrow morning when you go to Annon."

"Yes," Tali agreed, again not able to muster any enthusiasm. "But there seems no point to attending the hearing tomorrow since the outcome has already been fixed."

"It's not fair," Beth poured the coffee and placed the pot on a trivet in the middle of the table. "Have you noticed how well your furniture fits in this house?" She asked, changing the subject.

"Yes," Tali answered dully and then burst out in a half sob, "To have people think those things about me. When the Carters named my mother a loose woman, I wanted to hide. Now, I want to punch someone. To fight. And I have no idea how."

"Too bad we don't have a local physician."

"How would that help?" Tali frowned at Beth.

"Well, you know about wifely duties, etc." Her friend's eyebrows rose inquiringly.

"I don't know anything about being a wife. God knows Mama wouldn't even talk about her "deceased" husband, my father. I don't know the way of men at all. I quite understand the mechanics of the marital bed, but…"

Beth's expression became mischievous. "With the right person, the marriage bed is not mechanical. It's heavenly, a place of comfort and joy." Her friend looked so wistful Tali hoped there had been a lot of comfort and joy in Beth's brief marriage.

Beth continued hesitantly, "The woman's first time can be painful. You and Mr. Lonigan haven't been intimate have you?"

Tali blushed, remembering the hand climbing her leg during the kiss in the carriage. "Not really," she hedged.

"Kings and royalty used to haul out the white linen dramatically splashed with a maiden's virgin blood after a wedding," Beth told her as if a glimmer of an idea flitted through her brain.

"Too bad we don't live in those times," Tali said glumly dismissing the thought as insane.

"What if there were witnesses but not royal?"

"To what? Nothing less than a public bedding would suffice," Tali snorted.

"Maybe a private, public bedding." Beth murmured, "Why not? What's the worst that could happen, since the ugly rumors have already been circulated?" Beth leaned her chin on her hand, staring across the table at Tali her eyes sparkling with laughter.

"I could never do it. This is a ridiculous idea," Tali said.

"I can't see how there would be shame attached to either of you. You'd only be seeking justice and offering convincing proof."

Their conversation was interrupted by the sound of a wagon entering the ranch yard. "He likes tea. Not the iced kind, just plain hot tea with sugar and cream." Tali put the kettle on to boil water and addressed what was really on her mind. "Besides, he'd never do it."

Beth grinned. "You won't know until you ask."

Tali drew back in horror. "I couldn't ask him something like that." She could feel her face getting red just at the notion.

"Maybe you need to feed him a little sugar to sweeten the thought," Beth said, smiling as she set a plate of cookies on the table.

CHAPTER XIV

———◆———

There are three without rule;
a mule, a pig, and a woman . . .

*T*he lass had surely lost her mind. He blamed the
stress of all her tribulations and hoped the damage
wasn't permanent.

"It wouldn't be so bad," she assured him yet again.
"Only a few trusted women I know. People who are
respected, who will tell the truth of what they see."

He stared at her, wishing he had Murdock's bluidy
bottle of spirits to imbibe. He'd been that happy to see
the house set to rights while he'd been gone. And his
new wife had even readied a cup of tea for him, and set
biscuits by as a treat.

After Beth had taken her leave, riding beside Liam
when he drove the store conveyance back to town,
followed by Jack in the borrowed wagon, at last Kell and
his bride had been alone. He'd thought to down the drink
and the sweets quickly and move her from the kitchen to
the bed above.

When he would have pulled her onto his lap, a place
he more and more desired her to be, she scooted away
from him and he'd thought her shy.

"Is it timid ye be about the husband and wife
bedding?" he'd asked, thinking to reassure her of course,
before he whisked her up to the bed. Though he fecking

well wanted to consummate the marriage he set himself to patient wooing, thinking to coax her to his way.

"I want to wait until the hearing to be together the first time," she said in a rush, then added, "In front of witnesses."

He'd near choked when she'd proposed her plan for the morrow, which eliminated his hopes for the now. He'd stood, leaving the tea to cool and wrapped her in an embrace.

"Yer no' ta worry about the slander, ye hear? 'Tis as Murdock said, no one who knows ye will believe what's said."

"But others will," she shot back immediately.

Instead of the sad-faced beauty he'd left in order to fetch her beds, which he seemed destined to never use, he peered down into the face of a termagant. "I will not let them tell lies about me without fighting." And didn't she just fist her hands and glare up at him.

"And did ye think ta punch me in the gob, if I doona let ye have yer way?"

She slumped, losing the aggressive stance and resuming her woebegone look. He dinna like that so much. "Lass," he said softly, "do ye even ken the way of it?"

He thought to point out Tali's carnal ignorance—not that he didn't bloody well love that she was innocent. But his hope to dissuade her failed. In fact at his question, she perked up again, still pursuing her gobshite idea.

"Surely it's enough that you know how."

"Well, aye and nay," he'd told her. Of course he'd shagged his share of women and then some; but he'd never expected to make a holy show of himself tupping in public.

"I ken the way of it," he told her. "But I doona want ta scare ye ta death before others."

"I won't run screaming from the room," she assured him.

"We'll no' discuss this further," he told her. "Yer no' thinking straight and if I gave in ta yer plan, ye'd hate me later."

"I will not." She said. "But…" And her lips quivered, her eyes filled with tears, and the lass that had been so brave all day dissolved into sobs. Of course he held her in his arms and comforted her. So much in fact that his cock throbbed worse than his knee and his arousal pressed against her stomach wantonly. Unfortunately, the lass didn't seem to notice.

"They said I was a…whor…a…a whore, Kellan. I'm not. I deserve the opportunity to prove it."

In desperation, he asked, "Have ye ever touched one of these?" He placed her hand on the front of his trews pressing her palm against his blatant arousal. When she shook her head and tried to withdraw, ruthlessly, he shoved her hand beneath his waistband to touch the straining flesh she found there.

"Feel it. If ye persist in this crack-brained scheme,

ye'll be having all of *this* inside *yerself* on the morrow."

"Well, I feel it," she said. "What else do I need to know?" She quaked in his grasp but didn't waiver in her persistence.

He stared at her lips, so pink he'd wanted to take them with his mouth and quench the fever in him she roused. He scowled at her instead, fighting the urge to spill his seed with her fist closed around his bare cock.

"I should probably see it, too," she announced, undoing the laces that closed his pants. "So I 'don't run screaming from the room' tomorrow." And didn't she just beam at him as if she'd won a prize.

It was an Irish stand-off, neither of them willing to back down. He groaned, at the feel of her hand on his flesh and gave in, exasperated by her determination to go through with the proposed public coupling.

"If ye insist, then 'tis time fer yer first lesson in bliss," he told her. She listened and nodded as if agreeing to a picnic outing. He started to explain what he'd do and what she should expect, but changed his mind, deciding that showing would be better than telling.

"Have ye touched yerself enough to know where this goes?" He asked, freeing his surging erection so she could see what she held.

He didn't know if it was from his crude words or the fact that the stubborn chit realized she still clutched his stiff member while they conversed, but her face became diffused with color and she closed her eyes.

"Ye understand this show might all be for naught. There's plenty of lasses who don't shed a drop of red when they're tupped the first time. It doesna mean they're a bawdy. 'Tis just the way of things. You could be one such."

"Then hope that isn't the case," she answered somberly, still refusing to meet his glance. Kell had admired the dignity she wore like an old lady's shawl but it didn't keep him from telling her the truth.

"I appreciate yer desire to show your accusers wrong, but what yer suggesting is lunacy." And then he looked at her trembling lips and desperate expression and knew himself for a bluidy fool.

"We'll get through the morrow, tomorrow, lass," he said, removing her hand from his shaft and tucking himself back into his trews.

"What do you mean?" she asked, looking so lost, he was tempted to shove his dick in her hand again.

"I mean, fer now, ye've a starving man and a stove ready to cook his first meal. Are ye up to the task?" As if on cue, his belly rumbled and didn't she just smile, as if relieved to have something to do.

He sat at the table while she fussed at the stove and he felt whole. As if his journey from Ireland to the city of Boston and then to the wilds of Texas had been vindicated.

"I like the way ye look in me kitchen," he growled, openly admiring her as she fiddled with whatever she fixed on the stove.

He couldn't have testified to the quality of the food when she set the plate before him. It could have been shite from the stalls in town fer all he cared. She'd cooked him a first meal in their home and set it on the table she'd brought with her.

"Are ye no' going to eat yer own food?" he asked, when she set a singular plate before him and none for herself.

"I'm not hungry," she murmured. But given the state of the ensuing events during the day, he was sure she'd not nibbled a thing during the time.

"Would ye be trying to poison me on me wedding night, then?" he asked teasing her. "Share this feast before me or I'll no' eat a bite."

"That's coercion," she muttered, rolling her eyes, but taking up a fork anyway.

He cut a portion of pancake and lifted it to her lips. She grimaced but accepted the bite, poking a similar offering at him. It was a silly exchange that left them both grinning.

When they'd cleaned the plate, there remained the question of what next. The bed awaited upstairs, but Kell knew he'd not be able to refrain from making love to his wife if they ventured there.

She scraped the plate, fussing again at the sink, remembering the coming event more than likely.

"Since ye've denied me the right to show ye me

manly skills tonight, I've something to share instead," he announced, as soon as she'd rinsed the cutlery.

"What?"

"Come with me," he ordered her. And to ensure that she did, after he'd lit a lantern, he swept her along, out the door, and to the barn.

And there, he stripped his shirt off and flexed his arms for her. "Ye see my brawn, lass?" he said, and laughed at himself. "'Tis a mighty force ye've married. The pride of the ring." To show her his agility and strength he donned his thin gloves and pummeled the punching bag, relieving his unrequited lust at the same time.

He didn't know what he'd anticipated. He'd married above himself, decided to play the gallant, and was now expected to follow through. He'd married a lady, wanted to treat her as a wench, but gritted his teeth as he faced an untried virgin determined to prove her chastity in a public fashion.

"I'd like to do that," she said, interrupting his mental soliloquy about his pathetic state.

"Do what?" he growled, pausing from punching the bag long enough to give her a good stare.

"Hit the bag," she said further.

"Then do so," he invited, finding another reason for her nearness. She stepped beside him and he surrounded her with himself. "Now give it a shove," he told her. Of course, in order to push the heavy weight, she'd have to arch her back a bit, causing her rump to nestle against his groin.

The bag went flying under the force of her push, and as predicted her bottom caressed his shaft nicely. Before he'd enjoyed it thoroughly, the punching bag swung back with as much force. He caught it, stopping it from knocking her over. "Ye see, lass, what ye deliver can come back at ye if ye don't beware."

She nodded and removed herself from his arms. "I'll watch you," she said and seated herself on a bale of straw, perhaps the very one moved from his front room. He told her so.

"Ye realize, before ye brought yer dowry of chairs, stoves, and furnishings, I had not."

"There is only one stove," she corrected him, making him smile a tiny bit.

"I could show you how to hit," he offered, feeling less belligerent at the idea of fitting her against him for pugilistic instruction.

"I saw you once demonstrating a…a…"

"Ye spied on me?" he asked, feeling enormously flattered. "Where and when?"

"It was a Thursday, the day I usually come to town. You were in front of the livery with a group of men. I saw you bend your arm, then take another's arm to show them how to imitate you."

She flexed her arm to show him.

"Now, there's more ta it than 'twould seem," he

said, "The fighter only concerned with muscle will be bested by skill." He wanted her to understand that he wasn't stupid. He'd fought for a reason. But then he forgot that and simply preened in front of her interest.

"Show me the different moves," she encouraged him, standing close as he punched the bag using a right jab.

"There are four main types of punches, lass." Kell didn't mention the fifth, the knockout punch she'd delivered to his heart. "The jab, the cross, the hook and the uppercut." He demonstrated the jab and then laughed when Tali tried to imitate him.

"Yer too little to deliver a rowdy blow ta yer opponent that way. The best ye might hope for is a fool who leaves his chin unguarded." In order to properly demonstrate the uppercut, he sacrificed his manly stance before her, and moved to stand behind where he immediately molded his torso to her frame.

"The uppercut?" she reminded him wryly, after he'd sniffed her hair, kissed behind her ear, and tasted the skin that peeked out at him above her collar.

"Aye," he breathed against her neck. "'Tis a surprise attack. Not favored by brawlers to be sure, because to deliver a mighty blow, ye must be close and let down yer own guard."

He demonstrated, whirling her around to face him, standing close to her—very close. "Now what do ye do to send me reeling?" he asked.

The lass snickered, making him see the silliness of his demonstration but then she fisted her hands and punched his chest, wincing at the hurt she felt in her knuckles.

"Aye, ye do no' ken that the hand is made of wee bones easily broken. A fighter can no' waste himself on one mighty blow. What's ta be done then if his opponent does no' fall down?"

He took her hand in his, kissing the back of it as if to take the hurt on himself. Of course, his lips trailed higher until he'd reached her neck again, a place he'd come to crave.

"The uppercut?" she reminded him.

"Of course, lass. Mark me. A proper uppercut is short and crisp." He brought his fist up, but held the strength from it, and tapped her chin, much to her surprise. "Ye dinna expect the punch."

He took her hand and made a fist, then guided the trajectory of her arm until her knuckles rested under his jaw, demonstrating the how of it. "If ye accompany yer deadly angle," he tapped her fist against his chin again, "with all the force ye can muster behind it, ye can knockout yer opponent before he realizes yer intent."

Though it was a bluidy, damn, gobshite way to spend their wedding night, all in all, Kell considered it not a bad deal. She'd cooked his meal, he'd carried in her furnishings, she'd flattered his foolish pride and he'd flirted with her desire.

Aye, he told himself. *The lass is no' immune to me meager charms.* The silliness of that thought was overridden by the very real fact that he could feel her nipples stiff and eager pushing at him through the material of her dress.

And when they kissed, her slender fingers found their way to his hair, to stroke the back of his neck, and pull him closer to her lips. Aye, he decided, the lass had a tenderness for him. And since he'd not been able to deter her one whit from her plan, like any good Irishman worth his salt, he set to bargaining instead.

"It was a civil ceremony that married us. I did that ta protect ye."

"And I thank you for it," she said. And with a bit of aggression it seemed to him, she asked, "Are you regretting the decision?"

"Nay," he said, crowding her, letting his lust show for a moment. "Doona mistake me wish ta please ye fer indifference." And he kissed her, drawing her into his arms and molding her curves to his big frame.

It gratified and near maddened him to hear her soft moans of desire and feel the thrust of her perky breasts as she returned his heated embrace. By this time they'd moved from the punching bag to the bale of straw. She leaned against Kell, unselfconsciously cuddling in his arms.

"I'm of the Catholic faith," he said gruffly. "There are plenty of those who dinna approve me religion." His tone was defensive. It had been an issue he'd intended to work out during the courtship of his bride. But things had moved quickly and he'd let that important fact slide. But his being a papist mick didn't appear to bother her at all. In fact, she reassured him.

"My mother was born in the Catholic religion. But there isn't a priest or parish of that faith near enough to attend on a regular basis, so Sundays we prayed with our neighbors in the local Church of Christ."

He scratched his head, not knowing if that made Tali a lapsed Catholic or a Protestant. "Well then, if there be children from our union, I want them blessed by the Holy Virgin and raised in me faith."

"All right," she agreed, readily enough.

"And have ye considered children, then? Ye want bairns?" He almost groaned, thinking again of his huge bed just waiting for him to plant the next crop of Lonigans.

He claimed her mouth, not ending until her eyes sparkled with passion and her lips were swollen from his kisses. More than anything, he wanted to investigate the flush that flowed from her cheeks, down her neck and beneath the cloth of her dress.

"I do," she murmured in a husky whisper. "Want children. Many. I grew up alone. I want my children to have brothers and sisters to play with."

"So I should plan ta feed a dozen or so," he teased, wanting to start the process immediately but waiting because…well, because the lass asked it of him. And it didn't escape him that he needed to be strong for both of them, for the sweet lass was fair begging for his tupping.

Before it seemed much time had passed at all, the light outside crept in, announcing the coming dawn.

"We best get ready for the hearing," she mumbled, half asleep in his arms where they lay in the straw.

"Aye," he agreed, nuzzling the spot behind her ear he couldn't resist. "Or we could forget that idea and retire to our bed instead," he murmured hopefully.

That galvanized her into action and she scrambled up, ready to get the day's events behind them.

"I'm not at all sure what the proper attire to wear to a public bedding is," she joked, making him laugh at the same time he wondered uneasily if she really understood what was about to transpire.

CHAPTER XV

What is gathered meanly, it goes badly...

*B*arely past the first glimpse of sun, after Tali and Kell had bathed, dressed, and readied themselves for the court appearance, they sat at the table in the kitchen, her sipping her coffee and him drinking his tea.

The jingle of harness alerted them to a visitor that proved to be Mr. Murdock, driving his matched team of carriage horses into the ranch yard. The lawyer parked his buggy at the hitching rail close to the house and they met him at the door as he strode up the steps.

"Ah, good, you're ready," he said, looking relieved as if he'd anticipated the possibility of them not attending.

"As unpalatable as this event is, and as tempting as it is might be to avoid today's confrontation, after due consideration, I believe we should attend, armed not with a defense, but with our own attack."

Energized as she'd not seen him before, he followed them into the house, admired the furniture in its new setting, and accepted coffee instead of tea. In the kitchen, he listened to Tali's plan, and nodded, surprising her.

"The offer of proof should be enough to shame them into quiet." He paused to study the costume she wore. She'd chosen it because the peach color accentuated her complexion and its fitted bodice rose to a demure ruffle that tickled her chin when she ducked her head.

"It was a final gift from Mama," she told the lawyer. "Wearing it makes me feel as if she's with me today."

"It's a very good choice," he agreed. "You are the picture of sweet innocence." His gaze shifted to study Kell. "And you look," he paused taking in the white shirt and narrow tie that outlined the width of his broad shoulders inside the dark suit. His glance roved higher, noting the scabbed cut on Kell's chin and the dark bruise blacking one of his eyes.

Tali smiled inside as the two men measured each other in a silent duel. Murdock broke from the staring contest first and nodded his head. "You look fierce. That will do nicely."

They attended the hearing together in Mr. Murdock's surrey. Before they began, he handed Tali a linen duster, matching the one he wore over his own clothes.

"I don't have anything large enough to protect your suit on the ride," he said apologetically to Kell.

"Does no' matter. Me wife will brush me down afore we put on our show," he said in a brogue thicker than usual. He winked at Tali, warming her inside as he lifted her to her seat and climbed up beside her.

The surrey was a new acquisition the county prosecutor drove to and from Annon on court days. With the fringe on top waving in the wind and nearly matching the color of the sorrel horses pulling the open carriage, the rig was a riveting sight.

As beautiful as the open surrey was, as they entered Annon and traveled at a brisk pace toward the town courthouse, Tali wished for something less flamboyant. Preferable would have been a covered box she could crouch inside of and hide.

As if reading her mind, Murdock flicked the reins to increase the pace and said grimly, "Remember this in all things today. *You* and by extension, your friends, family and community, are the wronged. You are arriving with stalwart escorts, not to defend your honor, but to eviscerate the enemy and run them out of town."

In wonder, Tali stared at her mother's old friend who'd become a general leading his troops into battle.

Kell saluted the older man and picked up Tali's hand, kissing her knuckles.

"We do this together, luv," he said and grinned. "'Tis a scourge they've brought upon themselves ta be sure, with Lawyer Murdock on our side."

Not you or yours, but us and ours he always says. Tali turned her hand in Kell's palm, feathering her fingers through his to give his hand a squeeze. When he slipped his arm around her waist and pulled her closer in a quick hug, she leaned against his solid warmth, and relaxed her rigid posture.

Instead of releasing her grip after they arrived, Tali unashamedly held Kell's hand as he escorted up the steps to the courthouse and then inside the hall leading to the room where the hearing would take place. Although the proceeding should have been a private affair, clearly Simmons accusations the day before had garnered an audience.

Tali discovered it was a mixed crowd as they passed through it. Some had attended to lend her support. Beth stood with a group of five other Isaca ladies, including the minister's wife and Mrs. Pearson, the oldest woman in town. Their expressions were somber as they joined her trek to the courtroom door.

Not all the people loitering in the outer hall were there to offer support, though. More than one whispered accusation of *harlot* and *whore* were thrown at her.

As they entered the room itself, Tali braced for worse as she spied Celia Carter talking to Judge Stanley where he sat on the raised judge's platform.

Anthony Simmons caught her eye and smirked from his seat where he was flanked by her two accusers. As Murdock had predicted, they presented an image of professional businessmen, sitting at the table in their good suits.

Tali's heart thumped nervously as Judge Stanley studied her as she accompanied Horace to their table. Milford Stanley was a stickler for propriety and his expression indicated that he'd found Tali's behavior wanting. When the crowd outside began to fill the room, he stopped them.

"This is a closed proceeding today," he said.

"Anyone not involved in the case of Carter versus Fitzwilliam needs to clear the room."

Wearing a smug expression, Simmons popped from his seat and said, "We invite witnesses and have no need to cloak ourselves in secrecy."

"Nor do we," Horace said mildly, dampening the drama of the other man's statement. "In fact, we will soon call upon our own witnesses, citizens of Isaca as well as our friends in Annon who've come to support our cause against the chicanery being advanced today."

The judge harrumphed and looked sour but given the agreement of both counsel, he let the audience stay.

Once they were seated, Judge Stanley called the hearing to order and Anthony Simmons, the Carter's attorney wasted no time in going on the attack. His first witness, Celia Carter, wearing a gray tailored suit and veiled black hat, was every inch the grieving widow.

According to Celia, it had been a brief encounter between Cerise Fitzwilliam and Jeb Carter during the war. Tali listened to Celia's version which only differed from her mother's account in that they'd married.

"The woman bled him for the next twenty five years," Celia snapped, dropping her poise for a moment to announce her disgust. "Blackmailed him with the promise of revealing his wartime peccadillo if he didn't pay for her house and bastard child."

Tali winced at the picture drawn of her mother.

"Cerise was a kept woman he despised. I will not

allow the next generation to continue the extortion.

Murdock finally objected, pointing out that there was no extortion. They were discussing the bequest, not any past exchange of money between the two deceased.

"The bequest states that Jeb's daughter must maintain herself in a chaste and respectable manner. She has not. To let her reap the rewards of her mother's sins would continue victimizing Jeb. I won't allow it," Celia announced. Briefly she repeated the insults from the first hearing, adding this time that she wasn't surprised when she discovered Tali had not turned out well.

Simmons ended his questions and she stood, prepared to return to her seat.

Tali was reminded she wasn't alone when Kell squeezed her fingers inside his big paw; at the same time on her other side, Mr. Murdock stood. "A moment. I have a few questions."

Reluctantly, Celia Carter sat back down.

"Please state your name and relationship to Jeb Carter, the deceased." It wasn't that difficult a question. But Mrs. Carter became noticeably tense before she answered.

"He was my husband's brother."

"For clarity, please name your husband and explain where he is now."

"My husband, Nathaniel Carter, was killed during the Northern War of Aggression," she answered.

"And you make your residence where?" Murdock

persisted and before he finished he'd established that the witness lived on the Carter ranch, owned half of the Carter empire, and had shared Jeb Carter's home for over twenty years.

Tali wondered if everyone else had wrongly assumed the woman had been her father's wife. Apparently Jack's mother was dead because no mention of her was made. Tali chastised herself for not interrogating her half-sibling when she'd had the chance.

In her own defense, she acknowledged that she'd only known about her brother since the hearing four days prior. She'd admittedly avoided him when he'd helped Kell haul her furniture from cottage to house. She'd simply not been able to stomach learning more about his father's affair with her mother. The fact that they shared said father did not lighten her disgust.

Murdock ended his interrogation and Simmons guided Celia to her chair before calling his next witness. Although Celia Carter's motives had been put into question by Murdock's cross-examination, it went downhill from there. Simmons called his thugs to stand witness to Tali's depravities which they did with as much graphic detail as possible.

Tali braced herself, but nothing could have prepared her for the lurid account of her conduct reported to the court and those inside listening. The first man was hesitant as if it pained him to tell on her. Had Tali not known he was lying, she could have believed his story.

The next man was coarse of face and manners, vulgar in his descriptions of decadence that had the audience hanging on his every word.

"Offered to do us both, once. Said she needed extra money for some new knickknack or such. She's not cheap, you understand. If you'd see her furniture and cottage, you'd understand her tastes are exotic and expensive. Like mother like daughter, if you know what I mean." The man snickered as if he'd also had an intimate relationship with Cerise Fitzwilliam.

Judge Stanley slammed his fist on his desk and roared, "Enough. You've made your point."

"The bout is no' ended yet. Steady, lass," Kell murmured in her ear and regardless of the audience, slid his arm around her shoulders. She was grateful for the support. She thought she might swoon. It felt as if every ounce of blood in her body had drained to her toes. She shivered, though moments before the courtroom had seemed stifling.

Simmons cast a smugly pitying look at Tali and rested his case.

Mr. Murdock patted Tali's arm and stood.

"We offer truth to counteract the artful lies presented here today." He called a series of witnesses to defend Tali's reputation. Noticeably absent was Matthew. She was gratified to discover the preacher had made a trip to Annon to speak powerfully in her defense and to caution the audience against gossip and innuendo.

But when all was said and done, it was as Murdock had predicted. It came down to her friends against the Carter hirelings. And the thugs' words were so much more interesting and memorable.

"If that's all the witnesses," Judge Stanley said, looking tired and a little sad as he tapped the gavel against his desk. The room was still, a deadened shock settling over the crowd. Titillating as the stories had been, it was just another example of local citizens being ground in dirt. Tali gazed at the face of the crowd and read defeat.

Horace patted her arm and asked quietly, "Continue?" She quaked inside. Nobody expected Murdock to call Tali. Simmons couldn't question her unless her lawyer did first.

What could a young woman of now dubious birth, who had no known income, lived alone in a well-furnished but newly revealed kept home, who's recent beau had defected without excuse; a woman who just the day before had been caught in a closed carriage with a notorious brawler—possibly say to defend herself?

"Fight," Tali muttered between clenched teeth and as soon as she said it she felt better.

Mr. Murdock held up his hand as if to quiet the already silent room. Ignoring the Carter family and the audience, he faced Judge Stanley and announced, "We offer proof of innocence."

CHAPTER XVI

'Tis many a slip twixt the cup and the lip . . .

Simmons immediately derided Murdock's announcement. The audience, on the other hand, perked up. Perhaps it wasn't over.

Judge Stanley also looked interested. Seeing this, Celia Carter conducted a lengthy whisper with Simmons. The lawyer finally said, "We object. Here-say evidence is not enough to prove her innocence."

"We call for a public bedding." Mr. Murdock smiled as he delivered his statement which brought down the house.

Stunned surprise washed over Simmons who opened his mouth to speak, and then closed it again.

"Good ta see the gobshite at a loss fer lies," Kell growled loud enough to be heard by everyone in the courtroom. A snicker from someone grew into laughter as the audience joined in.

"That is a ridiculous request and we absolutely refuse," Simmons snarled.

The arse took it personally as intended. As Kell watched, the lawyer's face grew ruddy with anger.

"Not your call, Simmons." Judge Stanley interceded. "That would be up to me. And, frankly, after the pernicious stories put forth here today concerning Miss Fitzwilliam's character, Mr. Murdock, I believe your client has the right to do just about anything she wants to prove her innocence. As I understand it, she and Mr. Lonigan are recently wed."

"Yes," Horace answered.

"And the marriage has not been consummated?"

"No it has not."

"And you have women of good character ready to witness the event?"

"We do," Murdock said and pointed at Beth and the group of women standing with her.

"Request granted. We'll have a brief recess while you prepare." Judge Stanley said and banged his gavel. "I assume you've come prepared for immediate exposition."

"We have," Horace agreed.

At that point, Celia Carter stood, clearly enraged. "This is outlandish. They've assembled a hand-picked group of women to lie for them. If you actually allow this farce, I insist on being a witness."

"We have no objection to the presence of another witness," Horace agreed readily, at which Celia glared at the judge but sat down.

Every eye in the courtroom followed them, as Kell and Tali rose from their seats and walked toward the judge's private room. Kell felt Tali's shoulder trembling beneath his palm as he accompanied her into the chambers.

"Still time ta change yer mind, luv," he murmured

but, obstinate to the end, Tali shook her head. Then again, after the malicious filth that had just been spewed, Kell had just as much need to prove it lies. Nevertheless, he suppressed a groan as he looked at the grim faced women waiting by the screened area.

Ignoring the others in the room, he guided Tali toward the corner enclosure, and, hoping he'd be able to get his cockstand to the ready when called upon, braced himself for the coming do.

Bluidy fecking hell, I've never performed the deed for an audience let alone bedded a virgin. His glance swept over the lovely girl standing next to him and he pictured the moment he'd lie between Tali's sweet thighs.

A surge of heat settled in his groin, signaling his arousal—which under the circumstances was a bluidy miracle. Preparing for the task ahead, his shaft hardened into a solid length inside his trews. Kell concentrated on his bride and ignored their audience lest he shame his new wife by displaying a limp mackerel instead of a stiff rod.

✥

"This will prove nothing, Mr. Lonigan," Celia Carter hissed. "I'm here to observe this charade and establish forever that Tali Fitzwilliam is a whoring slut just as her mother was. The two of you suit just fine, trash calling to trash."

"Get the screeching *cailleach* out of here," Kell snarled.

"No, please, just finish this," Tali whispered, no longer sure that her idea had been a good one now that she lay with her skirts rolled up to her waist. As soon as her peach colored drawers were removed, her naked lower region would be on view.

Kell was grim faced and stern so after the first look at him, she closed her eyes. If she hadn't been so scared, she'd have been mortified.

This will be over in no time. It's nothing. I'll just pretend I'm doing something else. That didn't help a bit when she heard the rustle of skirts as the ladies moved around the cot to get a better view. Tali felt calloused hands remove her pantalettes and recognized Kell's unmistakable touch.

I will never live this embarrassment down. The cot sagged under her and then he was there, pushing her legs apart.

"Tali, look at me," Kell said gruffly.

"No," she whispered. She was shaking so hard the bed moved from the force of her tremors.

He leaned over and brushed his lips across hers, his message hushed and intimate as he said, "It'll be fine, luv. I'll try ta no' hurt ye."

Tali's eyes popped open at his words. It was all for show of course. They weren't really in love but she knew many of the women who'd volunteered to be observers and she was grateful for his pretense.

"They'll be no chicanery here, Pride Lonigan. I know you think you're going to spill your own blood somehow to make it seem she's virgin. I demand that you either show what you've got in your pockets or take off your pants." As the women watched, Celia Carter grabbed Kell, which, given his state of mind, seemed to Tali to be a mistake.

"I canna smack the lying smirk from yer face, but if ye doona take yer hand off me arm, I'll put ye on yer arse."

"Don't threaten me, you Irish lout." But Celia dropped her hand and stepped back.

Since Tali's lower extremities were bare with nothing between her and the women's stares, she drew a deep breath and ordered him, "Don't you dare hold back now, Kell Lonigan."

Without a word, he dropped his pants and climbed back on the bed, again situating himself between her legs.

"Oh, me lovely colleen, 'tis a fine gift ye bring yer husband today," he said in his lilting Irish brogue before he covered her mouth with his. Distracted though she was by his kiss, she still felt the head of his shaft part the lips of her cleft and brush across the opening of her channel.

He ended the kiss and sat back on his heels so the

ladies could see what he was about to do. Tali leaned up on her elbows and looked too. The heart of her womanhood was as dry as her mouth when he rubbed his manhood in the soft folds of her sex. She'd never envisioned her first time being this way.

"Natalia Lonigan, I'll be making ye me wife now." Tali felt a shiver of awareness as Kell murmured the words. As if trying to reassure her, he held her gaze but it had the opposite effect. Her flesh chilled and her breath stopped in her chest. She looked at the stranger kneeling over her and then in panic at the women gazing down at them.

Somebody stop this right now. The women's avid stares announced clearly they were not going to interrupt the proceedings. Celia Carter's eyes glittered with malice.

"Tali." Kell cupped her chin, angling her head so that she stared into his eyes. Below, the tip of his shaft nudged and stretched what had never been touched before. She gasped when he pushed harder, breaching her entrance.

He stopped; his expression became almost sorrowful. He stared down at her with his manhood half lodged in her narrow opening and witnesses waiting to testify *for* or *against* her purity. It was obviously up to Tali to take charge.

"Now," she whispered and thrust her hips upward, propelling his thick member through the veil of her innocence.

It was awful. It felt as though the walls of her channel were being scraped with sandpaper. Kell took back control, tilted her for better access, and plunged to her core. Her vow to be silent forgotten, Tali's gasp of pain echoed around the room.

"What the hell's he doing to her?" she heard someone on the outside of their enclosure say.

Kell shielded the view of her body from the others as he cradled her face in his hands.

"The likes of such loving will be but once, my sweet, sweet Tali." His gaze held hers as he declared, "I'll no' hurt ye again."

Their flesh remained joined when she stroked the back of her hand against his cheek. "It's all right," she reassured him. "I'm fine."

Tali watched his eyes crinkle at the corners in an almost smile and then he hugged her close for a moment before he began the process of withdrawing. It hurt worse. Pain ratcheted through her, necessitating that she bite her lip to keep from crying out again. She could feel a trickle of wet sliding down her cheek and prayed it was sweat and not tears. She would not weep like a child in front of Celia Carter.

⚬⚬⚭⚭⚬⚬

Kell held her gaze as he withdrew. Then he stood,

and with the red of Tali's innocence displayed on his still engorged cock, turned and faced the witnesses.

Celia Carter stood with her mouth agape, staring as Beth first displayed a clean white linen for the group to approve, and then handed the handkerchief to him. He blotted the blood from between Tali's thighs, and then from himself.

"Evidence," he said the one word and handed the stained cloth to Mrs. Pearson, the woman Beth identified as the oldest matron witnessing the event. She nodded her head solemnly and accepted it after which Kell pulled on his trews.

"My wife paid a grand price for that wee scrap of cloth. Mind it doesna get lost. Show those ye need ta show. I'll retrieve it on me next trip ta town."

He scooped Tali from the cot and carried her out the door where Horace Murdock waited beside Judge Stanley. To Murdock Kell said, "I'd be grateful if ye'd take care of matters here."

On the way to the exit they passed Anthony Simmons, smiling at them as if they were scurrying away in humiliation. Tali wiggled in Kell's arms and muttered, "Put me down."

As soon as her feet touched the floor, Kell watched his bonny wife march to where the miscreant attorney stood smirking. Without a word, she doubled her fist and brought it up hard under the gobshite's chin. Kell heard the crack as her wee hand met the arrogant sod's jaw.

Simmons teetered, his eyes rolled back in his head, and down he went.

Kell didn't bother hiding his grin of delight. The crowd hooted. One man yelled to him, "Best watch her Kell, she's got a mean uppercut."

"That she does," he answered. Kell had never delivered a more sincere bow then the one he swept low before her, catching her bruised hand to kiss her knuckles when she returned to his side.

When he slung an arm around her shoulder, ready to pick her up again, she said, "It's all right. I can walk. You don't need to carry me now."

"Do ye no' ken perhaps I *want* me arms around ye, lass?" With that said, she made no protest when he scooped her up. She curled into his embrace, hiding her face against his chest as he walked outside, cradling her in his arms.

Evidently, remembering she had things to worry about, though, she tugged on his shirt. "My house—"she murmured.

"Will be taken care of. Stop worrying now, and be easy. I've got ye, lassie, and I'm no' letting ye go." If his manner seemed gruff and possessive, his bride didn't seem to mind.

Beth stepped in their path, slapped something into Kell's hand and whispered in a low voice, "Use this on Tali."

He squinted at the tin and asked, "Fer her hand?"

"No," Beth answered and grinned.

Tali glared at her friend and grabbed for the tin. Kell shoved it in his pocket. "I will do as ye direct, Mistress Beth," he said and winked.

"*This* is for your hand," Beth said to Tali and displayed a bowl, a sack that already dripped, and a towel. "Judge Stanley contributed the ice for his afternoon sweet tea and said to tell you, 'Well done'".

Kell suspected he was grinning like a loon when he emerged from the courthouse to the steps. And didn't he feel like the fool once again, only remembering after he swaggered outside holding his bride proudly in his arms that they'd ridden to Annon in Horace Murdock's surrey.

Thankfully, Kell's old wagon hitched to his older horse, stood in the street with Liam and Jack beside it. The news from inside had obviously traveled quickly to the out because as he descended the steps with his bride in his arms, more than one congratulation was called out to them.

⚬ટ 9ૈ⚬

Tali felt stupid being carried from the building as if she were an invalid. But it was a convenient way to hide her face, so she didn't protest.

Beth followed beside them to the wagon and spotted the shaggy cat first.

"Where did he come from?" she asked pointing past

Liam and Jack to the seat of the wagon.

"Oh my goodness," Tali murmured. "It's the stray cat that I named Aloysius. He found his way to my cottage…" She looked accusingly at Kell. "It's your cat isn't it?"

He opened his mouth to deny it. She could see the struggle on his face. It sounded as if he half strangled on the truth when he muttered, "He isna mine, claims me no' and I the same with him."

"Then why is he at my cottage and here today?" The cat remained on the seat staring at them as if he knew he was the subject of the discussion.

"'Tis the horse, he came with the bluidy horse. I doona even like the beast," Kell growled and deposited Tali on the wagon seat beside the cat.

Instead of walking around, Kell looked across her at the cat and suggested, "Scoot that way luv. I'll sit this side to drive."

Obligingly she hid her smile and slid sideways, crowding the cat. The animal promptly jumped into her lap, looking up at Kell balefully.

"Behave," she told the both of them and urged the cat to the back of the wagon. He stood, bristled at her a moment showing his disgust, then jumped to the wagonbed, and curled into a ball, clearly waiting for them to start home.

Once they were situated, Beth handed Kell the judge's gift and he dutifully wrapped Tali's hand in the towel with the ice pressed against her knuckles.

"Now ye must keep it flat, palm lying against my leg to keep it steady," he told her.

"Your pants will get wet. The ice is already melting."

"Doona care," he growled, staring at her hand as if it was the most precious thing he'd ever seen.

"I'm sure it will be fine," she told him.

"Aye," he agreed. "Now keep it on my leg, as I said, and we'll be fer home."

She leaned against Kell and, as they left Annon, tried to forget what had just happened. He started several conversations, which she ended by remaining silent. Overhead, lightning flickered in an otherwise still sky.

"Perhaps it will rain," he said hopefully.

"It's only heat lightning," she answered and resumed her silence. After her euphoria from smacking the lawyer and defeating the Carter witch evaporated, she felt tawdry, as if she'd rolled in filth and come away wearing it. When she remembered the testimony of the two thugs, she couldn't suppress her shudder.

"Are ye well?" Kell asked immediately.

No I'm not well. I'm disgusted, humiliated and ashamed. Tali stared ahead at the dirt trail, refusing to meet his glance. He nudged her chin, tilting it up to meet his gaze.

"That wasn't so bad," he growled when she finally gave in and looked up.

"It was horrifying," she snapped and since she had no place else to hide, she buried her face in his chest again.

"Ye'll get over it," he claimed, patting her back. "People will only remember ye had the courage to prove yer innocence.

"No they won't," she muttered. "They'll remember I made a spectacle of myself."

But when he started laughing she quit hiding her face and demanded indignantly, "What?"

"The men will remember ye planted a facer on Simmons and put him on his arse." He snorted and laughed louder. "And doona fash yerself aboot the women," he continued, his accent so thick she had to strain to understand. "The ladies, lass, will remember the size of me shaft."

CHAPTER XVII

———⋅⋄⋅———

Let every man praise the bridge he goes over . . .

*P*erhaps I shoudna have reminded her of my size. Kell shifted uneasily on the wagon bench, wondering how soon he could finish the act and feeling like a right pervert because he wondered. There'd been pain. Not his of course.

Jesus Mary and Joseph, she was so tight. He tried not to think about the moment she'd taken matters in hand and impaled herself on his member; but too late, his shaft had no problem reminiscing and swelled in response.

She leaned into his embrace, her hand molded to his thigh, rubbing against his erection each time the old wagon hit a rough spot in the road.

"Why don't you drive around the bad sections?" she finally asked, the innocent not realizing he'd been enjoying himself.

"Are ye in pain?" he asked abruptly.

"Yes," she answered flatly. "My hand hurts." She lifted her palm from where it rested on his thigh, paid no heed to the ridge beneath his trews, and flexed her fingers.

"Ouch," she said and winced.

"We'll soak yer bruised knuckles when we get home." Kell slid his arm around her waist, pulled her close again, and flicked the reins, urging the old horse to move a bit faster.

"And," he paused, clearing his throat that had suddenly become constricted, "the other? Are ye in pain from the bedding?"

"No more than you, I suspect." And didn't she just flash a smile of mischief up at him and squeeze his thickened shaft beneath his trews.

"'Tis no' wise ta taunt a crazed man in the heat of rut," he warned her gruffly, leering down at her.

She giggled and the sound was an assurance that his bonny bride had no fear of him.

"We bollixed them, we did," he proclaimed, needing to crow a bit now that the deed was done and the event won.

"We did," she agreed. "Whatever that is."

"Lean up to me, luv, and I'll whisper the meaning in yer ear." Trusting him, which the lass would soon learn she could not do when it came to the hide and chase between them, she stretched, hugging ever tighter against his frame, tilting her head to hear his words.

And oh so easily his lips found the spot behind her ear to nuzzle the sweetness there, and his hand found her plump breast where her nipple stood erect and teased his palm. She moaned, a deep sound he caught when he kissed his way to her mouth.

"I want ye so much, luv, I crave ye night and day." It was the truth he murmured against lips that opened for him. Thank the good Lord the old horse wanted his oats and knew the way home. Kell enjoyed the rest of the trip holding his bride in his arms, promising her the wicked things they'd soon do while his trusted steed pulled the wagon without interruption to the ranch yard and into the barn.

The exchange of sunlight for the dim interior announced they'd arrived, and the hiss of the cat in the back, reminded Kell that there were better places to continue their loving. But it was the closing of the barn doors that got his attention.

"It took you long enough," Anthony Simmons snarled. "Couldn't you wait to fuck her until you got here?" The lawyer held a shotgun in his hand, pointing it at them.

"Get down from the wagon. And don't think I'll hesitate to shoot both of you. I'd prefer not, mind you. That is too quick a death." The lawyer touched his chin and smirked at Tali as he leveled his insult. "I've planned a more dramatic ending for the whore of Isaca."

"Ye've gone fecking headers, ye arse," Kell told him, scooting Tali toward the edge of the wagon seat with his hip.

"Not at all," Simmons disagreed, motioning them to get down. "I've been the Carter attorney for over ten years. For God sakes, I drew up the will eight years ago. Now get down." He walked toward them, holding the shotgun steady.

The bluidy cretin seemed determined to prove his brilliance as well as his aim. Kell agreed it was a good idea to let the lawyer run his gob. "Get ready to jump and roll," he murmured.

"If you think she'll escape, think again. The bequest states she must live with her husband at least a year before she collects. The important word there is 'live'; another instance of foresight on my part."

"Why do you want Mama's cottage?" Tali asked, calling Simmons' attention back to her. Kell tensed, ready to spring if the man got a step closer.

Simmons lifted the shotgun higher. "Don't tempt me." And then he continued his self-adulation. "Nobody cared about Carter's by-blow, including him. He paid for you dutifully for the first fifteen years of your life without apparent interest and tied the cottage up in excessive bureaucratic rigmarole Cerise couldn't afford to question." His smile insinuated that he'd enjoyed devising the red tape.

"I'll never know what spurred the change, but, four years ago he grew a conscience. Maybe he had a premonition of his death. Who knows? Anyway, he said it wasn't fair leaving so much to Jack and so little to you."

Simmons shook his head in wonder. "He hired a geology report to see if there was a way to tap into the artesian well on the property. With water levels low, he thought maybe it could be harvested and sold by the barrel."

"Oh for pity sake," Tali said. "The water's not even pure. I wouldn't drink it."

Kell didn't like the look of Simmons' smile. A bluidy flash of shark's teeth couldn't have gleamed whiter. "The geologist found a layer of natural gas and raw petroleum."

"And that is important why?" Kell asked, watching for the moment he could jump the gobshite while he gabbed. "Yer no' but a blood-sucking barrister, boyo. Ye get nothing from this."

"If you were not a dumb animal that climbs in a ring to get his brains beat out for money, you might be able to understand." Simmons held the shotgun before him, his finger on the trigger as he scanned the area behind them.

"Ah, yes. That will do nicely." He backed them to the cleared area where Kell's punching bag swung from the rafters. "Suffice it to say in the future it will be worth ten times Jack's land."

"Come here," he ordered Tali. "When you're dead, your estate reverts to Celia, hence me."

"Doona do as the greedy bastard says," Kell responded and grabbed her arm lest she try to obey.

"I'll blow his head from his shoulders if you don't." And then conversationally he went on, "It's too bad you have to die with her, Lonigan. I've nothing against you, at all. Really. I've won quite large sums on you in the past."

"She's no' moving unless it's out the door," Kell said and Simmons blew a hole in the punching bag, the sound of the blast reverberating through the barn.

"Next one turns his head into gray sludge on the wall," Simmons warned. "Come over here," he ordered her again.

"Nay, lass," Kell protested even as Tali twisted free of his grip and moved to stand in the spot where Simmons pointed.

The lawyer pulled a flask from his pocket, and sighed. "Such a waste of good whiskey, but..." He doused the straw in front of her and, after throwing the flask to the floor, pulled out a matchbox.

"A tragic affair, all around," he said, and grimaced. "Young newlyweds burn up in barn. We'll leave it to the gossips to figure out why you never made it to the house."

He lit the match at the same time Tali and Kell both lunged for him. But it was the cat, stalking them from above, who got to Simmons first. The wily beast dropped on the lawyer's back, claws unfurled for the attack.

The shotgun discharged its last blast, but hit nothing but the bales of hay stored in the back. Simmons screamed like a girl and dropped the match, which promptly ignited the alcohol soaked straw.

"Get out of the barn, lass," Kell shouted and jumped on Simmons, lending his fists to the mauling the cat was delivering.

Though he would have liked to end the bastard's hold on life, Kell left off pummeling the knave, when the fire began to gather strength.

Satisfied that he'd left the man senseless, he dropped him to the floor, gifting him with nothing more than a broken nose, bloodied eye, and perhaps a broken rib or two.

"I told ye to flee," Kell growled at his bride.

"We'll flee together," she sassed back, her expression grim as she beat at little flames that crept toward the hay mow.

"Fetch a bucket of water from the pump out front lass," Kell ordered, glad to see her obey this time. But when she opened the barn doors, the breeze fanned the embers into flames and carried sparks everywhere.

The dry wood of the ancient wagon ignited quickly and burned like tinder behind the horse. Old it might be, but the animal was not so far gone it wasn't squealing and rearing in panic where it stood in the traces.

Kell cast a last look at Simmons and left the sod sprawled unconscious on the floor. He turned instead to the task of rescuing the horse. He had to pull his shirt off and blindfold the beast to get it from the barn.

When flames from the wagon singed its tail and rump, it screamed and took off like a shot, running crazed through the flames. Kell rode its neck to the outside, fumbling in his pocket and retrieving his knife to slice through the harness.

That done, Kell collapsed on the ground, stunned but alive. He didn't realize he was on fire until water splashed over him and he heard the sizzle of his hair, a sound he for bluidy certain never wished to hear again.

And then Tali fell to her knees beside him, crying and kissing him at the same time.

"I thought you were trapped. I couldn't get the pump to work. I only got a little water. I...I..."

"It's all right luv. I'm no' damaged much, I think. 'Tis Simmons I must see ta now." He staggered to his feet as Tali clung to him, forbidding his plan to reenter the barn, now totally awash in smoke. A rumbling growl rolled from the structure before it exploded into giant flames, consuming the whole building and leaping toward the sky.

"We need to wet down the roof of the house," Tali said with a bucket in her hand, urging him toward the pump. Dazed though he was, her words mobilized him into action, and the two of them ignored the barn and the man they couldn't save and concentrated on their home. They'd not labored alone long, before riders began streaming in.

"Saw the smoke all the way to town," more than one neighbor explained. Buckets and containers started appearing and the men formed a brigade from the pump to the house. More ranchers arrived in wagons loaded with water barrels, burlap beater bags, axes and rakes, fighting the sparks lest they be carried beyond the bare ranch yard to the dry grass further out.

The barn burned fast and shortly after dusk collapsed in a shower of sparks that lit the sky. Kell sat on the steps of the veranda, hugging Tali to his side as they rested a moment together.

He stared at the grim faced men laboring on in the night and heaved himself from the step. Tali immediately stood as well. "Stay here, luv, where I know yer safe," he told her.

He smiled down at her soot stained face, knowing he'd never before seen such beauty. A tear cleaned a path as it trickled down her smudged cheek and Kell hugged her to him. "Doona cry, lass. 'Twas just a barn and can be replaced. The lawyer I canna grieve for."

"I'm not crying," she whispered, and almost reverently, looked at the sky. "It's raining."

꧁ ꧂

Beth arrived with the back of the store wagon piled full of food prepared by the ladies of Isaca. Many of the town women accompanied her to the ranch.

Tali wrapped an apron around her soot stained dress and stood in the rain beside them, serving up food to the tired men. Even after the light drizzle changed to a steady downpour, no one went inside and few seemed inclined to leave.

Liam and Jack arrived and joined Kellan in walking

a wide perimeter around the smoldering barn fire, lest a spark or cinder escape.

Though the mood had become almost party-like, and Tali had so much to be thankful for, it shamed her that she wished her friends and neighbors would leave. After the rain continued through the night into dawn, the fire was thoroughly extinguished, and the food was all gone, she got her wish.

She stood beside Kellan on the porch, peering through the rain as the last wagon pulled from the barn lot. She was wet, dirty, and suddenly cold when he removed his arm around her shoulders.

"That's it then, luv. The last of our friends have departed. 'Tis time to move inside." He took her arm and ushered her to the door, then lifted her in his arms before she knew what he intended.

"Kellan, what are you doing?" Her voice came out in an unattractive screech she abhorred, but he just laughed and bounced her in his arms.

"Carrying me bride into our home," he explained. "And seeing ta me lady's care the rest of our days," he added when they were inside.

She had no idea where he found the energy, because she herself felt as if she could sleep for days. Dirty, if need be. But he bounded up the stairs and to the bathing room with her still in his embrace.

"Ye'll feel much better when ye have the soot off ye," he explained, filling the tub, and divesting her of her garments as he spoke.

Soon enough, she sat in tepid water that felt glorious, and didn't care at all that she was naked before him. He rubbed soap on a soft cloth and washed her from top to bottom, handling her gently as if she was a child.

"Close yer eyes now, luv, so I can rinse yer hair."

Tali obeyed, and kept them closed even after he wrapped her head in a towel, lifted her from the water, and tucked her arms into her nightgown he'd found.

Only after he'd carried her to his big bed did she peek up at him. "Your eyebrows are gone," she muttered. So was a great deal of the hair on his head.

"I'll grow more," he assured her. "Now rest while I make meself presentable."

She closed her eyes, intending to listen for his return, but dozed until she felt the mattress sink under his weight. Keeping her eyes closed, she breathed deeply, feigning sleep.

"Rest, me girl," he rumbled, and slid under the covers, wrapping her in his heat, his arousal prodding her rump, as his hands came up to cup her breasts.

"I'm sleeping," she informed him as he wrestled her out of the gown he'd put her in earlier.

"Doona mind me, lass. 'Tis only checking to make certain ye are well, that I be doing. Rest and pay me no mind."

But since he conducted a running litany of what he found needed attending, from her 'wee perky nubs', to her 'bonny round rump', sleep was not in the offing.

When he'd teased her to the point where heat roiled in her stomach, her womb clenched in hunger, and she was ready to rise from the bed and thrash him if he didn't tend the ache between her thighs, he rose from kissing her belly, parted her legs and prepared to quench her desire.

"Hold onto me, lass, and let me show ye heaven," he growled.

And he did.

EPILOGUE

And a feinted blow finally lands . . .

As they entered the Catholic Parish in Clarksville, Kell heaved a sigh of satisfaction, surrounded by the elegant simplicity of the holy sanctuary. He was quite pleased with his wife, his brother, his brother-in-law—well perhaps not so much the last.

Jack had been present at the ranch since the barn burned and the cupidity of his relatives was revealed. He'd taken it well, seemingly having little affection for his aunt, Celia Carter, who'd claimed ignorance of anything but contesting the will.

When Kell had decided it was time to visit a priest and arrange for a more formal wedding than a quick gab in front of Horace Murdock, Jack had tagged along without being invited. Not that the formality would be today. In his head, Kell planned a lavish affair, which he was certain he could lure more than a few new friends to attend.

He wanted his bride to…

"Kellan," Tali whispered. "You're daydreaming again."

"Aye," he agreed, he did that a lot these days. But he jerked to attention when the priest walked in. He'd feared it would be troublesome getting the church's dispensation to marry, but Father Andrew welcomed Kell and greeted Tali as if she was an old friend.

"I'll just fetch the papers your mother left here for you," the priest said, wearing a smile as he hurried from the room.

"Do ye know this fellow?" Kell asked her, but he could see from her puzzled expression she didn't.

"No, but he must be the priest my mother visited once a month. As I mentioned, the rest of the time…" She became silent again when Father Andrew returned and set a leather folder before her.

"Your christening papers, her marriage lines—the first, I mean. The second, they took with them. I'm so pleased they worked it out."

Kell couldn't tell up from down. Jack next to him, cleared his throat and then said, "Excuse me, you must not have heard. Cerise Fitzwilliam is…" he stuttered for a moment, and then blurted, "she died."

The priest sank down on his chair before them and took up Tali's hands in his. "Oh I'm so sorry to hear that sad news, my child. They were so excited. Like children again. Did the ship go down?"

Well, it was a banjaxed affair for certain. After they'd gotten the tangled threads into a fulsome skein a few things became apparent. Cerise Fitzwilliam had married Jeb Carter when she was sixteen and he was twenty. They had not abided well together, and she'd ne'er gone back to the North after the war, but she'd not stayed with her husband either. And then there was Jack and Tali. They were twins.

The way the priest let on, it might have been the first and only time the young couple had—well—coupled. The confederate soldier and his northern wife had parted ways after the war when they couldn't come to an agreement on who was boss. And unthinkable as it was, they'd each taken a bairn.

After the telling was through and all seemed known, the last thing revealed was the worst—or mayhap—the best. Kell had thought he and Liam had knocked around and done some scurrilous things, but Tali's parents topped them all—after they'd duped their children, deceived their friends, and deserted their homes—the bluidy fools had eloped.

THE END

AUTHOR'S NOTE

Some of my ancestors immigrated to the United States in the first half of the 19th century during the Irish potato famine. As a result, there is more than a little blarney in my blood, which is to say, the tradition of story telling goes deep in my family. I've included as chapter subheads a few of the Irish sayings that molded (perhaps warped) my childhood.

In *Outrageous Pride*, I mention that although she was of the Catholic faith, Tali's mother attended the local Protestant Church because the Catholic Parish was too far to travel each Sunday. I based this story thread on anecdotal information from my own family's experience of changing faiths because of the proximity of a local church.

*Included free as a thank you for buying this book,
please enjoy the story of Tali's parents…*

CERISE
AMOUR

Book 2.5 in the
Unlikely Gentlemen Series

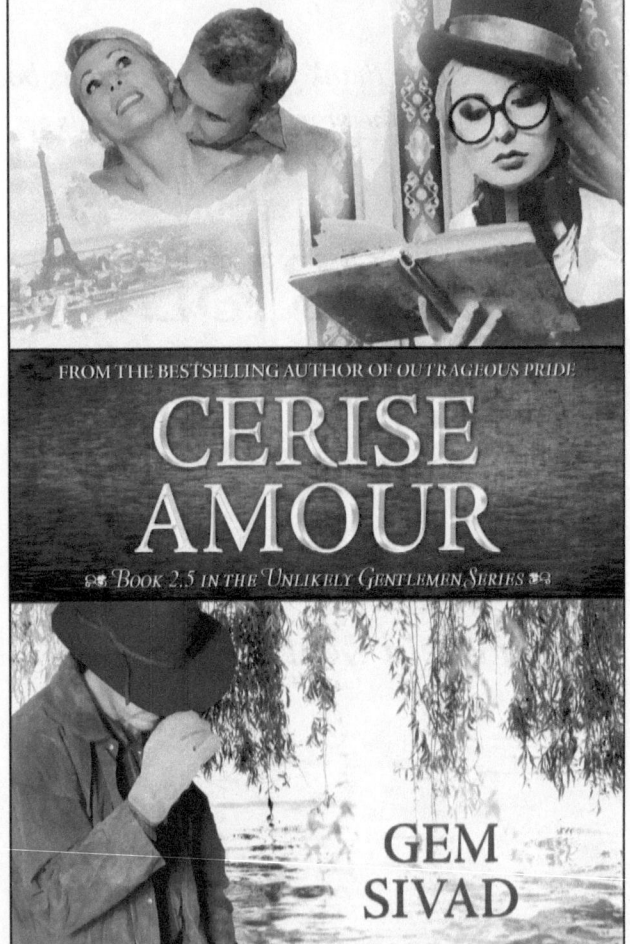

FROM THE BESTSELLING AUTHOR OF *OUTRAGEOUS PRIDE*

CERISE AMOUR

Book 2.5 in the Unlikely Gentlemen *Series*

GEM SIVAD

SYNOPSIS

After a hasty Civil War marriage to Confederate soldier, Jeb Carter, Cherry Fitzwilliam finds herself abandoned among strangers; over the next twenty-five years she carefully constructs a life based on lies.

Her neighbors and daughter believe she's a widow who lost her husband in the war. But Jeb is alive and prosperous and Cherry's one indulgence is a much anticipated monthly meeting with him that usually devolves into a shouting match.

When Jeb Carter becomes ill, perhaps even dying, discord changes to despair and he asks her to be with him to the end. Avoiding the questions of family and friends, they leave Texas on a journey that takes them to a love they've long denied.

CERISE AMOUR
Book 2.5 in the Unlikely Gentlemen Series

ISBN 978-1-62622909-9
Copyright © 2014 Gem Sivad
Published by Dark Mountain Books

Manufactured in the United States of America.

EDITOR
V.N. Johnson

COVER DESIGN
Michael Hart

PROLOGUE

Paris, France, 1889

*C*erise stretched her long limbs, enjoying the feel of silk sheets caressing her naked body. She'd retired the night before wearing a sleeping gown, which, as usual, had been discarded. Without looking, she knew it lay on the floor next to the bed—on *his* side. Her foot mistakenly, or perhaps not so accidentally, skated down Jeb's calf.

Her stomach clenched in anticipation when his breathing changed from a rumbling snore to a growl. In one fluid movement, he surrounded her, pressing his chest against her back and cradling her in his arms. Even though he emitted more heat than the smelting furnaces they'd viewed in Luxemburg, Cerise shivered.

"Cold, sweetheart?" he murmured against her hair as he tightened his embrace, and his arousal prodded her bottom. Wryly, she admitted to herself, she wasn't immune from its charm. Exasperated, she rolled over and faced him.

"I don't like pretending we're dead." She'd been trying to have this conversation for days. And likewise, he'd been avoiding it.

"Nor do I." Using her changed position to his advantage, he trailed kisses along her jaw to her ear where he paused to nibble on the tender lobe.

"We need to plan our return." Instead of the crisp voice she'd intended, her statement came out as a husky moan.

"No doubt you'll come up with one, soon," he muttered. "For now, let me enjoy our freedom." In a move he'd practiced many times in the last few weeks, he scooted her under him so his shaft nestled between her thighs.

"You're incorrigible," she accused; then whimpered, "no fair," when he cupped her breast, rotating his thumb against her nipple. Her body turned to liquid heat, and she arched her hips tangling her limbs with his.

"You want me as much as I want you." His tone held smug satisfaction.

More, I fear. Cerise met the gaze of the man she desired beyond comprehension. For years, they'd jousted for control with most of their combat carried on by letter or legal counsel.

Their physical encounters had ended in angry confrontations and harsh words. But always, lurking beneath the quarrels, she'd recognized mutual lust. During this recent time, while her husband had been hers alone, passion had blossomed between them.

But their escape from reality was quickly ending. Cerise faced either sharing Jeb Carter's world of influence and power, or resuming her separate quiet life. Either choice filled her with anxiety.

She tightened her arms possessively around Jeb's neck, pulling his head down for a prolonged kiss, trying to tell him through her actions how much she needed him.

Needed… That frightened her the most. With all that she had been through, she'd learned to temper her emotions with common sense and thoughtful intelligence. But prolonged company with Jeb Carter had a way of removing barriers to her heart—walls she'd spent years erecting.

Since her heart was already lost, Cerise focused on managing their coupling. She shifted beneath him, grasped his shaft, and guided his hard length through her soft folds.

Deliberately, he covered her hand with his and stroked higher bumping the bundle of nerves at her apex with his arousal. When she moaned and pressed against his touch, he laughed and rolled with her until she straddled him.

"Hungry for me?" he asked, smiling up at her.

"Yes." Shameless in her pleasure, she braced her arms on his chest, clenched the walls of her sex around his hard length, and rode.

Cerise lost herself in his attentions, meeting each of

his thrusts, and arching into the pleasure as he teased her nipples with his tongue and brought her to release again and again. She finally collapsed, sprawling bonelessly across his chest, too weak to continue though she knew he'd not yet claimed his own completion.

He flipped her onto her back where she lay replete, watching him. He wore a look of concentration as he put a pillow under her rump, lifted her knees, and situated himself between her legs.

Then as if her satiated slump gave him great joy, his gaze caressed her body as it moved upward. His manhood stood like a lance between his thighs, and his expression changed from lust to one of fierce determination.

"*Cerise amour*…by God that's right," he said gruffly, linking her name to the one French word he'd bothered to learn. "Cherry love, you are never leaving me again."

He delivered his edict, by sliding his manhood through her slick heat, its heavy length stretching the walls of her channel, marking his territory as he reached her core.

"Mine…" his ragged whisper accompanied each subsequent thrust.

"You're mine, too." Cerise wrapped her legs around his hips and felt prickles of heat skate over his flesh. She tightened her grip as his muscles tensed and then he came with a shout, filling her with his seed.

"I love you," she murmured as she pressed kisses on his chest. Whatever happened, she'd never again pretend to not want him.

Afterward, as they lay sated in each other's arms, Cerise began to fidget, unable to stop thinking.

"What's got you worried, sweetheart?" He caressed her hair, smoothing it from her forehead to peer at her.

"Remorse," she grumbled. She reached for her tortoise shell eyeglasses, set them on her nose, rose from the bed, and pulled on her robe as she crossed to the window. Once there, she watched the activities below, as if viewing the work taking place on the Champ de Mars would quell her anxiety.

"We were utterly selfish."

"Granted." The rustle of clothes being donned accompanied his agreement. "But then again, thanks to you kidnapping me, I'm alive instead of buried six feet deep."

"Kidnapping is a bit extreme, I think," she murmured. "In point of fact, we engineered this trip together."

"Nope, Cerise. I was too sick to plan anything but seeing you one last time. It's amazing what a big dose of the woman I love can cure."

It was more than remarkable. She'd come to their monthly meeting at the Clarksville Catholic Parish expecting their usual discord. He'd come to her with his proposal.

"I'm dying, sweetheart. Marry me again and let me spend my last days with you."

All of her grievances against Jeb had disappeared and Father Andrew had been more than willing to oblige their request. For the second time in her life, Cerise Fitzwilliam had become Jeb Carter's wife.

"After the ceremony, all I could think of was taking care of you. And given our past, I didn't think that would be allowed if we stayed at home," she admitted. And so, she'd done the unimaginable. She'd faked both their deaths and bought tickets on a passenger ship bound for Europe.

"I don't know what I would have done if you'd died." Her heart missed a beat even at the idea.

"Well I didn't. And I'm not planning on it anytime soon, either. I guess I wasn't as sick as I thought, because all it took was a long overdue vacation and your love to cure me in both body and soul. When we return to the hullabaloo at home, you'll have to own up to saving me—more than once."

They'd been away for six months. It was already a new year, and life had continued around them. The enormity of their deception hadn't penetrated her oblivion at first. Initially she was too focused on improving Jeb's health to consider how news of her own death would have affected her daughter, Natalia.

But, now here they were. His illness had seemed to abate, the farther they got from Texas. Jeb joked about her role as his rescuer, as she reluctantly admitted that the cost of saving him had been the destruction of her own artfully contrived life.

How could she possibly explain to her daughter that since the age of seventeen, Cerise's entire existence had been based on a falsehood?

She shuddered, aching with guilt and dread. Jeb joined her at the window, wrapping her in his arms to hold her close again, as she tried to disguise her trembling fear.

"Do you have regrets?" he asked too casually, resting his chin on her shoulder as if to share her view of the street.

"I regret that my father never got a chance to see La Tour Eiffel." She nodded at the iron lattice tower being constructed by engineer Gustave Eiffel, for the 1889 World's Fair. "And I regret that I don't own that keyhole desk we saw yesterday in the antique shop we visited."

"That's not what I mean and you know it," he said, nipping her ear.

"All right, I'm sorry I didn't see my son's first steps, that I let him believe me dead, that I mislead my daughter in thinking you dead." A sob escaped her throat in spite of her attempt to control her feelings.

He turned his head, pressed his lips against her throat for a moment as he hugged her tighter. "I'm guilty of all the above as well. Sweetheart, it was war. We didn't do everything like we should have. But, we're here, alive, and we have a second chance to get it right this time. I just need to know that you have no regrets about me... about us being together."

She turned in his arms to face him. "We've caused our friends and families great distress, and I wonder how we'll ever make them understand. But do I regret you?" With her finger tips, she traced the stern line of his lips and smiled at him. "Never."

"You ever think about the way it was when we met?" he asked gruffly, the harsh line of his mouth softening.

Think about it? "Every day for twenty-five years," she murmured.

CHAPTER I

*K*nocked from his horse by a lunging infantryman, Jeb Carter staggered on the ground, trying to keep his footing. He was choked and half-blinded by the billowing canon smoke, and he barely dodged a bayonet aimed at his belly. When he shot his attacker in the face, unexpected gore sprayed back on him; blinking through it, he didn't move fast enough to avoid the dying soldier's bayonet thrust that caught his thigh.

His commander, Brigadier General Henry E. McCulloch, had expected Walker's Greyhounds to encounter little resistance from the inexperienced Federal troops at Milliken's Bend. Instead, Jeb's division had found itself engaged in a bloody battle quickly devolving into hand-to-hand combat.

When a bullet grazed his skull, he fell to the ground, closing his eyes against the pain and fighting to stay conscious. It was still early morning, and dew wet the grass, though he couldn't be certain it wasn't his own blood soaking his skin and making him shiver. He didn't know how much time passed before he opened his eyes again.

A riderless horse galloped toward him, trumpeting its terror at the field of dying and dead soldiers. He levered himself up in time to catch the saddle leathers, letting the animal's frenzy pull him to his feet to stumble beside it as it cleared a path through those still fighting.

"Sonofabitch, sonofabitch, sonofabitch," he muttered, grabbing the horse's mane and silently thanking God for the times he and his brother, Nathaniel, had dare-deviled on the ranch.

His technique would have had Nate jeering, but Jeb scrambled up the fleeing beast and let it carry him from the field of doom. He rode slumped low in the saddle, clinging to his mount's neck.

Succumbing to the oblivion he'd earlier fought, he lost time, waking abruptly to discover the battle-crazed beast beneath him had become a placid animal grazing next to the river.

Not being from these parts, Jeb didn't recognize his surroundings, but he didn't need a map. Shots and the boom of cannon fire sounded in the distance, assuring him that somewhere in the distance the enemy still fought.

Even his hand ached when he unlocked his fingers from their death-grip on the horse's mane. He needed to assess his injuries, but when he dismounted, he almost blacked-out again. Steadying himself against the horse, he leaned for a bit until his head cleared.

"Gotta wash up before anything else," he muttered.

Holding tight to the reins with one hand, he knelt by the water and with his other hand, carefully, explored his scalp.

His head hurt as if a damned tom-tom beat behind his brow. But judging from the dried blood crusted on his head, Jeb decided the wound had quit bleeding. He splashed water on his face, washing and scraping the detritus of battle from his skin.

Feeling considerably more alert, he pulled the blood-soaked bandana from his thigh and inspected the hole in his leg. If it didn't go septic, he might even survive; but between now and that possibility, he had to find Nate.

Jeb ducked his head, mopping his face on his sleeve, ready to return to the early morning site to search for his brother. Raw agony pierced his shoulder and then the sound of the sniper's shot reached his ears.

Ahhh, dammit… Jeb fell into the water, hoping Nate survived to find his body since it didn't seem likely he'd be able to do the same for his brother.

The sound of battle coming from the direction of Milliken's Bend had ended Cherry's sleep at daybreak. She'd grabbed her glasses and hastily dressed, then dithered inside afraid to venture forth for fear of being shot or worse.

War. She hated it. Before her dad had brought them here, he'd assured her they'd be in a safe zone. Hah! Obviously there was no such thing to be had.

"I told him this was a bad idea," Cherry muttered, pacing from one side of the room to the other. S. M. Fitzwilliam, known to his peers as Fitz, was her only family, and wherever he worked became her temporary home. Right now her home was situated in a swamp.

When her dad's engineering skills had been needed in Louisiana, she'd accompanied him, even though both Union and Rebel troops had amassed where he planned to work.

"I think it's a foolish idea," she'd told him.

"We'll be safe enough," he'd assured her. "Remember the time we had…" and he'd meandered off into one of his many tales.

"War is different than—" she'd interrupted his story.

"The Union Army needs a canal built and we need money." He'd cut through her sass, his tone clipped, losing the edge of humor he'd usually displayed.

Had the project been successful, it would have connected Duckport Landing on the Mississippi River with Walnut Bayou and enabled the Federal troops to reach New Carthage by flatboat. Unfortunately, her ignored opinion had been only too true.

"'Twas a miserable waste of lives, money, and my

time; all in all, a farce," he'd admitted two nights before.

Site problems had made the Army's five month effort to cut a three-mile canal from the river to Cooper's Plantation an abject failure. General Grant, himself, had sent orders to quit the project that had been beleaguered by spring flooding, collapsed walls, and sickness among the troops.

"And will you be paid?" she'd asked. Her, 'I told you so,' was unnecessary and went unspoken because they were leaving.

"No problems there, luvie," he'd told her. "We'll have a tidy sum when I get paid and with government script in hand, we'll catch a north bound train to anywhere free of the fighting."

Having lived a nomadic existence for all of her sixteen years, she'd become accustomed to rough quarters and quick moves with her dad. But she'd never been smack in the middle of a war before. She didn't know whether to run, hide, or stay put.

This was the second day he'd been gone, he hadn't returned yesterday as expected, and now there was shooting close by. She had a feeling they'd have little time for discussion when he arrived. Cherry had already packed the old steamer trunk. Now she added the last of their clothes to the maps and books already there.

"Okay, Dad, all I need is for you to come get me,

and we can go." But, the morning dragged on, and Fitz didn't appear. Cherry chewed on her bottom lip listening intently. It was almost noon when the sound of firing died down and she decided it was safe to go outside the cabin.

But she'd barely stepped from the cabin when the quiet spell ended. The boom of cannon resumed, this time sounding from the direction of Young's Point.

"That's not good," she muttered, worried about her father more than she wanted to admit. It sounded as if the fighting had moved toward him.

No doubt her dad would have told her to stay hidden away on their patch of dry ground in the woods, but he wasn't here, and she could get a better view out by the bayou where the trees thinned.

She'd be glad to see the last of swamps. She didn't know where they'd travel next, but she had hopes it would be someplace with no mosquitoes and no alligators.

Swatting at blood sucking insects, she made her way to the edge of the waterway, scouting the area for noxious creatures before she turned her attention in the direction of Young's Point.

Her glasses steamed from the pall of sticky heat already blanketing the day, and she removed them, absently wiping the lenses with a handkerchief while squinting at the skyline where smoke hung like low clouds. The day's heavy humidity changed to a fine drizzle, and she returned her spectacles to her nose, preparing to retreat.

Suddenly, a hand snaked out of the weeds and seized her ankle. Cherry gasped, lurching backward, pulling loose from the weak grip.

Instead of fleeing, after she'd caught her breath, she peered down to inspect her assailant and met the fevered gaze of a Confederate soldier.

CHAPTER II

*eb heard the sounds of rescue before he stared up at deliverance. He'd been carried downstream by a torpid current, bleeding in the water all the way; finally he'd bumped against land and had just enough life left to crawl through mud and collapse in the marsh grass.

He was cold, and the water he'd swallowed had left him nauseous, not thirst quenched. But his eyes still worked, and, unless he was hallucinating, he was looking at a tall girl wearing glasses.

"It would be best," she suggested, enunciating her words carefully, "if you moved from those weeds before an alligator finds you."

"Help me up," he answered, extending his left arm toward her; too trustingly, she took his hand and tugged. If he lived another day, he'd tell her about the error of being too trusting. As it was, he struggled to rise, but fell back into the mud.

"You cannot stay here," she told him, her expression grim.

"Hurt," he groaned and closed his eyes, savoring the rain as it cooled his fever.

"Please wake up," she coaxed. When he ignored her, before he could warn her off, she grabbed his feet, inching backwards, tugging him through the weeds and away from the brackish water.

Though he lacked the strength to shout or even scream, his strangled groans must have registered on her finally. After a tortuous but short distance, she set his boots back to the ground.

"Sorry," she apologized.

"Leave me," he ordered, willing her to go away. He'd recover enough to move on or die in peace with raindrops pelting his face. He must have spoken the last aloud because she answered.

"If I leave you, it won't be to the mercy of raindrops. You'll probably be alligator food before you die. I don't know how you escaped the monsters already."

She squatted next to his body, speaking to him softly while she inspected him. "All right, I see the problem. You have two obvious weak spots—a nasty hole in your right shoulder and a wound in your upper left leg."

She paused and slid her arm under his back. "On the count of three, sit up."

Jeb grunted, obeying her command, and with her help, managed a sitting position.

"Now, this next part won't be so easy," she assured him and stood, looking down at him as if he were an interesting puzzle to be solved. Stalking around and studying him from every angle, she finally came to a stop next to his good leg.

Through a haze of pain, Jeb teetered in an upright position, listening to the girl who spoke to him with the authority of a drill sergeant.

18

"Give me your hand and bend your uninjured leg; I'll pull you up."

Since he'd been bracing himself with his good arm, as soon as he used it to reach for her, Jeb listed sideways.

She clasped his left wrist, gripped his hand in both of hers, and staggered backward. "Get up," she panted. As if his obedience was a foregone conclusion, she strained to pull him to his feet. Instead, his sideways slump forced her to her knees.

"You will get up now," she said, her tone steely, as if he'd insulted her by his inability. She leaned against his left side, avoiding his thigh, but circling his waist with her arms.

"As I lift, use my shoulder for support and your undamaged leg as a fulcrum to propel yourself upward."

He had no strength in him to do anything and tried to tell her so. But, she wouldn't quit pulling at him. Finally enraged by her pestering, like a berserker he heaved upward, trying to throw her aside. Ignoring pain, he staggered, leaned on her, and steadied his weight on his sound leg. "Now for the hard part," she said, sliding up his side to clasp him around the waist. "Let's go."

He cursed her most of the way. But in spite of his verbal abuse, she dragged, pushed, and carried him toward her destination. He made it to the cabin in the woods with little memory of how she achieved her goal. Sheer cussed grit if he had to say later, but however she did it, he lapsed into fevered oblivion once they reached her shelter.

The wounded soldier had helped as much as he could on the way through the swamp, and thank God for that. When his feet finally stopped taking orders from his brain, they were close enough to the cabin for her to maneuver his dead weight inside.

When she finally staggered through the door, she wasted no time hauling the wounded man to her dad's bed. He sprawled there unconscious and she collapsed on a chair to draw breath before she investigated his wounds. It felt as if an eternity had elapsed since Cherry had rescued him from the swamp.

He remained unresponsive when she cut through the gray coat and shirt to get to his injury. Even beneath his clothes, mud caked his body, and she had to wash the muck from his skin before she could proceed. Once she saw the extent of damage to his person, she thanked God for his oblivion.

She viewed the man she'd rescued with horror. Swallowing self-doubt, she raked the live coals into a small blaze and heated water to clean the wounds. Infection would probably kill him if blood loss didn't, but she had to try.

Growing up in frequently dangerous terrains, she'd learned to doctor her dad when he came home with cuts and bruises. But she had no ability to treat wounds of this magnitude. She filled a bowl with water and set it next to the bed.

"My apologies in advance for any discomfort," she told him. Since he was unconscious, she spoke to herself. After she'd washed her hands and meager tools, she began piece by piece tweezing the embedded cloth from the wound. Her patent's muscles twitched, but he made no sound.

Cherry thought he was unconscious, but once the debris had been removed from his flesh, he mumbled, "The balls still in there. You'll have to dig it out."

"All right," she agreed, trying to sound confident. "I can do that."

Unfortunately for her patient, her poor eyesight required close proximity. She washed the debris and blood from the tweezers and before she could lose her nerve, began probing the wound, leaning so close to him her cheek brushed his shoulder more than once.

But, except for the fact that her spectacles kept sliding down her nose, interrupting her work until she adjusted them each time, the surgery went smoothly. The soldier had been lucky; the bullet had glanced off bone instead of shattering it.

Her hands, steady during the procedure, shook as if palsied after she removed the lead ball and dropped it on the table. "Whew," she sighed, slumping down on the chair next to the bed.

"Douse it with whiskey, now," he growled, getting

her attention. Startled, she wondered if he'd been awake during the entire excruciating event.

"We don't have spirits," she answered. "You'll have to make do with the poultice we keep on hand." She and her dad used the salve she made from cattails on everything from mosquito bites to cuts. Fortunately for them, they'd never had to test it on anything more serious.

She applied the medicine, dressed the wound, and then sat on a chair to rest a moment before tackling the leg injury.

Later, much later, after she'd cleaned and stitched the gash in his leg, Cherry sank onto the chair again, closed her eyes, and frowned. "It will have to do. If you don't thrash around, maybe the stitches will hold it shut. The wound is deep."

She'd been muttering aloud to herself, but his grunt of agreement called her back to the here and now, reminding her to stay alert.

"While you're awake you need to drink water." The heat of the additional body in the cabin made it warmer than usual. Sweat drenched the sheet she'd pulled over him to hide his nakedness.

From necessity, she'd removed all of his clothing to access his wounds. While working on him she'd been unaffected by the fact that her patient was male. But holding a cup to his lips while he sipped suddenly became an intimate task that left her trembling.

She bathed his face, and after he drank, she left him, presumably sleeping; she really couldn't be certain of his state since he'd startled her more than once already.

After Cherry changed her dress, she sat by the bed and monitored his every breath. Her mind played misdirection games as she concentrated on her patient rather than considering why her father hadn't returned for her.

CHAPTER III

*O*ver the next days, Cherry steeped herself in the battle for the soldier's life. When the change came—the shakes, the chills, the delirium—she sponged his body, bathed his face, and trickled water through parched lips.

There wasn't much to his clothes worth keeping—gray trousers too damaged to repair and a tattered shirt of indeterminate color. She burned them both, just in case someone besides her father came to the cabin, someone like Union troops who might discover her rebel patient and take him prisoner.

While he slept and healed, she concocted a story about him being her intended and rehearsed the speech often enough mentally to deliver the lie with ease. It would be best if she never had to use the tale, but she tailored their imaginary alliance to her own desires.

He wasn't as old as she'd first thought, and without the dirt caking his skin, she found him handsome in a wild, rough kind of way. His thatch of dark hair, though shaggy and too long uncut, was sable, a beautiful blend of rich brown and black. And his eyes, when they weren't burning up with fever, were a wonderful deep blue.

Cherry discarded the rest of the soldier's tattered clothes but kept the soft leather boots that he'd worn laced to his knees.

"If you die, I'll take your boots as payment for all my troubles," she taunted in one of his lucid moments, trying to irritate him into staying alive.

He grunted, making a rough sound that might have been laughter. Then he answered in a gravelly voice, "If you get me well, I'll gift you with boots of your own."

Cherry smiled at his promise as she sponged water over his back before reaching lower beneath the sheet to wipe the sweat from his buttocks and thighs.

"Soldier Boy," she teased, giddy with relief that he planned to keep breathing. "I haven't lost a patient yet, and I'll expect payment of said boots in due time."

"Debt noted," he growled. "But it'd be best when you're fondling my ass to remember I'm a man, not a boy."

You certainly are. She twitched the sheet back over his flesh, feeling prickly heat ignite her cheeks in a fiery blush.

"Where are your people?" he demanded in a stronger voice than she'd heard before.

"Away," she answered, afraid to say more. He was, after all, a Confederate soldier, and her dad had been working on a canal to help defeat the rebels.

ꙮ

Jeb Carter didn't know what to make of the girl who

tended him. Without a doubt he'd have been gator food if she'd not come along.

In moments of lucidity, after she'd half-carried him to her cabin, operated on his wounds, and saved his life, he'd tried to ask questions. "Who are you?"

She parried his questions with silence or meaningless answers. "I'm the person who dragged you here."

"Where's your family?" That question brought an icy response that told him nothing.

"If you die, I'll have to figure a way to hoist your body, build a travois, and haul you to burial. And since I don't know how to dig a grave in a swamp you need to get better and then get out."

He didn't ask that question again. For a young girl, her language was frequently harsh as well as incongruously filled with industrial terms such as hoist, fulcrum and pivot points; but her touch was always gentle as she kept his body bathed in cool water and fought the infection that festered in his wounds. He became accustomed to watching her through half-slitted eyes that hid his awareness.

For days he wavered in an out of consciousness. Each time he surfaced, she was there, concentrating on her battle to save him. Gradually, there were more lucid times than delirium. She avoided giving him personal information, but boasted about her doctoring skills.

"Where do you get your medicine?" His shoulder

and thigh were on the mend, and he had no doubt healing had been aided by the salve she'd used on his wounds.

"I make it. I brought a book about medicinal plants with me when we moved here." Her satisfied answer brought a smile to his face.

"Moved here from where?"

"Everywhere," she answered and grinned at him.

"How old are you anyway? Twelve, thirteen?"

"I'm sixteen, for your information," she answered. Her smile disappeared, and she glared at him, folding her arms across her chest defensively.

At sixteen, she should have been blossoming into womanhood. But… Her tall figure was all angles and flat planes, she wore her hair braided in pigtails, and though they fit and were of a decent quality, her clothes were fashioned for a much younger girl.

"I'm Jeb Carter," he'd introduced himself. "What do I call you?"

"My name is Cerise Fitzwilliam," she finally answered and pushed her thick lenses higher on her nose.

"Cerise?" he repeated doubtfully. The exotic name didn't fit the bespectacled girl child in front of him.

As if she knew his thoughts she grimaced. "My dad calls me Cherry. You may call me Miss Fitzwilliam." She delivered her order in a haughty voice that made him reevaluate her age, putting her this time on the other side of sixteen. But it didn't take long for her to switch topics and become a kid again as she extolled her medicine-brewing talents.

"I make that poultice from cattails. It grows wild here. The other salves and remedies I concoct from roots and plants I gather. It would be just as well if you improved without my having to test any of them on you."

Jeb lay on his side, his good arm curled under his head, and thought about that. Her accent marked her as both educated and a Yankee. "You're not from here, Cerise. How did you end up living in an abandoned cabin in a Louisiana bayou?"

"Just lucky for you, I guess."

Since she shut down so quickly at personal questions, Jeb learned to keep his conversations geared to her daily tasks. To his chagrin, it didn't take long to discover that she hunted the food he ate. When she'd leave the cabin to check her snares, he'd worry until she returned with rabbit, or fish, or pheasant in hand.

Neither of them mentioned her vulnerable state as she went out daily to fend for the both of them. But he redoubled his determination to get better.

As his health improved, she produced trousers and a shirt for him to wear. Whoever it was who owned the men's clothes, he'd been gone a while; for whatever reason, Cerise was on her own. He was aware of her growing agitation and often listened to her pace the cabin at night when she thought him asleep.

The first day he made it out of bed she was gone, so he navigated his way outside on his own. He managed to stay on his feet long enough to scout around the place but not get back inside before her return.

"What do you think you're doing?" she screeched as she swooped down on him. "You're not healed yet."

"Dammit girl, I needed to use the privy, and that's not something you're going to watch from here on out."

"Good, you're on the mend." Her eyes sparked with mischief at the same time her face flushed pink when he embarrassed her, declaring his privy independence. On the one hand she was tough as shoe leather. But beneath all her bravado and sassy ways, she was a sweetly innocent girl.

But, her next words shocked him to the core. "You can move on soon."

Jeb knew he'd not leave her behind. She was strong, smart, fiercely proud, and too innocent to be on her own. If he abandoned her to survive, she'd die, and Yankee or not, that was unacceptable.

CHAPTER IV

*F*or days, sporadic firing sounded in the surrounding woods. Cherry spotted more than one gray or blue uniformed soldier when she ventured from her hidden shelter. Her dad had chosen well. Had the cabin not been tucked away in a copse of overgrown trees, it surely would have been discovered.

She tended to her patient, remained closer to the cabin when she scavenged for food, and fretted about the state of her father. Obviously something had happened to prevent his return.

Talking to her visitor became a treat to pass the days. But agreeing with him was an almost-never event. Cherry didn't argue though, when he declared himself fit enough to travel, nor did she turn down the invitation to accompany him.

Instead, she gave him another set of her father's clothes and explained how he could pay her back for saving him. Not that she'd done it for payback, but their close proximity had shown him to be a fair man.

He was twenty, and she judged him too young to be the limping, grim-faced warrior before her. His wounds were infection free and healing well, but in her opinion, her patient was too weak to rejoin his division. Nevertheless, he was determined to be on his way; therefore, so was she.

"I'd appreciate your help in getting to Young's Point," she told him. It had been over two weeks since her dad had gone, and she needed to find him.

"Who's in Young's Point?" he asked.

"My father." She'd curtailed her trips to the bayou and prayed her dad hadn't encountered an enemy on his way home. If he'd been delayed, she needed to get to the last place she knew he'd been.

She didn't know how much to tell Jeb. He wouldn't attack her because her dad worked for the other side. If he'd been going to hurt her, he certainly could have by now.

"Soldier?" Jeb asked.

"Engineer," she corrected him. "The project he worked on was abandoned before the last battle. He visited Young's Point to collect from the paymaster, so we could leave."

"Then what?" Instead of quizzing her about the canal her dad had worked on, he asked what her future held.

"Then we find a place to settle down. We've been saving, so we can have a real home. I'll keep house for my dad while he builds a business."

"You have particulars in mind for this place?"

"It has to be somewhere without giant lizards or sinkholes. " Cherry thought about her dream home and nodded. "Wherever it is, the house will have a porch, a small patch of ground for a garden, and a swing." She was hazy on the rest of what they'd need, never having had the opportunity to stay in one area long enough to collect furnishings. She added, "Inside, we'll have matched furniture."

"Might try Texas," Jeb drawled. "For the most part it's dry country with no alligators or swamps."

On the morning they set out, Cherry filled her knapsack with a change of clothes and the books she considered essential. The rest of her possessions joined her father's maps and equipment in the old trunk.

"That's it?" Jeb asked, sounding surprised at her light load.

"I'll be back with my dad to reclaim the rest," she told him confidently.

The girl knew her way through the woods better than Jeb, so he let her take the lead.

Let her. He snorted at that ridiculous notion. The kid had a mind of her own and did what she wanted.

Since she knew people in Young's Point and since her contacts were fighting on the other side, he had no compunctions about tagging along to pick up information.

His leg ached, and his shoulder was still sore; though he wished for a horse to ride, he recognized he should be thankful to be alive. More than anything, he wanted to find Nate.

When they reached Young's Point, they found Union troops in control. Dread settled in his stomach like a lump of lead, but he followed Cherry to the church in town and waited in the shadows outside.

"Father Andrew will know what's happened to my dad. It won't take me long if you want to wait."

For the first time since they'd set out together, her voice held a hint of fear.

"Go on then," he told her. "I'll be here when you get finished talking to the preacher."

"Priest," she corrected him. "This is a Catholic Church." She pulled a scarf from her pocket, covered her hair with it, and tied it under her chin. Before she left his side, she whispered, "If someone finds you here, tell them you're a friend of Fitz Fitzwilliam. That should keep you safe."

Her trust in her father's protection amazed Jeb. He must have displayed his skepticism because she wrinkled her nose at him.

"You'll see. It will be fine."

When she went inside the church, Jeb stayed quiet and hidden. There were Union troops in charge, and it wasn't safe to look around, but it didn't take Cherry long to return with news.

"More than a week ago, on June 15th, Generals Ellet and Mower defeated the Confederate leader, Walker and his troops. Father Andrew said afterward, the Union troops moved from here to Richmond, Louisiana where they destroyed the supply depot."

"And your father?" If Fitz Fitzwilliam was still alive, he needed to get Cherry to him so Jeb could be free to search for Nate.

Her grim expression didn't bode well. "He left his pay packet for me with the priest when the Union commandeered his engineering skills and put him on a navy vessel outside Vicksburg."

He looked at the skinny girl before him, wondering what in hell to do with her. Before he could decide, she said decisively, "I'm going to Vicksburg."

"No you're not," he answered gruffly.

"I have to find my dad and he's in Vicksburg," she said defiantly, fear lurking beneath her aggressive tone.

"Whatever's happening in Vicksburg is ugly. Worse than anything you've seen so far. You're staying here."

"Miss Fitzwilliam, I have to concur with your fiancé."

Startled, Jeb looked at the robed figure standing in the open doorway of the church. Then his words registered. *Fiancé? Since am I anyone's intended?*

"Bring your young man into the vestry," the priest invited, his glance skating from Cherry's mutinous expression to Jeb.

At the other man's grim look, Jeb's denial died on his lips.

◦◦◦

Cherry had her dad's pay packet tucked in her pocket along with the letter he'd left instructing her to leave the area by way of the Union controlled railroad. Father Andrew had been reluctant to hand over the considerable sum of money to her until she'd assured him she wasn't traveling alone. That of course had led to more questions which precipitated her often rehearsed engagement story spilling from her mouth before she could stop it.

The priest had looked suspicious and then relieved when she'd offered to introduce him to her intended waiting outside. Her rescued soldier hadn't denied her claim, giving her hope she'd be on her way soon.

As the priest ushered them inside, Jeb took her arm, leaned close, and growled, "You need to stay here where you can wait on your dad in safety."

"If I come with you, we can use the road between here and Vicksburg," she said softly. She'd prefer to travel with Jeb. The road would get her to her father faster than traveling through the woods. Either way she was going.

"I've managed to avoid trouble so far and will again.

But if Vicksburg is as bad as Father Andrew suspects, I'd like to have the protection of my intended in case I run into any two-legged snakes and gators while I search for my dad." She intentionally raised her voice so that her words reached the priest as well as Jeb Carter.

She'd been taking care of her father for seven years, since her mother went to heaven. Making her own decisions was a way of life, and she saw no reason to alter that now. Neither the soldier nor the priest stood a chance of changing her mind.

But, she'd underestimated Father Andrew's penchant for meddling.

"I'll listen to you say your wedding vows before you set out." With simple words, the priest forced both of them to an inevitable conclusion.

Cherry opened her lips to argue, and then, looking at Jeb, she didn't. They couldn't decline without admitting his reason for being with Cherry was a tissue of lies. She'd also failed to consider Jeb Carter's determination to find his Confederate brother.

"As soon as we're wed, we'll find horses and get to Vicksburg faster, Cerise." Her intended didn't hesitate at all.

CHAPTER V

*T*hey rode away from Young's Point mounted on horses Jeb paid for with Cerise's money. She'd been reluctant to hand over her pay packet until he'd reminded her they were husband and wife.

"We're not really husband and wife," she'd pointed out.

"What we are right now is married," he'd told her, maybe a little more harshly than he'd intended. "We'll worry about undoing it once we're on the other side of war."

She'd nodded, keeping back some of the bills before handing over the envelope of money.

It grated on his pride that he had to use her funds until he reminded himself that he'd married the girl as a means of getting to Vicksburg. He figured to locate her dad along the way and leave her with Fitzwilliam. He'd hand over the money to her father when that moment arrived.

Then, he'd continue searching for Nate among the survivors. According to the priest, after the battle at Young's Point, Walker's troops had moved to Richmond to defend the supply depot and been run out of there, too. He didn't want to strategize or think about jumping back into battle. Hell, he wanted to go home, herd cows, and forget about war.

But he couldn't. If Nate was alive, he'd be as close to

Vicksburg as he could get. His brother's wife was one, Cecelia Martineau, daughter of a local plantation owner. Her family's land lay west of Vicksburg.

Of course, her kin had kicked up a ruckus even before the war, considering a poor Texas rancher not good enough for their only daughter. War gave Nate a chance to put that complaint on hold.

In spite of Jeb's desire to stay out of the fray, Celia had harangued his brother until they'd driven their herd of cattle to Louisiana and sold them to Pemberton's troops, taking payment in Confederate script which was near worthless now.

Afterward, Jeb couldn't talk Nate out of joining Walker's Greyhounds to fight the Yankees. His brother had been determined to impress the Martineau family with his loyalty to their cause. When Jeb couldn't talk Nate out of his foolishness, he'd enlisted too.

He admitted the truth to himself—his heart wasn't tied to Dixieland and he wasn't fighting for a cause. He didn't have slaves and thought the whole damned business of owning people noxious. He'd come along to protect Nate, and when he found him, he planned to drag his brother back to West Texas by the scruff of his neck if need be.

"What is that awful stench?" Cerise asked. The air

was redolent with the smell, and the farther they traveled the worse it seemed.

"You smell death, Cherry—ripe, rotting flesh fouling the air."

She'd been anxious, not really frightened until she and Jeb passed a battle site and she saw bloated bodies littering the field. They'd once been soldiers dressed in blue or gray, but were now rotting corpses in tattered uniforms. Terror, the likes of which she'd never felt before, overwhelmed her. She had to find her father, so they could leave this awful war and go to a place of safety.

To avoid the Union sentries patrolling the site, Jeb led her from the open road back into the woods. The area was swampy; hanging moss brushed her clothes as she rode under the trees and she shuddered, her stomach roiling from the smell of putrefaction that permeated the air.

The oppressive heat bore down on them, and her feeling of impending doom increased. She stopped her horse behind Jeb's; he looked around for whatever danger had set her teeth on edge as though he felt it too.

"Let's go back to the road," she suggested too late. At that moment, a man dropped from the tree above Jeb and knocked him to the ground.

She kicked her horse into movement and plunged toward the two men but a second man leapt from his crouched position behind a tree and landed on her horse's back, sweeping her from the saddle and rolling with her to the spongy ground.

"Lookee here what I found," the soldier crowed. Cherry tried to scream but only managed a grunt of pain as a dirty hand clamped over her mouth, stifling her cry.

"You hush up right now," her assailant whispered in her ear, pressing his body down and pinning her beneath his weight on the ground.

"Please don't hurt me," she whimpered and went limp the way her dad had taught her.

"That's better, sugar. You and me are gonna be friends." The fetid stink of his breath washed over her as she tried to appear frozen in fear. She remained still when he pawed her breast, squeezing it roughly, deliberately causing her pain.

Mewling pitifully she felt real tears leak from her eyes, and when he grunted in satisfaction, shifting his weight so he could pull her skirts up to part her legs, she exploded into action, slamming her knee into his groin and bashing his chin with her head.

"Bitch. I was gonna treat you nice…" Instead of sending him into screaming pain, her attempt to knock him off only enraged him.

He straddled her, cursing and choking her. Cherry gasped when the pressure suddenly released, a gush of blood splashed on her chin, and her attacker toppled sideways.

"You okay?" After he cut the throat of her attacker,

Jeb kicked the body aside and crouched next to her, holding a knife coated in red. His words were calm, his actions pragmatic as he leaned over her and wiped blood spatter from her face.

"My dress…" she managed two words and stopped. Her throat was too sore to explain. She needed to change her shirtwaist. It was ripped down the front and the material soaked in blood.

"Told you to wear pants," Jeb muttered, pulling her roughly to her feet where she stood swaying uncertainly.

"Sorry." She removed another set of her dad's clothes from her satchel and stepped behind a tree for privacy. Her throat hurt and she couldn't quit shaking. When they'd begun their journey to Young's Point, he'd told her to dress like a boy; it would keep her safer.

She'd refused, wanting to look her best on the trip she was sharing with him. She knew their time together was almost over, and she didn't want him to remember her as a half-grown kid. It had been a stupid vanity that had nearly gotten her raped and killed.

I'm all right, I'm all right, I'm all right… While she changed her clothes, Jeb dragged the dead bodies into the brush to hide them. When she reappeared dressed in a man's shirt and a pair of her dad's trousers, Jeb grunted and motioned her over to where he stood holding the reins of both horses.

As she crossed to where he stood, her body suddenly began trembling as if with the ague, and regardless of her efforts to calm down, her rough gasps of terror escaped.

"It's all right, sweetheart. You did fine." Jeb drew her into his arms and muffled her face against his shirt while she struggled to control the wild hysteria that had suddenly overtaken her.

Finally, she calmed enough to catch her breath. She had no idea how much time had passed, but when she looked up again the natural sounds of frogs, gators, and swamp canaries had resumed.

The hand that had been patting her back, came to rest on her nape as she squinted at him. Then, she realized that her eyeglasses sat eschew on her face.

"Let me see if I can fix those." His voice seemed deeper than usual and she was reminded how close they stood when she felt his gruff words rumble in his chest.

"I can do it," she said, hastily stepping out of his embrace.

But, after she removed them, Jeb took the twisted frames, half-smiling as he straightened the bent stems. He used one of her father's handkerchiefs to polish her lenses and set her spectacles back on her nose.

"We both could have been killed today," she whispered.

"Yep. Best be on our way, now," he said, resuming his earlier grim expression. "We'll keep to the woods a mite longer until it's safer to use the road after dusk."

Cerise didn't argue, but as they passed the bushes where Jeb had dragged the bodies, she wondered if the road could be any more dangerous than their current path.

CHAPTER VI

—⋅⋅◈⋅⋅—

*T*hey made it to the outskirts of Vicksburg by the grace of God and Cherry's dad's reputation. There were so many in the crowded vendors watching the siege on the town, the presence of two more civilians wasn't questioned.

She and Jeb agreed to remain together until she rejoined her father. To that purpose, they rode to a field on the outer perimeter of the siege where tents had been pitched for the Union troops waging war.

She recognized more than one battle-weary face, but each time she asked for information about her father she was shrugged off. Finally, she saw Horace Murdock, a young cavalry captain who'd accompanied her father to their cabin more than once.

"Captain Murdock," she called to get his attention. When he returned her gaze, she dismounted and led her horse to where he stood.

"Miss Fitzwilliam, I'm glad to see you've made it here without harm," Captain Murdock greeted her, his expression somber.

Now that she had his attention, Cerise was at a loss for words. Murdock's arm was in a sling, he swayed on his feet, and he looked as if his wounds might soon get the better of him.

"Are you well?" she asked in concern.

"Touch of yellow-fever," he answered gruffly.

Jeb dismounted and remained by her side when she faced the Union officer. Instead of introducing them and delivering her usual spiel about the marriage, she couldn't spit out the lie.

"I'm Jeb Carter. Cherry's married to me now," Jeb announced, taking matters into his own hands.

Cherry should have realized something was amiss when Jeb's credentials weren't doubted. Later she understood that the dispatch officer was glad to have someone with her when he delivered his news.

"Miss Fitzwilliam, I'm sorry to tell you that Fitz was on one of the Union gunboats shelling Confederate troops during the Milliken's Bend battle. He died a hero."

It was the only time in her life she fainted.

She woke later to a pounding headache. Wincing, she automatically reached for her glasses. They were beside her on the cot where she lay. Light filtered through the tent flap that had been closed for her privacy. In the not too far distance she could hear the boom of cannons lobbing missiles at Vicksburg. Her momentary disorientation evaporated and she remembered.

Dad is gone. Grief mixed with panic and squeezed the breath from her as it blossomed in her chest. *I should have felt something, known somehow.* Instead, her father had been dead the whole time she'd been nursing Jeb back to life. She tried to stifle the sobs threatening to suffocate her.

I should have been out on the river looking for him instead of tending one of the rebels who killed him. She wanted to vent her anger and pain on Jeb at the same time she needed to cling to him, but he wasn't with her in the tent to do either.

She didn't know if he'd left her to the mercies of the Union army or if he'd return. She had to remind herself that she had no real claim on his attention. She couldn't blame him if he took the opportunity to leave her with the Northern troops and make his escape.

He'd introduced himself to Captain Murdock as her husband. She didn't know what to do about that either. If Jeb had gone, she'd have to make some excuse about it or tell the truth—she'd been helping the enemy.

She tried to parse her feelings, separating what she thought she knew from the reality of his being a Confederate soldier. The fact remained that he'd been wounded in the same battle where her dad had been killed. As if viewing a kaleidoscope of horror, she replayed everything in her mind, analyzing events that had happened before and since the fight at Milliken's Bend.

She tried to think of Jeb as the enemy but just couldn't do it. She had no allegiance to either side. Her father had been a transplanted Irishman who loved the

United States. Though he'd refused to become a soldier and make war against half his new countrymen, his engineering skills remained for sale.

"It's foolishness to fight against your own family. I want no part of it," he'd proclaimed two years before at the start of the war. But when projects dried up and the Fitzwilliam coffers were empty, he hadn't turned down engineering work for Grant.

Like a rat in a maze, Cherry's thoughts raced to her earlier accounting practices—could she have economized better, should they have lived more prudently? She tried to untangle the threads of long before, hoping somehow to change the current outcome.

She thought of her dad's last payment, the roll of bills from it in her pocket, and the remaining government script carried by Jeb. Had he taken it with him when he left? How would she explain her penniless state to Captain Murdock? How would she even live?

A series of loud booms interrupted her thoughts, and shame coursed through her. The poor people in Vicksburg were on the receiving end of the cannons' shells. She should be feeling gratitude that she'd gotten here and grief for the loss of her father.

There would be time later to worry about money. If Jeb had already left, she hoped he'd had sense enough to take the rest of dad's pay with him. He'd need legal tender to spend traveling through Union controlled territory.

The thought of not seeing him again brought a pang of sorrow nearly as harsh as what she'd felt for the loss of her dad. "He'll be fine," she whispered to herself. "It's best anyway for him to leave here while nobody's paying any attention."

But when her soldier boy walked in carrying a bucket of water and a platter of food, she had to clamp down hard on her muscles to keep from rushing across the tent floor and throwing herself on him. She covered her relief by peppering him with questions.

"Tell me what's happening," she said immediately.

"Good, you're awake." Jeb handed her the plate, scowling when she attempted to wave it away.

"Wash your hands and eat." His matter-of-fact attitude braced her as nothing else could have. Her stomach growled, adding support to his instructions.

Cherry washed her hands and then ate every scrap on the plate, even indecorously sopping up the last drops of gravy with a piece of bread. Finally she set the tin on the ground and looked at Jeb again.

"Now tell me what's happening," she said, wondering about the immediate circumstances of the camp they were in, but also asking about what would ultimately become of her, of them.

"Clean up first. You've got blood in your hair. Then we'll find a latrine for you; then we'll talk. That's the order of business."She shuddered, touching her forehead, feeling a crusty residue dried there. Her stomach churned, threatening to return the food she'd just swallowed.

It was a waste of time arguing with him. She accepted the rough cloth he produced and after wetting it, scrubbed the skin on her face, removing the evidence of her attacker's death.

"Bend over the bucket," Jeb ordered, taking the cloth from her hand.

The cold water shocked her but cleared her senses and settled her stomach as she dutifully dunked her head and let him wash her matted locks with a bar of soap.

"Pemberton's troops have been pushed back into Vicksburg and the damned Yankees are shelling the hell out of the city. I don't see how it can sustain much longer," he told her as he scrubbed.

"Be careful how you speak of the Union forces," she muttered. "In case you've forgotten, you're the enemy sitting in the middle of a Yankee tent city." She regretted her comment as soon as the words left her lips.

She felt worse when he didn't argue; as he patted her dry and then wrapped a towel around her wet head, he nodded agreement instead.

"I'm sorry it turned out this way, Cerise, but people die in wars, and your pa knew that when he came down here."

"He wasn't a soldier," she hissed, glaring at Jeb.

"Doesn't matter. He knew the risk working in a battle zone. But he should never have brought you along."

The last thing she wanted to hear from Jeb was criticism of her father. On the other hand, she didn't want him to leave her alone again, either.

"What day is it?" she asked because she had no idea how much time had elapsed since they'd left her cabin.

"Last day of June," Jeb answered quickly. "I need to get you settled somewhere safer than here. Then I can be on my way to find Nate."

She was appalled at the notion of their separation though she'd been angry at him moments before. Terror replaced grief. There were no relatives to turn to, and though she had many acquaintances she'd met as she'd traveled with her father in their nomadic existence, she'd made no close friends.

"I have nowhere to go," she whispered, closing her eyes as the raw truth burned her throat.

"We'll figure it out," he promised. "Don't cry now, sweetheart."

Instead of watching her devolve into the tears she fought, he pulled her to her feet. She hadn't realized how badly she needed to use the comfort station until she'd stood upright.

Clutching his arm as though he might run away, she walked beside him as he ushered her outside. Captain Murdock was nearby and escorted them to a row of blankets hanging from poles.

"Ladies facilities," Murdock explained.

"I'll wait right here for you," Jeb assured her when she released his arm to hurry behind the curtain.

His promise didn't stop her anxiety. Cherry finished quickly; terrified he might leave during her short time away.

CHAPTER VII

During each of the battles he'd fought, a cold detachment had taken over Jeb's mind. But nothing of those moments matched his steely determination now. He'd played his part with the Union boys, none of them inclined to worry about Fitzwilliam's daughter now that she had a husband to take charge.

He'd carried her to the tent Murdock provided, then, after the captain left, reconnoitered the enemy camp, coming back to the tent to check on her as she slept. When she'd begun to stir, he'd borrowed a bucket, filled it with water, begged a plate of food for Fitz's daughter, and did what he was supposed to do—took charge.

Now, waiting for Cerise to reappear, daylight faded and campfires began dotting the landscape. If the continued boom of cannon fire hadn't punctuated the twilight, the evening would have seemed almost serene.

When they'd first met up with Murdock, before the captain had delivered the bad news, she'd smiled at the Union man, looking pretty damned relieved to see him.

Murdock didn't look so good himself. But he'd hung around the tent checking on her condition while she'd been asleep, and he'd hurried to her side when they came out. Jeb had nodded at him but kept moving toward the latrines. Murdock had joined them and walked on her other side.

It was good knowing the girl would have someone to take care of her after he left; the thought should have made Jeb happier. But, when her head poked from behind the curtained blankets, and her gaze skated past Murdock to settle on him, pressure eased in Jeb's chest.

It was second nature to welcome her back with a hug, and it felt more than right to keep his arm around her shoulders as they returned to the tent.

"You have to leave, don't you?" she murmured as they walked along.

"Yep." There was no sense lying to her. He should have been gone already. Nate was out there somewhere in that mess of soldiers squaring off with each other, and he needed to find his brother

"I'll come back for you," he promised rashly.

"No, that would be too dangerous," she whispered. "Once you're gone, stay gone and be safe."

He ducked inside the tent, sweeping her inside with him. He was tense, as anxious to stay with her as he was to leave.

"I'll be fine." She tried to reassure him, but tears filled her eyes and spilled over.

He thumbed one away; then, although he had no business doing it, he leaned closer and brushed his lips across hers. She didn't kiss him so much as cling to him, her arms going around his neck and her body pressing against his for support and comfort.

He walked her backward to the corner of the

enclosed space. When her knees met the cot, she sat on the edge and pulled him down with her.

Jeb thought briefly that the makeshift bed was too narrow and might not hold their combined weight. And then he stopped thinking at all.

"Stay with me just for tonight," she whispered, stretching out on the cot and squirming sideways to make room for him.

He nodded and lay down beside her. It was hot inside the tent, but she pulled a blanket over them anyway.

He wasn't sure later who seduced whom. He remembered saying, "It's too hot in here for all these clothes."

It was too dark by then to see her expression, but she nodded her head and fumbled with his buttons instead of her own.

Up to that moment, Jeb had been in denial about his physical attraction to the girl who'd saved him. She was only sixteen and quite clearly innocent. He'd planned to be gone before giving his imagination permission to think about her that way.

He'd taken his dad's advice early on. "Son, don't bed a woman you're not willing to wed. You might wake up next morning harnessed to a pig."

There weren't many females to choose from in the rough country back home, and none of them had sparked his interest. Being only twenty, he'd figured he had plenty of time yet to find the right woman—plenty of time if he survived the war.

But, hunched under the blankets, with Cherry's fingers nimbly opening his shirt, desire and proximity robbed him of common sense. Besides, the priest had seen to it that they were married.

⋅ೞ ꩜

It seemed to Cherry as if every fiber in her being was atremble. And yet, her fingers were steady as she undressed Jeb. She needed to press her body against his, to touch his skin, to hold him tight. Her father was gone and tomorrow Jeb would leave too. But she had this moment. She had right now.

"Have you done this before?" His voice was gruff as she removed his shirt and started unbuckling his belt.

"Undressed you?" she asked and laughed softly. "A hundred times and more, soldier boy."

"You know what I mean."

"You mean have I ever lain with a man?" she asked, feeling desperate. If she said yes, he'd think her a woman of loose morals. A no might cause him to quit what she'd started before it had really begun.

He caught her hand, blocking her attempt to unbutton his pants. "Have you?"

"Yes," she said quickly.

"All right," he said, releasing her to continue. He

didn't ask who or when, thank heaven, but Cerise thought she heard a touch of disapproval or maybe it was disappointment in his tone.

His manhood swelled beneath the buttons closing his trousers. When her fingers pressed against the rigid length, he groaned.

"Did I hurt you?"

"No."

It was dark in the tent and she couldn't see his expression but she was sure this time she heard laughter in his voice.

"My turn," he said abruptly and took charge, making quick work of divesting her of her clothes until she lay naked under the blanket next to him.

Suddenly he rose from beside her and she could hear him fumbling with something in the dark. "What are you doing?"

Her only answer was the smell of sulfur and the snick of a match when he lit a candle and came back to stand over the cot. Before she knew what to expect, he tugged the blanket from her, exposing her bare body.

"Give it back," she said and tried to grab the cover.

"Nope. You've seen me. Now I'll see you."

Instinctively, she threw one arm across her breasts and used her other hand to cover the soft nest of curls at the juncture of her thighs.

Whether on purpose or accident, she couldn't tell, the candle tipped, sending a drop of hot wax to splash on her stomach.

"Ouch." Outraged, she sat up and blew the candle out. But not before he'd seen her pasty-pale skin, flat-chested upper form, and long, bony hipped torso below. She was still scowling when he bent over the cot, and kissed the flesh of her belly.

"Sorry," he murmured against her skin. The brush of his lips sent a rush of heat sizzling through her that eclipsed the burn of the candle wax.

"You need to quit fooling around now," she gasped, both embarrassed and aroused by his intimate attention. Instead of obeying her, he sat on the edge of the cot and continued to tickle her with butterfly kisses that trailed upward.

She was shocked when he visited her nipples. After he'd licked and kissed each turgid nub, he pulled one into his mouth, alternately sucking on it, then teasing it with his teeth and tongue.

Finally he continued his upward journey stopping to nibble her lips before deepening the kiss.

Cherry writhed under his attentions. Her body needed, needed, needed… She pulled on his shoulders and he came fully onto the cot to lay over her.

His chest pressed against her breasts, and he groaned again, rubbing against her, mixing his sweat with hers. He still wore his unbuttoned trousers. She parted her legs, liking the way it felt when he settled between her legs and the swell of his erection pressed against her mound.

"Take these off," she said and tugged at the waist of his pants.

"Shhh…" He hushed her by covering her mouth with his. As his fingers delved between her parted legs, he stroked her folds, sending more hot waves of desire coursing through her.

"Good," he grunted. "You're wet for me." Sliding one finger through the entrance to her body, he stroked her there until her clenched muscles relaxed; and then he used two fingers, pushing deeper. She whimpered and gasped when his digits tore through the veil of her innocence.

"You lied to me," he growled, his voice gravelly rough.

"No I didn't. I lay in the bed beside you when you were sick." She didn't pretend ignorance of his charge nor give him time to reflect on her answer. "Kiss me," she ordered him.

He didn't resist when she pulled his mouth down to meet her lips. During the kiss, he resumed teasing her with his intimate invasion.

She was ready to scream with frustration by the time he shed his pants and, naked this time, knelt between her thighs. Leaning on her elbows she peered at him, but because of the dark, the experience was really more about feeling what Jeb did than seeing what he might do.

She braced herself, going rigid when he replaced his

fingers with his shaft, fitting it to her entrance.

"Easy sweetheart," he murmured as he reached between them, making her wanton as he stroked the bundle of nerves at her apex.

Her hips thrust upward following his touch. His own thrust carried him steadily through her channel until he was fully seated.

The walls of her channel flexed and clenched, squeezing his manhood as if to hang onto it. She wanted him to do anything that would soothe the incredible tension building in her.

He began a slow glide and withdrawal, his shaft moving in and out of her slick passage in an ever increasing rhythm. When she thought she couldn't stand another moment of the coiling need in her womb, a cataclysmic wave of pleasure flooded every nerve in her body.

Jeb made that exquisite feeling happen for her twice more. When she sprawled beneath him, her body sated and her mind completely fuddled by sensation, he began thrusting into her with renewed vigor, continuing until he shuddered and she felt the hot pulse of his seed spill inside her.

They slept in a tangle of limbs with Cherry's head resting on his chest and his arm curved protectively around her body. When they woke at dawn, everything had changed.

CHAPTER VIII

*T*hough Jeb fully intended to be gone before the Union camp came awake the next day, he lingered in the tent with Cherry. He increasingly disliked the idea of leaving her under Murdock's care, but no other reasonable option presented itself.

Nate still needed to be found, and, though Jeb had successfully infiltrated the enemy's camp, he didn't believe in pushing his luck.

"I'll accompany you to Murdock. Then I'll be on my way." He wanted her to understand that he was still leaving, that the night before hadn't changed anything.

"All right," she answered. "Thank you for staying this long."

If he had to choose one word to describe Cherry's morning attitude, it would have been stoic. She kissed him on the cheek, hugged him briefly, and said nothing more as they went to find the captain.

Where order had ruled the day before, organized chaos met them when they stepped outside. The place was a cacophony of sound. The camp followers laughed and socialized with infantrymen who were folding tents and loading them on two-wheeled carts. Army mules brayed, saddles creaked, and metal stirrups clanged in noisy accompaniment to the not so distant boom of canon fire.

"What's happening?" Cerise asked one of the soldiers they passed.

"We've been ordered to engage Pemberton's troops in battle."Grant was escalating the conflict against Vicksburg, determined to breach the Confederate stronghold.

Jeb witnessed the death of his plan to leave Cherry with Murdock. He almost turned to leave camp with her that moment. But she insisted on saying good bye to the cavalry officer so they continued to the spot where his tent had been the night before.

Someone had propped Murdock against a tree. The tent was missing altogether. Jeb guessed that regardless of what Grant had planned Murdock's soldiering days were done.

"Sick," he whispered from ashy lips when Cherry rushed to him, spouting questions. He'd been weakened by his half-healed wounds and collapsed from a bout of the yellow-fever he'd suffered before.

Jeb commandeered an army wagon, acting as if he had every right to use the vehicle. Nobody challenged them when he loaded Murdock in the back, or when he drove the wagon to the bayou cabin to pick up Cherry's trunk.

It irritated Jeb when he sat on the front bench alone, while Cherry sat in the wagonbed next to Horace, draping wet cloths over the sick man in order to cool his fever.

Once they had the trunk, she insisted on sweeping the floor, and lingered in the cabin a while before coming back out and closing the door. He guessed she'd been saying goodbye to her dad as best she could. When she climbed into the wagonbed, Jeb didn't know how to comfort her from where he sat on the bench.

When he drove the rig out of the woods and onto the main trail leading to Vicksburg, he kept his mouth shut and his head down, hoping to hell nobody recognized him or asked why he wasn't dressed in Union blues. The road was crowded with foot soldiers and mounted infantrymen. Ahead, army wagons carried canons closer to the town under siege. Nobody and nothing moved faster than a crawl.

"You keep on drivin' in that direction, you'll get Captain Murdock and his lady killed," an infantryman yelled at Jeb.

He wanted to correct the soldier walking beside them. No doubt, the man assumed since Cherry sat with Murdock's head in her lap, she was his woman. But Jeb kept his comment to a question. "What's slowing things down?"

"War. Fighting already started up head. Best take the captain and his woman to the train station. His kin hale from northeast Texas. If'n ya take him to the supply depot, and load him with the gun crates, he'll ride home in style. "

Jeb didn't know there was a train depot or cargo

trains running on tracks close by. But he nodded agreeing that the idea sounded fine.

"Which way to the train?" Cherry got right to the point while Jeb had been trying to decide if the location was somewhere obvious he should already know.

"That way." The soldier pointed ahead to the path branching off to the east.

Jeb slapped the mule into a trot, and as the wagon creaked and its occupants bounced, he used brute force to push through the crowd. He reached the path going toward the train station, and yelled thanks to the helpful infantryman.

As an afterthought he shouted, "Good luck to you," and then wondered if he'd wished ill fortune on his Confederate comrades.

He drove and mulled that thought over as he followed the man's directions to the army train depot. Once Jeb confirmed that the railroad company had a spur running northeast and a supply train that could get them within fifty miles of Murdock's home in Isaca, Texas, he talked to the station master, secured spots on the floor of a car, and helped Cherry get Horace onboard.

After situating the sick man on a pallet, Jeb knew he should wish them luck and leave. But when it came time to climb out of the railroad car, he sat down instead. It was time to consider his options.

He didn't dare hope for any more good fortune. Fate had already served him a full portion. Out of uniform as he was, if the Yankees discovered he was a Johnny Reb, he'd be hung as a spy. He wasn't going to get anywhere near Vicksburg unless he joined the Union troops marching there. And that he wouldn't do.

Nor was he willing to leave Cerise to fend for herself with only a sick man to look after her. No doubt she'd be the one taking care of Murdock, having gotten plenty of practice in soldier nursing just recently. But Jeb convinced himself that wasn't his reason for traveling with the cavalry captain rather than setting out alone.

He planned to use the time during the trip to catch up on his sleep. He'd even half hoped that Cerise might curl up with him. But she seemed oblivious to him for the most part and only intent on keeping Horace Murdock alive. When the train stopped at the first military depot, she begged a bucket of clean water from one of the railroad workers unloading crates of weapons.

The man she spoke to was sweating and bare-chested. He took his time answering and when he did, he flirted a little with Cherry before he agreed to fill the bucket. Jeb wanted to wring his neck. But when the strutting peacock returned with the clean water and handed it to her with a grin and a flourish, Jeb stood from the corner he'd claimed and strolled to the edge of the open car.

"Best watch yourself," he warned the man. "That lady's my wife and you're being too free with your attention to her."

"Sorry," the railroad worker said looking at Jeb. But the wink he offered as he left was directed at Cherry. Jeb stayed on his feet next to the car opening until the train lurched into motion and they were on their way. Then he walked back to his corner and sat down.

"Mind who you talk to," he told her on the way past where she sat by Murdock. "The less people know about where we're going the better off we are." He should have stopped there when she nodded, indicating she understood. But he couldn't keep his mouth shut.

"Next time you need something, don't be flirting with strangers, ask me." The words spilled out of his mouth in a possessive growl.

"What?"

"You heard right. Ask me next time," he repeated.

She closed her mouth and didn't argue, but her nostrils flared and her chin angled at a mutinous tilt.

Her nonverbal actions—pursed lips and arched brow as she peered at him over the spectacles perched on the end of her nose—irked him as much as her limited conversation.

Guess Cerise doesn't like me bossing her around. Too bad. After last night we're truly married. Unfortunately, he'd be gone before she even settled into the fact she was a wife and under his dominion.

As the train chugged along, he considered what to do with her, finally deciding he needed to take her back to the ranch to live . She could wait there for him to get home. She wouldn't be by herself. He'd be leaving her with Celia, Nate's wife.

After he settled that in his mind, he turned his attention outward and stared at the other two occupants of the train.

He hadn't asked Cherry why she needed the water, because she'd been wiping Murdock's brow all day. But when she started unbuttoning Horace's shirt, that ended that.

"Hell, no." Jeb took charge. There was no way he was going to sit by and let her look at another man's body.

"You're being stupid," she told him. "His fever is soaring. Horace needs to be sponged down. I did it for you. It saved your life."

Yes, you did. If I recall, you also patted my ass a time or two. "I'll do it this time," he said brusquely. "Take the other blanket and curl up in the corner. Close your eyes. Get some rest."

The train made stops every fifty miles or so to drop crates of weapons off at roughly constructed depots. Nevertheless, they made good time and three days later they were in Texas and close enough to Isaca to depart from the train.

Murdock had been fevered and oblivious most of the trip but on one occasion during a lucid moment he suggested sending a telegram to Annon, the closest telegraph office to his kin.

"My family will be most grateful, sir if you could let them know." Before he lapsed into delirium again, Murdock scribbled a name to be contacted.

When the train stopped at the Annon depot, Horace's grandmother, his father, and his aunt all waited on the platform. Their wagon had a pole attached to the side with a Mounted Troops Guidon flying high declaring their pride in their Union cavalry officer. Dead or alive they were ready to take their soldier home. Esther Murdock crawled into the railcar and crouched over her grandson.

"Horace—are you alive boy?" Horace woke up enough to give a feeble smile before closing his eyes again. But it was enough to put a big grin on the old woman's face. "He'll be fine," she announced to the waiting Murdock clan.

"Yep." Jeb helped the Murdock elder out of the train and then carried Horace to the edge of the car and handed him into waiting arms.

"Come along you two," Murdock's father said to Cerise and Jeb. "There'll be plenty of food at our house and a decent place for you to spend the night before you travel on."

Jeb hopped to the platform below and reached up to lift her down, but Cherry ignored his proffered help and jumped from the car by herself.

CHAPTER IX

*C*erise stifled the urge to punch Jeb in the nose, though she wasn't certain if she would be able to control the impulse for long. He'd risen from their night of pleasure with nothing more to say than he'd be leaving.

Fine. She could take care of herself. She'd hugged him, given him a kiss goodbye, and prepared for him to go. Then she'd mentioned her decision to talk to Horace Murdock, and Jeb suddenly decided he'd stay for that conversation.

When they found poor Horace collapsed and abandoned, she was glad to have Jeb's help in getting the cavalry officer to the rail line. She had no doubt it would have been far more difficult and dangerous without his aid. It was his attitude which made her want to jam her finger in his eye.

He scowled, growled, and acted with arrogant authority in matters that were clearly none of his business. She'd saved his life for heaven's sake, not the other way around. But still, when she remembered the two men who jumped them in the woods, she suspected Jeb had likely saved hers too. But that, by her count, made them even. It didn't give him rights over her life.

She knew he would leave as soon as he could foist her onto someone else; and she also knew that she didn't intend to be foisted. She had her dad's money. She'd find a little house with a garden and a nice porch, and live happily ever after by herself.

That was her plan. Jeb's plan seemed to be evolving by the hour. First he was leaving, then he was seeing her to the army depot with Murdock, then he climbed on board and said he was accompanying them to their destination in northeast Texas.

That was all fine. It was safer with him onboard, and easier to care for Horace, too. Especially since Jeb took over his nursing and relegated her to the corner of the train car where she was supposed to sit and close her eyes.

After he threatened the railroad worker at the first stop, she began to realize Jeb's problem. He was jealous. As flattered as she initially felt, it wasn't long before his possessiveness irritated her.

When Murdock's family members were at the train station to fetch Horace home, Jeb introduced her as his wife. Technically she was. Of course, they'd stepped across a line when they'd coupled that night, but, she wouldn't tell and she figured he'd forget about it as soon as he left. From the beginning they'd agreed it was to be a marriage of convenience, and in her opinion, it was no longer convenient.

He, on the other hand, acted as if it was real and as though it gave him say-so over her decisions. When the family urged Jeb and her to come to their family celebration, he hadn't asked her opinion before accepting the welcoming committee's invitation. That irritated her, too.

He's leaving and soon. Who does he expect will do my thinking for me when he's gone? Cerise had no intentions of having him plunk her down somewhere that made him feel secure so he could run off to get shot again while she fended on her own.

She'd had enough of his possessive nonsense. If she was to be on her own, she'd start by making her own decisions.

When they arrived at the Murdock homestead, she let him segregate her from the Murdock males who were all intent on discussing recent battle news. That was fine. She didn't want to talk about the war. It only reminded her that her father was dead.

She hadn't really had time to grieve and like a wounded animal, she needed a den to crawl into where she could mourn and heal.

Jeb relegated her to the kitchen with Horace's grandmother, Esther Murdock, along with the other family women. A conversation lull gave her a chance to inquire about availability of property around Isaca.

"The Murdock's have been in this part of the country since before it was the State of Texas," Horace's grandmother assured her. "Some of my antecedents were scoundrels who ran afoul of the law and took root here." She studied Cherry's face and whatever she learned there, she seemed to approve. "They found it to be a good place to start over. Maybe you will too."

And with her help, before they'd even finished the supper dishes, Cherry knew of several properties in the area standing empty at the moment. One in particular at the edge of town, interested her greatly.

"Last winter, I fell and nearly broke my leg, and though I hated to leave my house by the road, my son decided it would be better if I recuperated here with him." Esther frowned in thought a moment before continuing.

"I've been fussing about moving back in, mainly because I don't want the house to sit empty. And Kevin's been fussing about me staying on here, mainly because I'm a better cook than he is." She wiped down the counter, folded the dish cloth, arranged the towels, and handed Cherry a cup of tea before she again spoke.

"Horace is home, and I suspect he's still alive because of you and your man. Tomorrow, since we've got something to celebrate this year, I'll go into town for my Fourth of July fixings. Why don't you ride along in the buggy? The main trail to town runs right by the cottage. We'll stop and you can inspect it."

After the kitchen work was finished, Cherry drooped with fatigue, reluctant to return to the crowded front parlor where Horace's relatives had congregated.

"Hinny, take the hip bath to your room and fill it for Cerise; the poor child's about to drop on the floor. After she bathes, she can curl up in the spare bed in your room until her man remembers she's here."

Esther's wry·observation didn't skim over Cherry's head. But she was just too tired to care. She accepted the offer and retired. She didn't see Jeb again until next morning.

She only knew he'd slept curled up in a blanket on the back porch because Horace's dad mentioned it over breakfast eggs. After they all ate, she carried the dirty dishes to the kitchen, helped with the wash up, and then slid out the back door, intending to join Esther on her trip to town.

"Wait up," Jeb called to her before she could escape the porch. Without preamble, he delivered his version of her future. "I'm taking you to the Carter ranch. You can wait there with Nate's wife while I hunt him down and bring him home." He'd worked it all out, and in his mind apparently, it was all settled.

"No," she said, stepping around him.

"Dammit, I can't leave you on your own, Cerise. Hell anything could happen to you."

"We'll talk when I get back from town," she promised and kept walking.

By the time she returned, she'd found her future dream home. Mrs. Murdock's house was old but solidly built.

"Oh it's rough looking now," the old lady told her as they walked through the rooms. "I haven't had time to keep it dusted and cleaned proper."

Cherry thought the front porch adequate and the inside rooms promising. She'd already decided to see if she could afford the rent before they went through the kitchen to the backdoor and stepped onto the open veranda. It was love at first sight. The old lady's garden had gone wild, but the tiny natural pool in the corner and the aroma of honeysuckle and hyacinth clinched the deal.

"I'd like to rent this property from you, Mrs. Murdock," she said, fingering the money she held in her pocket. "How much will it cost?"

"You don't think you need to talk it over with your husband?"

"No."Cerise hesitated then blurted out the truth. "He plans to take me to a place I've never been, and leave me with people I don't know, while he goes back to fight alligators and make war. I'll wait here, thank you. I'll be closer at hand if he needs rescued again."

"I think there's a real interesting story tucked inside that complaint." Esther Murdock's eyes sparkled and her face lit up with interest.

Cerise realized she'd blabbed too much. From the flag they flew on the wagon and the other two she'd seen decorating the homestead, these were Union supporters who hated the other side. If Jeb got caught right now, he could be put in prison or even hung for a spy.

She shivered at that idea. She was mad at him, but she didn't want him dead. "I'm missing him already," she told Esther. "And I'm mad that he's going back into danger looking for his brother. He thinks Nate might be with the troops at Vicksburg."

Esther patted her hand, accepting her explanation. "You already know folks here, like you said. If you want the house, we'll find a way to work it out."

CHAPTER X

Isaca, July 3, 1863

*J*eb was pretty sure that Cerise was the most stubborn girl child ever born. She wouldn't listen to his advice and didn't recognize his authority. He was the man, and that meant he was supposed to make the decisions for them. But, apparently nobody ever told Cherry that's how being married worked.

He gave up trying to reason with her and decided to just throw her over his saddle and haul her to his ranch if he had to. Crazy as that notion was, it was clear that he needed to get her away from the Murdocks, who more and more seemed intent on keeping her.

Horace was doing better at home thanks to all the pampering of the family women. That was a good thing because Jeb sure as hell didn't want to see Cherry heading for the room with her sponge bathing tools.

He'd lingered here coddling her longer than he should have because she'd just lost her dad. But he'd decided as soon as the Murdock Fourth of July shindig ended, he was taking his new bride with him and they were leaving. Someplace between the cabin in the swamp and the cot in the tent, Jeb had developed feelings for her that ran deep.

The whole damn situation leading up to their current circumstances, including the wedding that was supposed to have been a charade, was bizarre. Even their meeting had been a fluke.

And yet somehow during their time together, the skinny, mouthy, stubborn brat had captured his heart. She was only sixteen but he already knew she'd mature into a strong woman.

Admitting that he wanted to spend his future with her meant also acknowledging his growing suspicion that she didn't want any part of the ranch or a life lived with him. It hurt.

While they were visiting with the Murdocks, he wanted her to lean on him and let him take care of her. But, hell, most of the time, he couldn't even locate her. Cherry had disappeared with Horace's grandmother all day, and when she'd finally returned, she immediately stationed herself in the kitchen among a clutch of Murdock kin. He didn't have to be a genius to know she was avoiding him. He didn't catch up with her until she stepped out on the back porch after supper.

"Time for our talk," he growled, catching her by the arm before she could scurry away. And that was odd behavior on her part, now that he thought about it. Cerise didn't normally dart around.

He liked the way she walked with an unhurried, confident stride. Now all the sudden she made a dash for the nearest door every blasted time she laid eyes on him.

"We're married," he blurted out as soon as he had her by the arm. "Now you need to listen to me." It wasn't what he'd intended to say and he could see it was the wrong thing to have said. But he couldn't unring that bell, so he just kept going. "I need you to get your things and meet me at the barn."

"Why would I do that?" she asked. "I'm not ready to leave here."

"Well get ready, because that's what's happening."

"No," she said trying to step away from him.

"Yes," he answered and stepped closer, walking her backward until her back rested against the side of the house. And then, he did what he'd been needing to do for days. He kissed her.

Her lips were stiff under his, and as soon as he lifted his head she whispered, "We aren't supposed to be doing this."

"This?" he murmured and pulled her close again, pleased to feel her arms slide around his neck and her lips soften under his. He couldn't stifle his groan as she relaxed. He slipped his hand behind her to better adjust their fit, but her height being near his, her mound snugged up against his groin as if they'd been built for each other.

When she opened her mouth to him and he mimicked with his tongue how he wanted to use his cock below, her nipples were so stiff against his chest he could feel them through both layers of their clothes, as her soft moans roused his need to a fever pitch.

Neither one of them were exhibiting good sense.

God knows what would have happened if a rider hadn't come tearing into the ranch yard waving his hat and yelling at the top of his voice.

"Vicksburg fell. Vicksburg fell."

The Murdocks poured out of the house from both the front and back, passing Jeb and Cherry on the porch as if they were invisible. Hastily they ended their embrace and the moment of intimacy was over.

"Come on," Jeb told her, pulling her with him to the clearing where the messenger remained mounted, ready to carry word to the next ranch over. Before the man resumed his ride, he accepted a jug, drank deep and then delivered the rest of his news.

"Pemberton's quit. Sent a note to Grant. Haven't heard yet what's to be done with the rebs that's been caught. Lotta prisoners to feed if he keeps 'em all penned up somewhere." He wiped his mouth with his sleeve before saying, "Much obliged."

As he left to deliver the news to the Prescott ranch, bottles and more jugs materialized in the hands of the Murdock men, and a bonfire blazed high as the family started their Fourth of July celebration early.

Jeb stood with his arm around Cerise, trying to catch all the information flying around so he could figure out what to do. If he could find Nate among the prisoners, he'd get him loose somehow.

"We can't go to the ranch yet. I've got to get to Vicksburg," he told Cherry. Then he realized he couldn't take her into that mess with him. He looked around the clearing helplessly. "Maybe you can wait here until…"

"I've got a place already," she told him. "I used my dad's money to rent a house today. It sits right outside the town. I'll be fine."

He didn't know whether to be pissed or glad she'd acted without telling him. It didn't matter. Either way, he was going and at least she had a place to hole up while he was gone.

"I'll find him quick and be back before you know it. Afterward, we'll go home." Then he remembered they'd ridden a train most of the way and the Murdock's wagon the rest.

"Dammit, I don't even have a mount or a saddle to put on it," he muttered.

Cherry seemed to understand the state of panic he was in and took charge. "Use some of my dad's pay to buy a horse from Mr. Murdock," she told him. Only then did he remember he was carrying the rest of her funds.

He pulled the money from his wallet, fumbling with the cash to hand it over.

"Buy the horse then give me half of what's left. Keep the rest to help get your brother free."

He felt hollow inside, like someone had just pulled his guts from his body. There was no way in hell he wanted to leave Cherry alone. "I'll be back for you. I promise," he told her.

With the decisions made, getting the horse was easy.

He didn't care who was watching or what they thought. Before he mounted to leave, he pulled Cherry into his arms and hugged and kissed on her like there was no tomorrow because quite possibly there wouldn't be.

He left before dawn and he felt her gaze follow him as he rode away. The thought of his bayou girl kept him going when things got bad and then fell apart.

ⱷⳡⳡⱷ

Cerise didn't want to stay on with the Murdocks after Jeb left. She slept in the bed next to Hinny that night, but rose early the next morning to negotiate with Esther over breakfast.

After they agreed on the amount to be paid each month, Cherry handed Esther cash to cover the first month's rent.

"It's hard times and a good thing that your man left his pay with you; but you be careful letting folks know you have money," Esther cautioned her on the drive to the house.

Cherry nodded agreement. She'd been in charge of her dad's pay packet when he was alive. She knew how to set up temporary quarters and lay in supplies. But as she accompanied the older woman through the house, watching her choose the furniture she would leave, a feeling of permanence, and security crept over Cerise.

"Odds and ends I've collected, Cerise." The older

woman smiled as she walked through the rooms, touching a piece now and then, her gaze lost in memories. "Leftovers from a life well lived."

Cerise didn't want her to change her mind about moving, and breathed a sigh of relief when Esther entered the kitchen, pointed at the stove, and said, "It's old, still works, but it'll need replaced soon. I won't miss cooking on it. It burns hot, so be careful. The back door is cracked and needs repaired, and I'll send Kevin over to take care of that."

She opened the cupboard doors and looked at the dishes inside. "I'll leave you a pan and a skillet. You'll need glasses, cups, and two place settings."

"Jeb's gone, he won't be back for a while. One will do," Cherry said quickly.

"He'll be back. And besides, when I come to visit, what will I drink my tea in if you don't have a spare mug or two?"

In all, Esther left an overstuffed chair in the sitting room and the old scarred table and chairs in the kitchen; she claimed she had no room for either in her son's house. Cherry suspected she was being kind.

Esther marked to go, the rosewood bed set from the big bedroom, but left the rocking chair and a smaller pine bed in the side room.

"It will be fine if you want to move this into the bigger sleeping room. I'm not parting with the bedroom set. Kevin might need it at some point. But, you can use it until you get something better."

With the business part settled, Cerise was anxious to begin claiming the space for herself, and Esther was in a hurry to be gone.

"Dad and I were happy here, Cerise. But he's gone, and I'm of an age now to want to be closer to my family. I'll send Kevin to bring your trunks tomorrow and he can fix your back door while he's here. Hinny can come with him to help you get settled."

Cherry followed her to the buggy out front, said goodbye, and watched her drive away.

Once she was alone, she tackled the kitchen. The pump spewed rusty water at first, but she kept pumping until it eventually ran clear; and the box of soap powder under the sink made it possible for her to clean.

After she'd scrubbed the counters, and wiped out the kitchen drawers, musty from disuse, she emptied the cupboard of the dishes, stacking them on the table for Esther to retrieve.

Halfway through the cupboard, she found the tea caddy with enough loose Earl Grey inside for a hot drink. She wasn't much of a tea drinker but she could almost hear her father say, "Put on the kettle, love, and make yer dad a cuppa."

It was Esther's kettle, so she added that to the list she was making of items she'd soon need to buy. There was no sugar left or cream to be had, but she found a corner of honeycomb and dripped sweet gold into the hot drink.

After she'd made a ritual of the preparation, delaying the moment when she had no one to serve but herself, she carried her tea to the veranda. It was late afternoon, the first time that she'd been alone in over a month. The solitude felt odd when she sat down in the two-seater swing on the porch.

"Hope this is solid," she muttered, propelling herself tentatively back and forth. She watched the breeze blow through the tree at the end of the garden, and listened to the wind chimes someone had tied to a branch.

From the swing, Cherry could see the river that lay below her house, so different from the bayou where she'd lost her dad and found Jeb. She looked away from it, not wanting to think about any of that right now.

Instead, she watched crickets in the garden as the creaking swing with its swaying motion lolled her senses. The heavy afternoon air, redolent with the scent of wisteria and honeysuckle, soothed her spirit as the hot tea loosened the knot of misery inside of her chest.

Back and forth, back and forth, back and forth. She sat in the swing long after dark, trying not to think, or remember. Finally, she cried.

CHAPTER XI

*J*eb had greatly overestimated his ability to retrieve Nate. By horse, even pushing it to exhaustion, it took him twice as long to return to Mississippi as it had taken to leave on the train. He didn't arrive in Vicksburg until July 11th. And by that time, Grant had pardoned the Confederate soldiers and sent them home.

Jeb thought he'd hit pay dirt. He'd find Nate, pick up Cherry on the way back, and head for the ranch. He ran into one of Walker's soldiers and got the information that instead of taking his pardon and using his head, Nate had joined Gen. Braxton Bragg's Army of Tennessee.

Jeb didn't catch up to him until after a battle at a place called Chickamauga. Bragg's troops were celebrating the day's victory.

It was mid September, cold already and the countryside had been stripped of anything edible long before. Jeb stumbled through the ranks of soldiers who all looked the same—walking skeletons wearing bloodied gray.

He found Nate, and his brother wasn't any better off than the rest of Bragg's army. Nate didn't even make sense most of the time. He'd become a half-mad, killing machine. At their initial reunion, Jeb was careful how he hugged his brother for fear of crushing the starved form.

When he couldn't get his brother to leave, Jeb

stationed himself by his side, determined to wear him down and change his mind. He tried not to let himself worry about how Cherry was managing alone. Instead, he made Nate listen when he told him stories about her.

"She's too young to be a wife. I know that. But damn, Nate, she saved my life more than once. She's smart and funny and…" He grinned, remembering their arguments, "She's real independent, too." He'd choked up thinking about her, wondering why he wasn't with her and again tried coaxing Nate to go home.

"You've got a wife waiting at the ranch for you and this war's played out. There's no winning it, Nate. Gettysburg followed by the fall of Vicksburg turned the tide. The South lost. Come home."

"You think I want to be the one to tell Celia we lost?" Nate snarled. "I'm in until the last man drops."

Unable to convince his brother to quit the war and go home, Jeb fought by his side; both of them followed Bragg's troops through October and into November, scavenging off the land to survive. Near the end of the month, they ended up near Chattanooga where rebel troops had Rosecrans's Union soldiers pinned down.

There wasn't much action. Every now and again soldiers from both sides would exchange fire, but for the most part nothing much was going on. They'd been there two weeks, with semi-regular meals, and a chance to sleep safe.

He'd started to get through to Nate and had him

talking about leaving and getting home in time for Christmas. Nothing warned them but the whoop of Union troops yelling, "Chickamauga! Chickamauga…" as a tide of blue swarmed Missionary Ridge.

It was a battle of brutal carnage between two war weary and desperate crazed forces.

The battle ended for the Carter brothers when a canon shell exploded and sent Jeb flying out of the hole. He landed with a thud, but conscious enough to slap out the flames on his shirt.

Though singed and scraped, he was all in one piece. When he mustered the strength to crawl back to the spot where Nate had been, he found that the wall had collapsed covering the whole area.

Jeb dug with his hands, frantically removing the rock and rubble until he found his brother beneath the dirt. He pulled his brother from the rubble, cleaned the dirt from his nose and out of his mouth, and pounded on his back trying to get him to breathe.

"Thank God," he groaned when he heard Nate's choked cough. His brother was alive.

Once he had the dirt cleared away, he tried to help his brother move. But Nate couldn't lift more than his arms and said he couldn't feel anything below his waist.

Jeb didn't wait for Union troops to find them. It would be a bullet or prison and neither appealed. He gathered his brother in his arms and carried him away from the battle field and didn't stop walking until he'd found a farm with a barn, a horse and a wagon.

He waved away the old man who braced him with a shotgun. "I'll pay you. I've got Union script. But I'm taking my brother home, and I need your wagon and horse to do that. Kill me or get out of the way."

He probably was out of his head too. He had no idea why the old man didn't blow a hole in him and take all of the bills he'd pulled from his pocket. Instead, the farmer peeled off what he thought was fair and handed the rest back to Jeb.

The farmer's wife brought a pan of food and two blankets to the barn. After he ate and tried to get some broth down Nate, he laid his brother on one blanket in the back of the wagon, covered him with the other, and set out for Texas.

———✦———

"Damn, brother, you're jarring the meat off my bones," Nate yelled at him from the back of the wagon.

"Can't drive much slower than this," Jeb called back but pulled the horse to a stop.

Nate didn't complain much and slept a lot. It was clear from the time he opened his eyes, some things weren't working right on him. He said his legs were numb and he couldn't seem to lift more than his neck and arms.

Jeb finally found a doctor and used Cherry's money to pay him for the bad news.

"Looks like your brother twisted his spine. You need to keep him stretched out where he can lay still, with no bumps or undue jolts. You never know. His back might heal."

Going slow over the best trails available, it was late January 1864 when Jeb drove the wagon into the Carter ranch yard, relieved to see that the house was still standing.

His pa came out with a shotgun in his hand, not even recognizing them until Jeb called out.

It was halleluiah they were home and all good. His ma cried and his pa latched on Jeb with a hundred questions and a thousand ranch needs.

John Carter had managed to keep a small herd of cattle bunched near the ranch but there were more cows running wild to be gathered and brought home. Jeb's father had kept the ranch going—barely.

The morning after they arrived, Jeb spent the day by his father's side, and promised himself he'd leave the next to fetch Cerise.

"I have a wife to bring home," he told his dad. But when he explained his need to be gone for a while longer, his pa turned white.

"A week or two more can't hurt, Son. I need your help right now. With two of us working together, we can gather a herd and get 'em back on Carter land. If our luck holds, we'll have a crop of calves to add to our herd come spring." His pa's words were imbued with enthusiasm that didn't disguise his desperation.

"Three weeks, then," Jeb agreed. "End of this month, I'll leave to bring my wife home." That was the only night Jeb spent in his bed and instead of sleeping, he spent the dark hours thinking about having Cherry in it with him.

In the morning, he loaded provisions in the wagon bought with Cherry's money, hitched two horses to the back, and he and his dad headed for open range where stray cows and wild cattle roamed.

He and his dad found the time to catch up on past events while they hunched over campfires at night and branding fires during the day. Jeb heard all about how the ranch had withstood an Indian attack, rustlers, and drought.

"We just couldn't have made it through without Celia's help." His pa praised Nate's wife up one side and down the other and expressed his doubts about Jeb's choice. "If this Yankee girl you're so set on is half the wife your brother brought home, you'll be a lucky man."

"I wouldn't be here right now if that Yankee girl hadn't saved my life." Jeb didn't hold back sharing Cherry stories and by the time he finished telling his dad about her hauling him from the swamp to the old shack, catching food for them, and nursing him back to health, his pa had thawed considerably.

"All right, Son. You need to go fetch your woman," his pa said three weeks to the day later. That morning, they broke camp, bunched the beef they'd rounded up into a tight herd, and set out for home.

It was the last week in February when they reached the Carter ranch. Their jubilant return quickly changed to despair.

Though his health had rallied when he first arrived home, Nate's condition had worsened while they were gone. Celia, crowded out their ma and claimed her right to do the coddling and nursing, but none of her tinctures or cures seemed to do much good.

As if he'd waited for one last conversation with his brother, Nate held on long enough to hand Celia's care over to Jeb, making her his brother's responsibility.

Jeb sat on a chair by the bed and leaned close as his brother struggled to speak.

"She's to have my share of the ranch. Ma and Pa have agreed." Nate paused, gasping for breath. "Swear to me that you'll look after her, Jeb, so I can move on and get shut of this pain."

"I swear that I'll always take care of your wife, Nate." Jeb bent over his brother's blue-veined hands, the fingers twisted, the nails oddly ridged with white lines. He held them in his own tanned and healthy grip as he agreed to everything Nate requested, whether it was a wise thing to do or not.

He couldn't bring himself to leave with his brother fading more each day, but at the same time, he hated himself for resenting the situation that kept him from fetching Cherry.

Nate lingered until the tenth day of March when he died in his sleep. After Jeb dug a hole in the family graveyard and helped his folks with the burial, he walked with them back to the ranch house where he made his announcement.

"First thing in the morning, I'm leaving to bring my wife home."

His pa had been expecting it.

"I don't know how you can consort with a Yankee, after just burying your brother," Jeb's ma said. His mother put up a fuss, even suggesting that somehow Cherry's being from the North made her the cause of Nate's death.

"You're grieving, Ma, and I'll take that into account. But I'm bringing my bride home, and I expect her to be made welcome when she's here."

Then Celia inserted herself into the conversation, soothing Jeb's ma and asking if she could ride along with him as far as the train depot in Clarksville.

"I received a letter from my cousin weeks ago. Before Nate's passing." She paused and dabbed her eyes with one of those filmy handkerchiefs she favored.

Jeb's mother answered for him. "Of course you can go with Jeb. We don't want you missing a chance to see your kin. God knows with this war dragging on, who knows when you might again get news from your parents."

"Thank you, Mother Carter." Celia beamed at Jeb's ma and then began to make plans. "I have clothes and personal items to transport to the depot so it would be simpler to drive the wagon to the eastern part of the state. Your young lady will surely have need of transporting her own things back here."

"No." Cherry's possessions were a concern, but it stuck in his craw that Nate's widow had suddenly decided to manage his trip to suit herself. "Driving a wagon, it would take me three times as long to get there."

He didn't say it aloud, but he admitted to himself he didn't want the task of listening to Celia's endless chatter all the way. He'd made a pledge to his brother, but by damn it didn't include playing nursemaid to the widow.

"But Jeb," she protested, dabbing her eyes again.

He hardened his heart. "Celia, best be saddled-up and ready at dawn. We'll rest the horses when needed, but I don't plan any overnight stops. If that's too much for you, I'm sorry. It's the best I can offer."

His ma started to argue but Jeb's pa stepped into the fray and shut it down. "He brought his brother home to us at the expense of leaving his wife behind. He's going to make that right now, and Celia's need to visit with her relative doesn't count."

Jeb's ma deferred to her husband though her lips were tight. Celia grimaced and sighed, but seeing Jeb intended to stand firm, she nodded agreement.

He left the Carter spread at dawn the next morning.

Celia rode beside him. Jeb tried to ignore his sister-in-law's advice and warnings.

"Jeb, you've been gone quite some time. Your young lady may have moved on."

"Nate was away a long time, Celia. Did you move on and abandon him?"

"That's different, Jeb, and you know it. Your mama and daddy were there to look after me. A gently bred woman needs the support and consideration that rougher elements don't understand." She'd cast an inquisitive glance his way and added, "Your young lady is gently bred isn't she?"

Jeb thought of how Cerise had navigated the swamp, laying traps to catch supper, cooking it and then coming home to sponge-bathe a wounded soldier. "My wife is as gently bred as she needs to be, Celia. And she'll be waiting for me right where I left her."

For the most part, he shrugged away his sister-in-law's persistent nay-saying; but by the time they'd reached Clarksville, his anticipation at being with Cherry again had given away to unease.

CHAPTER XII

*H*ad it not been for the Murdock family, Cherry's acceptance in the small community of Isaca might have been quite different. But Horace recovered from his illness in time to vouch for both her respectability, and her Union sympathies. Esther sang her praises as well.

The house situated on a bend in the road leading to town, was in easy walking distance of the general store. It wasn't a grand shop, but it stocked essentials she much appreciated. It had been, after all, not that long since she'd existed on fish and game she'd caught in the bayou.

Jeb didn't return immediately, and she had no way of knowing when, or even if, he ever would. Sometimes she dreamed and woke to find her body clenched in need, poised on the pinnacle of the release he'd called from her. She didn't really understand the man and woman thing they'd done together. But it wasn't a subject that lent itself to conversational inquiry, so her questions went unasked.

She moved into the little house at the beginning of July, 1863; on the fifth day, to be more precise. She had no income and no money other than the remainder of her father's pay. The practical side of her nature took charge after her initial grief and shock abated.

Fitz Fitzwilliam had performed surveying work

when not engaged in engineering projects. His tools, a surveyor's transit with a telescope sighting bar on it, and a plane table attached to a jacob-staff, were in one of the trunks she'd brought from the cabin.

When she remembered them, she crouched on the floor by the big leather and brass bound box, removed her father's books, and set them aside for the canvas wrapped instruments in the bottom.

She wasn't sure how or where to sell the equipment but felt certain both pieces were valuable assets. She leafed through her father's books, accumulated from his education at Union College in New York and his continued study at the Rensselaer School of Engineering.

Sentiment would have had her keep the heavy tomes, but she felt certain Fitz would have pointed out her disinterest in learning the subject matter and advised her to liquidate these, too.

It was odd. She lived more or less in a cocoon. Once she took up residence in the little house by the road, it became her cottage, her bulwark shielding her from loneliness.

Esther kept her informed as to the progress of her grandson's health as it improved. Though Esther urged her to visit Horace during his recuperation, on the two occasions Cherry accepted, war dominated the conversation. After that, she declined.

She knew from the older woman that Horace was thirty, almost as old as her dad, and she felt no compelling need to pursue his friendship. Overall, Cherry refrained from visits to the Murdock home. Her heart wrenched whenever she saw the spot on their back porch where she and Jeb had said goodbye.

Though Jeb had never seen the little house that she'd rented, she waited within its comforting walls, sometimes suffering a disquieting sense of panic, wondering if he'd be able to find her when he returned.

By late August, when she'd heard nothing from Jeb, she began to make her own plans. Her father had always told her, "Assume a position, lass, and it will become."

"Well I'm certainly not assuming a position of defeat and poverty, dad." Her conversations with her father sustained her as she pulled the seams from her good quality but childish dresses.

"You always treated me as if I could do anything," she murmured. "But you dressed me in little girl clothes." She sighed over her memories as she remade her childish pinafores and dresses into vested shirtwaists fit for a lady engaged in commerce. In her own mind, she'd become a business woman of sorts.

"That's a dress style much better suited to your height and age, Cerise." Esther inspected her costume when she'd completed her first transformative sewing project. Cherry grinned with elation when Esther approved her effort.

In mid September, Cerise was invited to the Murdock's for their Sunday meal. It came as no surprise, when the Battle of Chickamauga dominated the conversation.

"The blasted rebels are beat but won't admit it," Kevin Murdock said gruffly.

"You'd be hard pressed to find a man at Davis' Cross Roads who'd agree with you," Horace had disagreed.

Cherry listened as father and son discussed the war's progress, and her heart soared at the possibility it would soon end; at the same time she feared the worst for Jeb in the final days.

"I need to sell some of my father's possessions, Esther," she told her landlord and friend on the way home. She needed a means to support herself if Jeb never returned.

"No, child, you want to part with a few items taking up too much room in your home. Never admit to anyone you need." The old lady gave her a sharp look and patted her arm.

She took Esther's advice to heart, but want or need aside; selling her dad's things would provide additional funds, though not enough to live on forever.

After she'd decided which of her father's books and equipment to part with, she gathered information from the general store owner about business establishments in Clarksville and planned a trip to visit book stores and resale shops.

It was before dawn on a week day in late September

when Horace Murdock backed a wagon up to her house and loaded her father's steamer trunk, filled with his books and surveying equipment.

"You look very nice," Horace's compliment reassured her that her needlework would pass muster in the shops she'd be visiting.

The Murdock conveyance had two rows of seating instead of the standard one. Horace and his dad sat up front and Esther and Cherry sat behind them on the back bench. Once they got started, Esther handed Cerise a hat to go with her outfit. "Now you look like a prosperous lady ready to conduct business."

"I like how you see me," she told Esther as she pinned her hat in place. Later, Cherry realized that Esther had handed her more than a hat. She'd given her a goal, something Cerise could work toward instead of focusing on her father, Jeb, and her past.

With that in mind, she scoured Clarksville, visiting both used and new book sellers, talking to the owners and showing them her father's engineering texts. Before she entered each establishment, she tilted her hat at a confident angle and prepared to listen. She found that many of the proprietors seemed lonely, especially in the dusty book shops.

The first book store was empty of customers and the clerk, who turned out to be the owner, showed great interest in her engineering tomes although he made no offer for either. On the other hand, he had several suggestions on where she might obtain a good price, so her time wasn't wasted.

Neither was his. While she'd kept him talking about possible places to sell the articles in her trunk, Horace Murdock had been busy.

"These will give me a place to start." Horace pointed at the two books he'd put on the counter. "I've decided to read the law and become an attorney."

From his father's look of consternation, evidently Horace hadn't discussed his decision with his dad.

Esther, on the other hand, nodded her agreement. "It's a fine idea. You can study at night and help Kevin around the place during the day. It'll be a while before you're ready for the law exams."

Cherry wondered if Horace and his grandmother had planned the moment of revelation. She didn't doubt it at all when Kevin Murdock cast a murderous look at his mother.

"I suppose I have you to thank for encouraging him," Kevin muttered, glaring at Esther. "We need help on the place; not a blood sucking lawyer in the family."

Cherry tried to think of something to say that might diffuse the situation. Before she could murmur a word, the heat of the building, the musty smelling books, and her lack of food since early breakfast, rolled over her in a tide. The pleasant words she had intended changed to a sharp rebuke.

"Mr. Murdock, my dad liked your son but he said

Captain Murdock wasn't robust enough for soldiering and doubted he'd survive the war." Her burst of words piddled to a stop and a flush of embarrassment heated her skin when she realized all eyes were riveted on her.

"Well Dad was wrong, Horace did survive, but he didn't get any more robust. He's never going to be able to do farm work. But he's smart. He'll pass the law exams with no trouble." She tilted her hat a little more and added, "Then you'll have a blood sucking attorney on your side."

She directed her attention to the shop owner."Mr. Morris, will you trade my books for those two?" She pointed at the books next to Horace.

"Yes, ma'am," the book seller agreed, eager it seemed, to move the discord out of his store.

"Then we've concluded our business here." Cherry scooped up Horace's books and led the way to the exit. When they stepped outside, she handed them over with a grin.

"Consider this a retainer for services yet to be rendered. I know my dad would say I got a good deal for his engineering texts." She hadn't made a dime on her first business transaction and yet she felt flush with success. "I'm hungry. Let's find someplace to eat."

During the meal Cherry became a reluctant witness to the heated conversation between the Murdock men. To her relief, the argument finally dwindled to thoughtful dialogue.

"The girl's right, you know, son," Kevin Murdock admitted, pointing his fork at Horace. "You don't have the stamina of a working man."

"The doctor says I'll likely have bouts of yellow-fever the rest of my life and quinine can only help so much." Instead of taking insult from the conciliatory remark, Cherry was happy to see Horace had good sense and agreed.

Before the end of the meal, the humor of the Murdock family had shifted back to positive, while her mood dipped. She needed to find a buyer for her father's surveying equipment.

When they set out again, they agreed to double their possibility of success by separating. While the Murdock men talked to the owner of a hardware and equipment store, Cherry and Esther entered the shop next door, Edna's Treasures. There, they walked through aisles of household items and furniture that ranged from scratched and worn to elegant and new.

"Where do things like this come from?" Esther asked, reverently tracing the lines of a magnificent armoire.

"War prizes," a voice answered, and an older woman stepped out from behind an exotic, hand-painted screen.

"Oh my," Esther murmured. "Stolen?"

"Not at all," the woman answered briskly. "The world is in flux, even the most fervent rebel sympathizer sees the end of the conflict is near, and they know they aren't going to win."

"Well of course they're not. And it can't end too soon," Esther answered firmly.

"Amen to that," the woman agreed. "I'm Edna, the owner of this treasure trove." While she and Esther exchanged names and opinions on the war, Cerise wandered through the furniture, most of it a fine quality she'd never hoped to own. She returned to Esther's side in time to hear the shop owner's remark.

"Certain estate owners situated behind enemy lines have found it necessary to liquidate their assets."

"But how…"Cerise motioned at the fainting couch, Persian rug, child's crib, bedroom set, and a few other items that caught her eye among the oddly assorted pieces.

"Auctions," Edna answered and then lowered her voice to a conspiratorial whisper to continue. "As discreetly as possible, the Southern plantation owners are raising money, gathering up whatever they can spare, and hauling wagon loads to centralized warehouses to be sold."

"How sad," Cherry murmured.

"Their loss is my gain. I figure after all the bloodshed that's happened someone ought to get something good out of it. Why shouldn't it be me?"

Cerise made no sale at Edna's Treasures, but the shop owner recommended a particular hardware establishment.

"Brown's your man. He sells to the army engineers, railroaders, and that ilk so…"

Edna was right. Caleb Brown inspected the contents of the trunk, and when she named the deceased owner, the shop owner nodded in recognition and smiled.

"I knew Fitz. A good man and a fine engineer. I'm sorry he's gone." After he reminisced a bit, he offered her more than she expected to get for the equipment, and then patted the lid of the old steamer and asked, "This for sale, too?"

A pang of loss struck her at the thought of parting with the sturdy trunk that had accompanied her wherever her father had taken them. But she suppressed the feeling and nodded. "Of course, if we can agree on a price."

She enjoyed the bargaining, or dickering, as Mr. Murdock called it. Both her mental state and financial affairs reflected a positive balance as they traveled home. More than that, she'd discovered a taste, and she felt strongly, a talent, for business.

"You did very well today," Esther told her and patted her arm affectionately when Kevin pulled the wagon up in front of her house to drop her off.

Horace jumped down and stood by the back bench, ready to lift her down.

"I can manage if you let me use your shoulder to brace my step," she assured him, putting her hand on his arm to ease her descent.

"I will render services as needed," he said and

laughed. Whether she needed it or not, he retained hold of her arm and walked her to her front door. She wished it was Jeb beside her instead.

"Good night, Horace, no—good night, Captain Murdock," she told him when they reached her porch. "I've decided it's unseemly of me to address you by your given name."

He frowned at her and then his mouth curved into a smile. "If you've been improper in calling me Horace, in the name of my advanced years, my past friendship with your father, and our new client-attorney privilege, I give you leave to continue."

She smiled at the diplomatic nonsense he spouted in his sedate, old-fashioned voice. "You are not that advanced, Horace. And I thank you for my privilege. You will certainly make a fine attorney."

She watched him return to the wagon and take his seat before she called, "Thank you all so much for your help. You are true friends."

Once inside, she walked to the kitchen, made a cup of tea, and carried it through the backdoor to sit on the porch swing where her thoughts lingered on Edna's shop. Cherry hated the idea of people so desperate they were selling their household goods.

"On the other hand," she muttered. "The truth is, I just dragged my trunk all over Clarksville to do the same." Her business trip had solved her immediate need for capital and given her an idea for a future, discreet, money-making enterprise. She focused on the possible when what she longed for each night seemed more impossible.

Cherry wished Jeb would return. In her mind, after this point she became vague on what they'd do or how they'd move on together. In the swamp cabin, he'd been a good listener and companion while he'd recuperated.

She would have liked to hear his opinion about her budding enterprise but remembered that his return would mean she no longer needed an enterprise. Her thoughts, when they included Jeb, left her frustrated and sad.

So, because it did no good to wish, and it wasted her time as well, she pictured the furniture at Edna's Treasures, especially the antique armoire.

Later when she retired, she tried holding onto that thought. *I need to find out when the next auction occurs.*

But as soon as her eyes closed, it wasn't an image of furniture that filled her mind. She saw instead, Jeb standing on the Murdock porch, holding her close, and promising he'd return.

Tears prickled behind her lids, her breath caught in her throat, and she lay sleepless, trying to recapture the excitement of her new venture and quell her heartache.

CHAPTER XIII

*C*herry dove into her new enterprise with vigor, attending any auction to which she could arrange transportation. At an event in late November, labeled an "estate sale," a polite term for a bank foreclosure, Cherry stood between a beefy farmer on one side and a matron of advanced years on the other.

She'd arrived at dawn, strategically choosing a spot close to the auctioneer's box. But the temperature in the enclosed space climbed as more people gathered; by mid morning the room was stifling.

She was distracted when she felt an odd motion in her stomach. She attributed it to indigestion, but revised that opinion when it felt as if a fish rolled over in her tummy.

Surreptitiously, she rested her hand on her belly. Startled, she felt a touch from inside press back and it flustered her so much, she missed bidding on a velvet covered fainting couch.

Being young and ignorant of most women's health issues, she'd put her lack of menses down to grief and stressful living. She'd experienced no morning sickness or loss of appetite and had attributed her exhaustion to her new business schedule.

But in the midst of a teaming crowd of bidders and the sing-song chant of the auctioneer, she realized that she had a new life growing in her womb; she carried

Jeb's child.

Stunned though she was, she still accumulated a hand-loomed carpet and two matching Windsor chairs before the auction ended.

She used some of her capital to pay for her goods, and paid a freight wagon carrier to let her ride with her furniture to Clarksville.

At Edna's shop, she traded the two Windsor chairs for a crib and layette and sold the rug outright. Behind her pragmatic business conduct, her mind raced, teaming with preparations that needed to be made and problems that needed resolved.

The freight driver had other stops to make, so she paid him to deliver the baby furniture to her cottage, gave him directions, and made her way to the stage depot where she bought a ticket to Isaca.

She collapsed on the coach seat, amazed that she'd managed to take care of business with her thoughts in chaos. Alone and finally able to analyze her discovery, she resolved to keep it a secret until she was certain. But in her heart, she knew she carried Jeb's child.

Cherry's height and willowy stature, plus the cooler season that made wearing a loose cape possible, helped disguise her condition until after the Christmas holiday. By then, she'd begun discreetly making plans for the birth.

"You'll need a crib and nappies ready, and

clothes and..." Esther's excitement bordered on panic after she discovered Cherry's secret. Bright spots of red burned on each of her otherwise papery white cheeks. "You can't be here alone, either," Esther fussed.

"I'm fine on my own, and as for the baby bed, I already have one." Cherry ushered her friend and landlord to the smaller bedroom and proudly opened the door, showing off the crib and chest of drawers.

"I'm glad to see you've been planning," Esther said, patting her arm. "But if your man hasn't returned, when it gets closer to your time, you'll come back to the house and stay with us for a spell."

Cherry had no inclination to move out of her cottage, even for a short time. But in late February, she changed her mind when an astonishing surge of growth made her almost double in size, rendering her cumbersome and awkward. Although, by her calculations, the baby shouldn't arrive until the end of the month, Cherry accepted Esther's invitation and moved back to the Murdock place on March 9th.

Two days later Cherry's labor began in the morning, and though her pregnancy had been easy, her delivery was not. She suffered birthing pains until the evening of March 12th, 1864, when her first child, a daughter, arrived. Her son quickly followed, surprising the midwife, the Murdock clan, and his mother.

Jeb escorted Celia to Clarksville and left her in a hotel where her male cousin, Mark Stevens, awaited her. With the assurance that Nate's wife would be cared for until he returned with Cherry, Jeb visited a livery stable, intending to return it after he dropped her trunks at the stage depot to be hauled home. It didn't occur to him that he should have cleaned up some until after he drove the buckboard toward the Murdocks.

"Hope she recognizes me," he groaned, scratching the stubble of beard covering his chin.

Nothing worked out as he'd planned when he arrived. Cherry was still at the Murdock's all right. In fact, she was sitting in a rocking chair on the front porch when he drove into the ranch yard.

Horace Murdock occupied a chair next to her, and to Jeb's mind, the two looked cozy as could be. All of Celia's warnings and dire predictions came to the fore and, without thought or investigation, Jeb leapt to the conclusion that he'd lost his bride to the Yankee cavalry officer.

When it was all said and done, he couldn't remember stopping the carriage, or tying the horse to the hitching post. His memories started with him standing toe-to-toe with Horace Murdock.

"You didn't waste any time, did you, you Yankee sonofabitch?" Jeb knocked Murdock's proffered hand away, letting his gaze shift to Cherry.

He was enraged, sure that all of Celia's insinuations were true. Cerise looked so content, sitting next to Murdock on the porch, Jeb felt good punching the stupid smile off the bastard's face.

"I expected better from you," he snarled, glaring down at her. Only it wasn't just her staring up at him.

"I'm glad you're alive," Cherry said. "It would have been a kindness to let me know." And then the baby in her arms began to cry.

Later he couldn't explain his actions other than to admit he'd gone a little crazy when Cherry handed him the swaddled bundle. The kid blinked up at Jeb from eyes just like his own. And then the baby burped, sighed, closed his lids, and lapsed into sleep.

"Is he all right?" Jeb asked anxiously.

"I just fed him. He'll sleep for hours now if you quit jostling him around. Give him to me." Cherry stepped closer and held out her arms.

"No, I think not." Jeb backed down the porch steps, unwilling to part with the baby in his arms. "You can do what you want, as it appears you have. But I'll not leave my son to be raised by another man. Come away with me now and we'll talk."

"I can't right now," Cherry answered. "You need to stop acting a fool. Captain Murdock and his family have been true friends while I've been here alone."

Jeb felt a twinge of guilt that she'd been forced to

rely on other than him. But hell, he'd been to war and back. He didn't listen to her pleas or the threats of Kevin Murdock when the older man emerged from the house with a shotgun.

"Leave now or you'll be in the stockade tonight. The Union troops will be interested to know we've got a rebel in our midst."

"Cherry, I'm taking my son with me to the Ellison Hotel in Clarksville." Cradling the baby in one arm, Jeb climbed onto the buckboard seat. "If you've a mind to see him again, you come visit him there. I'll wait two days. If you can't tear yourself away from your good *friends* by then, don't bother coming at all because we'll be on the Carter ranch. The rest of you," he glared at the Murdocks watching from the porch. "You can all go to hell."

Jeb's son slept all the way to Clarksville but began crying as soon as he opened his eyes.

"The kid's got good lungs," he said, as he carried his son past the front desk.

"He's probably got wet nappies," the clerk suggested. "I know when my boys were young, they bellowed when they were wet. If you'd like me to fetch a chambermaid to take him I can."

"Nope, we're good."

"Sounds as if the babe might be hungry, too," the clerk remarked, helpfully.

Of course, Cherry fed him hours ago. "Do you know

114

of a wet nurse I can hire?" Jeb jostled the baby but the cries grew louder.

"I do," the clerk assured him. "The hotel has these requests from time to time and we have a list of mother's who are willing—"

"Fetch one here and I'll pay you for your trouble." Jeb interrupted him and carried the squalling baby to his suite. Neither Celia nor her cousin was in the room.

Jeb laid the baby on his bed and removed the wet nappy, washing the kid's bottom before he improvised a diaper from a hotel towel. An unfamiliar tenderness filled him as he inspected his son, amazed at the soft skin and sweet expression the baby wore when he wasn't crying.

"Nathaniel Jackson Carter, howdy, son, I'm your pa," Jeb introduced himself. "From this day forth you'll carry your Uncle Nate's name."

Jeb held the baby and paced the floor, worrying about the fool he'd made of himself at the Murdock place. Gradually though, as he focused on the baby, pride and love replaced his anxiety.

Cherry and I made this boy. He meant what he'd told her. If she wouldn't come with him, so be it. But he was keeping his son.

A clean but poorly dressed wet nurse arrived. She stated her fee up front and Jeb paid for Jack's feeding with Union greenbacks from Cherry's money. After the woman finished, she tucked the sleeping baby into a cradle provided by the hotel.

"I'll need you at least for the next two days," Jack told her. "Do you have to go home to feed your own?" He didn't know how else to find out if she could stay. His blunt question brought tears and she shook her head.

"No," she whispered. "I'm available."

Jeb gave her his bedroom so she could be with the baby if he woke. He paced the sitting room floor, waiting for Cherry to arrive. But it was Celia and her cousin who returned. Jeb didn't ask where they'd been because he didn't care.

Celia immediately started complaining. The first night, Jack fussed a good long time. Jeb cradled him as he paced the floor, rocking the baby in his arms until the little fellow went back to sleep.

The next morning, Celia said the baby's crying set her nerves on edge, and she left with her cousin to visit other relatives in the area.

After two days, when Cherry didn't show, but Celia returned with her sympathetic remarks and sad gaze, Jeb bought an extra stage ticket for the wet nurse and paid her to travel with him and the baby so she could feed Jack on the way to West Texas.

Celia wrinkled her nose at the idea of traveling with a crying baby and a poorly dressed widow. Jeb was grateful to her cousin when Stevens offered to escort Celia to the Carter ranch on a coach leaving later.

⋰⋱

After Jeb left, Cherry packed the valise she'd brought with her to the Murdocks and asked Esther to drive her to her cottage. She planned to gather up her essentials and the babies' needs before she left for Clarksville.

"So you're following after him?" Esther asked, her expression set in disapproval.

"Of course I'm following him. I can't leave my son alone with a maniac." In spite of the virulent quarrel that made no sense at all to her, her heart thumped with joy. Jeb was alive, he'd come for her, and they were going to be together.

Her vision of happiness was interrupted with the sound of another visitor entering the Murdock ranch yard.

"I hope it's not your mister come back because Kevin might blow a hole in him." Esther hustled to the window to peer out. "Now who in tarnation is that?"

Fearful that Kevin might have gone to report Jeb's presence and brought back Union troops, Cherry stopped packing long enough to ask, "Is it the army?"

Before she received her answer, a knock sounded on the bedroom door, followed by Horace's announcement. "Cherry, you have a guest in the front room."

"I'm Celia Carter." Jeb's sister-in-law hurried across the room, introducing herself as soon as Cherry entered.

She presented a picture of fragile elegance, a widow in mourning.

Celia's black dress billowed around her, emphasizing her delicate frame. As she folded back the veil from her wide-brimmed hat, she confirmed that her face was as beautiful as the rest of her.

Pretty though Celia was, her eyes were cold as ice and her head tilted just enough to let everyone in the room know she was better than the rest of the world.

"My name is Cerise," Cherry corrected her. "And if you're looking for Jeb, he's on his way back to Clarksville."

"Jeb sent me," Celia assured her.

"What were you doing? Lurking outside the ranch waiting for him?"

"We thought it best to let him speak to you first," Celia admitted.

"Is the baby all right? Have you seen him? Is he crying?" Cherry didn't know this woman and kin to Jeb or not, she already didn't like her. But she needed to know about her son.

"I'm sure Jeb has the situation in control. Clearly he's taken the baby because you're not fit to raise him. Why you're no better than poor white trash. It won't do. The Carters won't sanction a liaison between Jeb and a girl such as you." Her lip curled with disdain as she noted Cherry's faded gray muslin attire.

"Marriage, you mean," Cherry corrected her. "We

didn't have a liaison. We got married. What do you want? It's clear you're not here to tender a welcome."

The cry of her baby girl interrupted the confrontation. Without explanation, Cherry left the woman standing in the middle of the room and hurried to the bedroom where Natalia had been asleep.

She lifted her daughter from the cradle, cuddling her close until her cries ceased, hoping that Celia Carter would take her absence as a hint and leave. But when Cherry returned carrying the baby, she found that the Carter woman had remained in the room.

"Twins? Oh for pity's sake," Celia snorted. "You're a conniving strumpet who took advantage of a wounded soldier. And now I suppose you think these children will firm your claim on Jeb."

As Cherry and the Murdock's listened, Celia Carter denounced Cherry as a no-good Yankee, a camp follower, and a loose woman.

"Jeb and I were accompanied on this trip by our cousin, an attorney." Celia turned to her escort who until that time had remained silent. "Jeb insisted on doing the honorable thing and checking on you, but we brought Mark along to put a stop to any legal claims coerced from Jeb during his illness."

"Here now," Kevin Murdock interrupted the verbal attack. "I've heard enough. You need to be on your way before I set the Yankee army, the one you're busy blaspheming, onto you."

Feeling like a hulking draft horse, Cherry cradled Natalia protectively and seconded that suggestion. "You and your lawyer can leave now. And don't worry. If that's what Jeb wants, he and the Carter family won't have to suffer my presence. But I'll have my son back."

"Oh, I think not," Celia murmured and then laughed. "After all, there are two children. I would have preferred the girl myself, but you know how men are. A man wants his son, so Jeb's mama and I will have to be satisfied with the boy."

"You can't have him," Cherry snapped. "He's not a box of candy to be passed around."

"You're missing the obvious. We already have him. Mark, explain." By the time Mark Stevens finished outlining Jeb's rights as the father and the non-rights of the mother, Cherry trembled in fear of losing her daughter too.

"Horace, is what he says true?" Cherry asked her untrained legal representative, hoping he'd contradict what had been claimed.

"Well, if you're married then I suppose he has a legal right to expect you to live with him. He'd have jurisdiction over any children born of the union. And if you're not married, I suppose he has a legal right to claim your child as his own unless you can prove the boy's not his son..."

"But he's *my* son," Cherry protested.

"He belongs to both of you in as much as you are the

parents. But, I'm afraid in a court of law, being a man tilts the odds greatly in his favor and—barring Jeb being hung as a rebel traitor—he'd probably win custody," Horace admitted and shook his head.

"I told you so." Celia clapped her hands and laughed, making an incongruous sound amid the solemn conversation. "The Carters will raise Jeb's son. You needn't worry about the baby's future. Better that you spend your time taking care of the one we've let you keep."

"And Jeb sent you to tell me this?"

"Of course."

"I don't believe you," Cherry told her. "Now if you'll excuse me, I'm in the middle of packing."

"Could I have a private moment with Cherry before I leave?" Celia asked Esther.

Cherry would rather have bedded down with a rattlesnake, but taking the matter out of her hands, the Murdocks hurried to vacate the room, as did Celia's cousin.

"Believe this," Celia said as soon as the door closed behind the last Murdock. "The Carters are true Southern patriots and they've lost one son, as I have a husband."

Celia retied the ribbon on her elaborate hat and paused to smile and give Cherry a final warning, before lowering the heavy, black veil. Her voice dropped to a quiet hiss.

"Neither the Carters, nor I, will accept a filthy,

Northern bitch living in our midst." She paused and shrugged before adding softly, "Follow Jeb and I'll see you dead; and if the second brat over there survives, I'll be raising two of your children, not one."

Cherry believed her. After the horrible woman left, instead of readying her things to join Jeb in Clarksville, she had Esther drive her to the cottage where she sat on the back porch swing, rocking her daughter.

"It's probably for the best," Esther tried to soothe her. "For today, just stay here and wait. If what that vile woman said is untrue, your man will be back. If not..."

The unthinkable, *if not,* came to pass. Jeb didn't return, and, as it turned out, Cherry developed a high fever, her stomach began to cramp and she collapsed. Her delirium abated enough for her to hear the doctor when he arrived.

He was furious with Esther. "What were you thinking? The girl just birthed twin babies four days ago and nearly ripped herself apart. She had no business being up and around at all. Now we'll be lucky if we don't lose her to childbed fever."

He left a bottle of medicine behind and prescribed bed rest and constant supervision. Esther stayed at the cottage and divided her care between Natalia and Cherry.

It was a week before Cherry recovered enough to think about Clarksville again. Remembering Celia's threat to take Natalia too, Cherry remained at home. At her request, Horace wrote the first of many letters to Jeb

Carter, this one demanding the return of Cherry's son.

The reply came in a matter of weeks. The single sheet of paper held one word. "No."

When it became evident that without storming the ranch she'd never retrieve her son, she focused on caring for her daughter and tried to forget Jeb all together.

"She'll not carry his name, nor will I," she told Horace. But at the last moment, she relented to the demands of her heart. "A middle name will call no attention to our *liaison*. Register my daughter as Natalia Carter Fitzwilliam, father deceased."

She resumed her business, doing her best to convince herself of what she told others—she was a widow with one child whose father was lost in the war.

CHAPTER XIV

Jeb stared at the woman who'd captured his heart twenty-five years before. They'd become adversaries instead of partners after the war. His fault. He knew that for sure. He'd handled everything wrong.

"The war remains hell in my memory," she said now, as if reading his mind.

"It *was* hell."

They'd ordered room service and moved from inside the suite to the private balcony.

Instead of facing each other across the small table, he set Cerise's chair next to him so they could share the view of early morning Paris. And truthfully, with memories, not all good, flying around the way they were, he wanted her close enough to hold onto if need be.

They ate breakfast while they watched workmen constructing Eiffel's arch. Jeb's steak was seared on the outside, rare inside, and so tender he could cut it with his fork.

"To my mind, this is the best I've ever had." He pointed at the piece of barely cooked meat. "Think I could lure the chef to Texas?"

"Trade this place for red dust and cactus? Not if the chef has any sense." Cerise paused to sip coffee and nibble a fancy pastry she'd drizzled with warm honey from the tiny pot on the table. "Have you ever seen anything so beautiful?" she murmured.

"You, when we made love the first time." Ignoring her astonishment, he offered her a bite of steak. "You'll be hungry in an hour. Better have some of this."

"I don't understand how you can say something like that and then offer me a piece of bloody meat." She arched her eyebrow and pushed her glasses higher on her pert nose.

"You don't eat enough to keep a bird alive. In fact, in those new spectacles, you remind me of an owl," he murmured, pretending to misunderstand her remark. Truth was, he'd seen her preen in front of the mirror, studying her new glasses when she thought he wasn't looking. "They give you a sophisticated, scholarly look," he complimented them and her. He didn't mention that they intensified the color of her lavender eyes and emphasized her fringe of dark lashes.

"Remember when I held a candle up and checked all your parts?"

"You splashed wax on my stomach," Cerise said, her expression indignant.

Jeb grinned back at her; twenty-five years later he was still unrepentant. He reached into the pastry basket, took up a croissant, dipped it in honey, and ate it before continuing.

"I'd been wondering how your brows and lashes could be almost black, while your head hair was so pale it was almost white. I wanted to see what color you were down below."

Chewing slowly, he relived the moment in his head. "It was your idea to consummate the marriage. I figured it was a good time to appease my curiosity."

Her glare changed to a half-smile and she rolled her eyes at him. "I was sixteen and filled with romantic notions."

"You were scared spitless of being alone and figured to make our marriage real," he corrected. He had no illusions about why the younger Cherry had wanted him.

"And I had Union greenbacks you needed," she answered wryly.

He shrugged. "Not the first wedding that happened because of mutual convenience." But it wasn't so. The girl who'd rescued him had called to something inside of him. Her father's pay packet had only been a bonus.

"The truth is, sweetheart, I wanted you from the moment you sponged the sweat from my body and ogled my ass." He leered at her and grinned when a pretty blush tinted her cheeks pink. "And, I don't think I'm wrong when I say, you wanted me too."

"Well, for all our mutual wanting, we made a mess of things," she murmured, her expression changing from laughing to sad.

"Not really," he disagreed. "I built the ranch into a prosperous spread and toadied up to enough men of law and state politicians to amass some power."

"You're a ruthless man. And was Horace Murdock

one of your toadies?"

"Never fear, Horace has always remained loyal to you." Jeb waved away her frown. "And I'm ruthless because I've had to be. Not that it ever worked with you. Admit it. You've enjoyed the life you wanted in a house you wouldn't leave."

"You connived to get it from Esther and bought it before anyone knew about the deal." Though she'd won that conflict, her anger at his past behavior was palpable.

"Believe this or not, sweetheart, that dear old lady approached me. When she sold me that house, she considered herself looking after you. She wrote me and explained. Though she knew you were smart enough to pay the taxes and the upkeep, you didn't have the money to buy the house. She said she couldn't afford to give it to you and she was afraid even if she did, without the protection of a man, you might not be able to hold onto it."

"Horace would have told me—"Cherry interrupted fiercely.

"Murdock didn't know," Jeb assured her. "I was eager to buy, and she was eager to sell once we met and talked."

"She thought you were a scoundrel. Why would she have sold it to you?"

"I don't want to impugn the character of your friend, but I've done well, Cerise and money sometimes has a way of smoothing over discord."

"I do not believe for one moment that you bribed Esther with money. What did you offer her she couldn't resist?"

"She asked if we were really wed, and I assured her you were my wife, the only woman I'd ever marry. I admitted the truth. I loved you, but you didn't feel the same."

"Nonsense," Cerise muttered. "She knew I was head over heels in love with you; I just wasn't willing to live with a jackass."

"I've been called worse," Jeb admitted and saluted her with his coffee cup.

"As soon as you coaxed the deed from Esther you threatened to evict me." Cerise scooted her chair away from the table, ready it seemed, to leave breakfast and the conversation.

"Stay, there are things best said here, and then forgotten." Jeb laid his hand on her arm to keep her with him. "Esther wanted you to leave."

When Cerise gasped and gave him a disbelieving look, he took her hand in his before continuing.

"Sweetheart, Esther Murdock loved you, and if she could, she would have welcomed you as Horace's wife. She came to me on a fishing expedition, so to speak. If we weren't married, she planned to press Horace's suit with you, since he didn't seem to be able to get the job done."

"Don't be foolish," Cerise muttered. "Horace and I

have never contemplated being more than friends."

"Maybe that's the way you see it, but that's not the way Esther wanted it to be. If Horace couldn't have you as a legal wife, she wanted you to leave so he'd find someone else."

"You're saying that Esther sold you the cottage to get rid of me?" Jeb hated the hurt and bewilderment that tinged her question.

"Nope. I'm saying I wanted my wife and our daughter to live with me and our son. And Esther wanted her grandson to marry and give her some grandbabies to play with. Was that so wrong, Cerise?"

"You took my son from me and left your daughter behind." She clenched her hands into fists and it was clear to Jeb she'd like to use them on him.

"Yes I did," Jeb admitted. It probably wasn't a good time to reminisce, but he still got a tingle when he remembered his first glimpse of Jack.

"I'll be damned if I ever forget the way he gazed up at me from a face that looked like a miniature Nate."

"Don't be dense. He looked just like you, which is why I called him Jeb, Jr.," she disagreed. You knocked Horace down, accused us of adultery, took the baby away, and changed his name."

"Yep. At the time I didn't know his name or that I'd fathered twins. If I had, my sweet daughter would have come home with me, too."

He'd never forget his wild ride carrying a sleeping

Jack. He'd held his son in his lap and drove the buckboard hell-bent-for-leather back to the livery stable in Clarksville.

He'd been crazy; nursing a mixed bag of jealousy, pride and grief, sure that he'd lost his wife to another man, but determined to keep the son who looked just like his brother. And too, he figured whether Cherry wanted to be with him or not, she'd come after her baby.

"You never came for him. I understand now; you had another baby to tend and couldn't leave her behind, but damn, Cherry. I never thought you'd let me take our son."

๏๛ ๛๏

"After we quarreled and you left, I started packing. But, your sister-in-law's visit ended that."

"What visit? I didn't send her."

Cerise forced herself to remember that awful day. "She arrived with a lawyer in tow, shortly after you left."

"You're saying she followed me to the Murdock place?"

"Yes. She told me you didn't want to be married to me and intended to legally sever our relationship, but you wanted your son. Her lawyer explained that the Carter family would take Tali if I came after Jack." Cherry didn't tell him the rest. It was even hard for her sometimes to believe her life had been threatened.

"It appears my brother's widow has a lot to answer for. And as for not wanting to be married to you, hell, I've spent my life trying to get you back." From his amazed fury, Cherry couldn't doubt the truth of his words or his vow. "In years gone by, I've made allowances for Celia's weak character; but trust me, sweetheart, this time she'll pay."

Cerise stood and pulled Jeb from his chair. "I don't intend wasting any more time on Celia or the past. Why should I when I have what I've always wanted right now."

"And what would that be?" he asked, pulling her into his arms again.

"You," she told him. "I've wanted you for myself ever since the day I wrestled you out of an alligator infested swamp."

"Speaking of alligators…" He laughed at her words and holding her hand, returned with her to the sitting room of their suite.

She didn't know what to expect when he left her standing and crossed to the armoire to remove a box wrapped in ornate paper.

"I picked up something for you the other day while you were poking around in that antique shop," Jeb told her.

"What's the occasion?" she murmured as he handed it to her.

"Paying a debt long overdue," he drawled. "Open it."

She had no idea what to expect as she removed the fancy wrapping. Inside the sturdy box, she found a pair of suede boots handcrafted to fit perfectly.

"Thank you. I coveted yours greatly. Now I have my own. But it took you long enough," she chided him, adding a grin to her scold when he seated her on a chair, knelt in front of her.

After he'd laced the soft-soled leather moccasins to her knees, she elevated her leg, admiring the new foot gear. Then she leaned forward and planted a kiss on his mouth.

"I bought you something too," she murmured against his lips. "Tickets."

"And where are we going now?" Jeb asked, sitting back on his heels.

"I booked passage for us on the German ship, Bremen, sailing in two days for Galveston."

"You didn't think you should consult me?" Though his expression was enigmatic, she knew him well enough to sense the anger simmering beneath the false calm.

"I wanted it to be a surprise."

"And when we reach Galveston, where then?" A frown wrinkled his forehead as he lost his look of indifference and glowered at her. "I'm not letting you go back to living in that cottage while I ramble around alone at my ranch, so forget that. We are not separating again. If you think I've been ruthless in the past..." he began a growled warning.

"Hush." She covered his mouth with her palm. "We'll figure it all out when we get where we're going. It occurs to me, that we did this to ourselves before. I didn't believe enough in you and me, and you didn't either. It's different now. We're really together this time."

"Are we?" he asked, holding her face between his hands as he peered in her eyes. Whatever he read there must have reassured him because he grimaced and then grinned. "Guess I'd better get my explanation ready for when I meet my daughter the first time."

"I have no idea what to say to Jack, either," Cherry admitted.

"I'll let you do the thinking on this one," Jeb drawled evidently mollified by her words. His wink confirmed it. "You can figure out our story during our voyage; then tell me what to say when we get there."

Cherry laughed and stood, pulling him up too. After she stomped her feet into her new boots, she wrapped her arms around Jeb's neck and whispered, "I'm ready. Take me home, soldier boy."

THE END

ABOUT THE AUTHOR

Gem and her family live in a rural area where wild turkey, bear, and deer wander the country roads. Watching them is inspiration for her muse. She enjoys writing all genres but has a particular passion for steamy historical romance and twisted paranormal tales.

Although she has hermit tendencies, she loves hearing from fans. For updates (or if you're an avid Words With Friends junkie) follow her at any of these places:

GEM'S WEBSITE
GemSivad.com

E-MAIL
Gem@GemSivad.com

NEWSLETTER
GemSivad.com/Dreamcatcher

LIKE HER FACEBOOK AUTHOR PAGE
Facebook.com/GemSivadAuthor

FOLLOW HER ON TWITTER
Twitter.com/GemSivad